DEADLY CADENCE

A DIAMOND DUST MYSTERY

DEADLY CADENCE

A DIAMOND DUST MYSTERY

PAMELA L. HARRIS

An Imprint of Roan & Weatherford Publishing Associates, LLC
Bentonville, Arkansas
www.roanweatherford.com

Library of Congress Cataloging-in-Publication Data
Names: Harris, Pamela, author.
Title: Deadly Cadence/Pamela L. Harris | Diamond Dust Mysteries #1
Description: First Edition | Bentonville: Rogue River, 2025.
Identifiers: LCCN: 2025933825 | ISBN: 979-8-89299-009-7 (trade paperback) |
ISBN: 979-8-89299-010-3 (eBook)
Subjects: BISAC: FICTION/Mystery & Detective/Cozy/Paranormal |
FICTION/Mystery & Detective/Women Sleuths | FICTION / Romance / Sports
LC record available at: https://lccn.loc.gov/2025933825

Rogue River trade paperback edition May, 2025

Cover Design by Casey W. Cowan
Interior Design by Staci Troilo
Editing by George "Clay" Mitchell & Don Money

DEDICATION

To Jamie and her Smith & Wesson

DEDICATION

PROLOGUE

HER FINGERS TRACED the contours of the Warrior's autumn face, then moved to the sable hair that brushed his bare shoulders. The Sun's passion had melted his topaz eyes into lustrous pools of gold and burnished his skin from pale bronze to blazing copper. As his life force flickered, she gazed up at him for the last time. Then he, too, was gone. Her heart squeezed with agony.

Who had done this to them? Ripped him from their bed. Given him to the Sun so she might dance her fiery flames across his velvety skin. Seared him with unimaginable pain.

The One who'd left her mother for dead? Her father had told her only of his beginning with the Enchantress—never of his ending. He'd never revealed the One—the chosen mortal—the only human powerful enough to bargain lives away.

She fought off the Moon's icy caress for as long as she dared. The blur of images that had marked their time together whirled before her in eddies of time—the meadow and mustangs, his warm smile and deep laugh, their bodies melding as one.

In the moments before the Moon destroyed everything that defined her—before it turned her feet to lifeless ash, her arms to dusty chalk, her heart to a dying ember—she freed the last of them into the universe, then surrendered to her bondage.

CHAPTER 1

A WELL-UPHOLSTERED JULIE Easton shoveled granola into her pie hole with the alacrity of a charwoman accepting an invitation to the queen's garden party.

Across the road, Logan appraised her rival. Her brow puckered with confusion. Julie's racing bike—the Silver Bullet—lie on the road beside Julie's size-ten booties.

Julie's coach, Tim Richard, stood at the bottom of the starting box, fawning over Julie's teammate, Taylor Sherman, as he made last-minute adjustments to her bike, helmet, booties, and skin-suit. Taylor's slender frame didn't pose much of a threat in today's time trial—the *race of truth*, the only cycling event that disallowed drafting off another rider's slipstream. It pitted the cyclist against the clock, against herself. Victory went to the racer with the fastest time over twenty-five miles—not the skinniest or the nimblest or the craftiest.

Today's race at Moriarty in New Mexico featured an out-and-back record-qualifying course—win the race, win bragging rights. Logan had trained hard for her chance to crow.

Reilly sat cross-legged on the ground, inflating a tire. "Now, what is *she* thinking? Julie has packed on at least a stone of fat since last month's race in Tennessee." She licked her finger and held it up to the wind. "With the winds buffeting that rack she's shaking, today's race is going to be hard enough for her to win without packing more suet onto those

Herculean thighs she's rocking." Reilly took the wheel in hand, rose, and locked it into the front fork of Logan's bike. "You're good to go."

Logan pressed her thumb into the rubber, checking the tire for full pressure. "Gosh, it's hard as a rock. Thanks for taking care of me."

"Hey, that's what best friends do."

"Then, in the spirit of caring, promise me you won't tell Simon he pinched my inner tube."

"Heck, no. No good ever comes of calling out your team mechanic for anything, and that goes double for one who's a curmudgeon like our Simon."

"Great. Now for my other favor."

"Julie?"

"Yes. Don't underestimate her. Pot belly aside, she still has her Brobdingnagian thighs. I'm begging you—*do not*, I repeat, DO NOT say a word to her about anything. She doesn't need any added incentive to beat us." Logan placed her hand on her hip, frowning at Reilly. "And need I remind you to play nice with everyone else while I'm out on the course?"

"I always play nice."

"Then why do you bring a gun to a bike race?"

"It's a cop thing. Someday you'll thank me." Reilly tapped the timer on Logan's bike. "T-minus three minutes. Best get a move on."

Logan steered her bike toward the starting box as Taylor and Tim moved up the ramp. Taylor was her minuteman, she was Julie's minuteman, and Julie was Reilly's minuteman. Julie clomped across the road, blocking out the official's countdown as she made her way to a sandy-haired man on the other side of the box. The man, dressed in a lightweight three-piece suit that stuck out in the crowd of jean-clad spectators like a Christmas tree at the mall in July, only had eyes for Taylor.

Logan zeroed out her timer as Reilly joined her beside the ramp. "Who is that man ogling Taylor?"

"Some guy from Sapphire Rose."

"What's a Sapphire Rose?"

"Some startup sports-apparel outfit."

"And Mister Suit is here because?"

"SR is considering a cyclist for its new cover girl."

"How do you know that?"

"I got a sniff."

"Are you interested?"

"Only if it comes with a diamond-studded holster." Reilly's foot nervously tapped out her pre-race jitters.

In the box, Tim continued to fawn over Taylor—sliding the zipper tab of her skin-suit shut, smoothing the cuffs on her shoe covers, zeroing out the timer on her bike. Logan took her final sip of water and tossed the bottle to their coach, Grant Kingston, who moved in alongside Reilly. The moment Taylor sailed onto the course, Logan ran her bike up the ramp and set the front wheel behind the start line. With the official gripping her seat post, she mounted the saddle, clipped into the pedals, and twirled her feet into the ten and four positions of a clock.

"Ten," the clock official counted off.

His "nine" came with her deep breath.

"Eight" brought a gust of wind that jiggled her bike.

On "seven," the retching sounds of Rachel Hapsburg donating her breakfast to the brambles floated past.

"Six" moved her feet a full circle.

She zeroed out her timer on "five" and tightened her grip.

"Four."

She straightened her legs.

"Three."

She cocked her knee.

"Two."

She stopped fidgeting.

"One... you're off."

The official dropped his hands, and she sprinted down the ramp.

The moment the wheel of her bike hit the tarmac, she lowered herself into the aero-bars, clicked into an easier gear, and spun up her cadence to ninety-two rpm. The tree-lined roadway swiftly gave way to bushes and rocks, then a blur of sand and scrub.

Patrol cars parked on either side of the roadway warned of the upcoming turnaround. When the orange cone that marked the halfway point rose up, the timer flashed 25:32—ninety seconds better than her guesstimate, forty-two seconds better than her out-time at her last race. Clear of the turnaround, she dropped the bike chain into a harder gear and powered down the descent at a speed in excess of forty mph. On the other side of the road, Julie rocked side to side, battling the climb.

As her pedals spun out, Logan's legs became a blur. On level road, she cruised at twenty-seven mph, clicked the chain into the most difficult gear on the rear cog, decreased her cadence to a comfortable ninety-two, and fought to maintain twenty-eight mph as her heart rate spiraled into her red zone. At the mile-to-go-marker, she spun up her cadence to ninety-six and her speed to twenty-nine. A half-mile out, she eclipsed Taylor and then Taylor's minuteman in quick succession. Two hundred feet out, the crowd urged her on. She rose up on the pedals and pumped her legs, sprinting for the finish line. Her front wheel was within a foot of the piezoelectric sensor when a silver bike streaked past and tripped the timing strip fractions of a second before Logan's front tire did the same.

Julie's victorious cackle haunted her for weeks.

CHAPTER 2

LOGAN STEERED HER Jeep through the front entrance of the Diamond Dust ranch on a crisp autumn day in early September with Julie's haunting laugh still ringing in her ears like a Wiccan chant. The clock on the dash read 2:18 p.m. When Grant had first penciled the championship onto her racing calendar, she'd balked. Her inexplicable phobia of the moon had driven her to target races held in early to late summer—when sunlight was at a premium, and moonlight was stingy—but when the Cycling Federation had selected a ranch in Montana to host its marquee race, she'd given in. A land where the northern sun ruled with an iron fist late into the night sky posed little threat.

She eased the Jeep to a stop in front of a Craftsman-style house done up in warm greens and rusts. A spry old man with bronzed skin and a silvery ponytail paced to and fro across its veranda. The personalized license plate BIG GEAR on the SUV parked a few feet away warned of Julie's earlier arrival.

She turned off the engine, slipped out through the driver's side, and freed her suitcase from the rear seat, as a younger man with hair the color of raven feathers bounded out of the shadows with all the enthusiasm of an abandoned litter of puppies. He jogged up to the Jeep and planted his worn boots inches away from her sneakers.

The familiar nausea bubbled up inside her. She shrank away, inching backward until the cold steel of the bike rack pressed into her back, forcing her to skip her pale eyes over his dark face and inky eyes until it blurred into the sinister shadow her mind made of him and every other man who got too close. Her affliction had reared its ugly head the night of her senior prom. She'd gone with a neighborhood boy—someone safe. In the end, even he wasn't. The sensation of his roaming fingers on her bare arms had made her skin crawl, but his probing goodnight kiss had triggered the revulsion that continued to plague her whenever a man came too close. Over the next decade, a parade of ominous shadows had rendered her a practiced hand at brushing off a man's advances. Either that or die.

It wasn't until this shadow had receded that the man with the demon eyes came back into focus.

She forced herself to breathe. "Hi, I'm Logan."

His hand skimmed the rim of his black Stetson. "Jake Erde, ma'am."

"Erde—Spanish?"

"Blackfoot. Means 'of the land.'"

Sudden movement near the Craftsman brought Julie out the front door and onto the veranda. As she passed the old man, he cast a mournful eye on her white toenails, then vaulted the railing onto the dying lawn. Julie scowled at his back, then traipsed down the staircase and disappeared behind the house.

Jake's boot sought purchase on the bumper of her Jeep. "My family has raised cutters on our tribal lands for more than a millennium."

His closeness set her head whirling. She groped for something to grab onto, stumbled forward, and fell against him, choking on his spicy scent. She pushed away and forfeited her lunch to a patch of lavender growing in the front yard.

He rushed toward her. "Are you okay?"

She held up her hands to fend him off. "Don't come any closer—please. I caught a bug on the drive up. I'd hate for you to catch it too."

He backed away. "That's too bad."

"I'm sure it's nothing a good night's sleep won't cure."

"Must be awful eating takeaway, fighting traffic, and sacrificing sleep."

"Every job has good and bad points." She thrust her helmet underneath her arm. "If you tell me which cabin is mine, I'll get out of your way."

"Seeing that you're sick, it's probably best if I go with you."

She made the mistake of reaching for her suitcase at the same time his hand closed around its strap. Snatching it back, she moved around to the passenger seat, collected her gym bag, and inched backward—right into the shadow of the old man.

His soft brown eyes jumped to Jake, then slowly focused on her face. "Different," he murmured to an invisible playmate. "The ancients did not know of the betrayal."

Jake extended a hand toward the Craftsman. "Dad, go check on the electrical cabling we ordered. The invoice is on my desk."

The old man quelled him with a belligerent glare. "You must go. To remain portends the death of your bloodline." He fled up the staircase and disappeared inside the Craftsman.

"Don't mind Jeremy. He jumbles up his timelines."

"Is your father a history teacher?"

"No, a keeper of knowledge."

"Oh, a librarian."

"Something like that. If you're interested in history, the ranch is steeped in it. The old stagecoach route runs across our northern ranges, as do the makings for wooden tracks Union Pacific left behind when it aborted its effort to connect the northern and southern parts of the state. Wasn't until the Great Northern steel tracks came through at the turn of last century that Seattle and Chicago finally linked up." His eyes fell to the far horizon where a prison of crimson brush interred a riot of golden trees. "The tracks run through a tunnel a stone's throw northwest of your race course. I can give you a tour sometime if you'd like."

"I appreciate the offer, but my schedule is pretty tight."

He pointed toward a series of ragged peaks rising in the distance. "Surely you'll want to clear some time on your busy schedule to drive into Two Medicine. It ain't much, but it's quaint. Art galleries, cold

brews, ice cream—hand-churned. Library's a hole in the wall, but ol'
Betsy at the laundromat will treat you right."

"How far?"

"Twenty miles and change." He extended a hand. "Your lodgings are
around the next bend."

Gigantic logs framed the walls and ceilings of the rustic cabin. A
chandelier made from rods and horseshoes bathed the rustic timber in a
flaxen glow. A rug in a Native American weave hid the polished oak
floor. A quilt of similar ilk draped over the bedpost of a twin bed. While
he offloaded her gear, she ducked into the bathroom. A soft-green rug
eased the starkness of the white tiles, and the invigorating scent of pine
conjured up memories of her aunt's ranch in Colorado.

He pointed out a meal schedule on the bookcase, as well as the spare
blankets and towels jammed into the cubbyholes. "Nights get chilly this
time of year."

No television, microwave, or computer in sight.

He drew back the curtain draped across the picture window, slid
back the windowpane to expose the screen, and pointed to a satellite dish
atop a shabby timber building sitting less than fifty feet away. "Wireless
broadband." He slid out the drawer to the nightstand. A stack of
stationery and a pen set sat front and center. "Snail mail."

He reached underneath the bed and came away with a carryall. Made
of pale-blue canvas, the front displayed the silhouette of a black stallion
rearing up on its hindquarters. Dark sequins glittered at the animal's
feet. "Compliments of the Diamond Dust ranch, ma'am."

"I'll accept your gratuity on one condition."

"Ma'am?"

"That's the condition—stop calling me ma'am."

"Sorry... Logan."

"That's better—and thanks, it's lovely... and thoughtful."

"My pleasure. Good luck on your race."

When he was gone, she thrust the carryall back underneath the bed,
reached for her old gym bag, and scooped peanut butter cups and

sinfully dark chocolate bars into the drawer of the nightstand. A small refrigerator tucked away in what passed for a closet—a thin bough strung across an alcove—held cans of pop. She helped herself to a Diet Coke and moved to the picture window. A framed collage of tumbling waters, elephant-ear plants, and snow-capped mountains gave her a feeling of *deja vu*.

She tossed the empty can into the trash bin by the door, then wrapped herself in the velvety quilt, laid down on the bed, and let the caress of the afternoon breeze help her catch up on the sleep she had sacrificed.

SHE AWOKE IN a panic, scrambled over to the window, and peered out at the indigo sky. A wispy moon hung in the northeastern sky. She flopped back down on the bed, curled into a ball, and fell back asleep.

Her second awakening came with a hot shower. She ran a hairbrush through her long, dark hair, then snatched up the map on the nightstand. It was a diagram of the ranch. The building rising up on her doorstep was the dining hall. A stable and corral sat some distance behind it linked by a dirt road. In the far distance, a workshop, surrounded by numerous lakes and rivers, hugged the mountains. More cabins littered the ranch, all within walking distance of the dining room. A circle of hot tubs lay west of the Craftsman. The out-and-back time-trial course, marked in green ink, started and ended on a narrow road beyond the hot tubs and reached north.

Still sluggish from her long drive and short nap, Logan donned jeans and a sleeveless blouse, framed her wintry eyes in a dark fringe, secured the windowpane back in place, and banged out the screen door, relinquishing the safety of her sanctuary with a heavy heart.

A PAIR OF mangy dogs snored blissfully on the front porch of the dining hall. Her first step onto the splintering boards brought the old hound doddering over to sniff her jeans, its whip-like tail twitching back and forth like a pendulum. Her next step prompted the shaggy beast of snow-dog lineage to lash out his monster paw and block her egress.

"Another time, Fido."

He pulled back his paw as his floppy tail accepted her promise. Logan stepped over him and reached for the door handle. Struggling against the weight of the thick slab of wood, she caught her toe on the sill, pitched forward, and slammed into a man heading out. His arm shot out to keep her upright, encircling her waist as his face twisted with pain. He untangled his arm and pushed her gently away.

A sharp ache in her heart took her breath away. "I'm so sorry… uh, stranger."

"You do not know me?"

"No… maybe… I don't know. Your touch is… it… you feel…." She braced for the familiar revulsion to bubble up, but nothing happened—nothing unpleasant. In its place, a memory stirred.

She blocked out the sunlight and stared at the man astride the pale stallion—the one bronze of skin and yellow of eye, the one whose waves of dark hair danced down his back like turbulent waters. He was naked to his lean waist, his lower half cloaked in pelt. He'd painted his face red—the blood red of a warrior—the color that symbolized power, strength, energy.

She closed her eyes for what seemed like only a breath, her heart hammering. When she opened them, the stallion was gone, and she was in his arms again. His cheekbones were high, his face chiseled, his skin velvety. His shingled hair fell only to his shoulders now. His finger traveled along her jaw. She closed her eyes, drinking in the excitement his touch sparked inside her, longing for more of him, yet dreading the moment they went their separate ways. She opened her eyes to find his face twisted in agony. He dropped his arms and backed away from her—from the pain her touch caused him.

He cloaked himself in oblivion—mirrored sunglasses, dark jeans and shirt, and an ankle-length coat with a hood but no fastenings. The coat's impeccable tailoring clung to his broad shoulders and nipped in at his slim waist as if originally stitched for a warrior chieftain. She'd seen photographs of similar Native American blanket coats or *capotes* in art books. First Americans had worn them as a form of identification.

"Please go," he said.

She backed away from him, her heart aching with each step. "I'm truly sorry I'm not the woman you think I am."

Then, she turned on her heels and fled outside into an angry sunset.

———

THE TRUTH OF her homecoming brought him to his knees. His invisible pain reminded him she was forbidden, yet it had done nothing to diminish the love he'd harbored for her throughout the ages. *Why had she called him stranger?*

———

WITH THE MOON still a faint circle in the heavens, Logan picked her way through forests and meadows, over creeks and streams, and across rocks and sand. Her escape ended at the stable, where a turn-of-the-century buggy decorated with a red-satin bow imparted a festive mood to her otherwise tremulous evening.

Unlike the ramshackle dining hall, the stable was light, bright, and modern. White flashing highlighted a dark-green roof, mint walls, and copper doors—now shut to keep out the chilly evening breeze. Overhead lighting lit up the corral, where hundreds of horses stood neck-to-neck and nose-to-nose. Gray mares flanked chestnut stallions and white yearlings mingled with black three-year olds. When a colt trotted over to nuzzle her palm, she was pleased. She liked animals, especially dogs and horses, and they seemed to like her back. Primarily white in color, the colt's head, ears, belly, and rear hindquarters were sable. Threads of white combed through its dark tail. His blue eyes gave her a measured look, and his newborn fragrance—tempered by saddle soap—mingled with that of her own almond-scented lotion.

"Sabino traits."

She stiffened as the old man's singsong voice intruded into her peaceful retreat. She turned slowly around, hoping he'd vanish as softly as he'd materialized. He didn't.

She threw herself against the railing to distance herself from him. "Sabino?"

He shuffled a dozen steps closer. "Small color traits."

She climbed onto the top rail, gripping it until her knuckles whitened. "His markings are stunning."

His next step set her heart pounding. She coughed, struggled for breath, and coughed again. Still, her curiosity bested her discomfort. "Who is this woman you've mistaken me for?"

"You bear little resemblance to her in flesh and bone, but my heart…."

A deafening crack of thunder drowned out his words. Then, the heavens opened. He dashed to the garage doors and punched a switch. The copper doors chugged upward. He scampered through the opening, motioning her to join him. She shook her head. His gestures came harder. She clung to the railing, letting the rain seep into her skin, hoping a good soaking would cleanse away her ever-constant apprehension she wasn't of this time.

When the old man stopped gesturing, she loosened her grip on the railing and stared down at the puddles of rainwater running in rivulets on the ground, until an overwhelming sensation of being hunted flowed through her. Too late, she realized he'd moved in beside her. She stared into his sharp eyes. Again, she braced herself against his touch, but when he gathered up her legs and yanked her off the fence, nothing happened. She didn't fight back when he threw her over his shoulder, slipped inside the barn, and set her gently down on a bale of hay. Seizing her chance to escape, she dashed to the rack of gardening tools on the far wall and yanked off a pitchfork.

His eyes flirted with the weapon, but his mouth broke into a smile. "You return strong of spirit and cunning of mind. You will need both to face your ordeal." He lowered himself onto a neighboring bale and beckoned her to join him. "Come, child. Do not fear me."

She perched on the edge of the bale and set the pitchfork between them. "Your words make no sense to me... before when you greeted me or now when you have trapped me."

"I am not a hunter like you. I am a teacher. My task is to nurture others to discover their purposes. Each purpose carries with it much responsibility. Those that cannot accept this vanish into the outer world and are forever lost to us and themselves, leaving a void in our world. You are different in that you did not leave us willingly. The Great Creator knows this and so has granted you this journey of choice."

"I've lived here before?"

"You were born here and found purpose here."

"But I have no memories of this place, of any people or family or my life here."

"My heart binds only to the hearts of the people who chose to remain. Our past link allows only for shared memories. You have battled the heavens to come back to the land that holds your heart. You need not fight any longer." He laid the pitchfork on the ground. "Your time runs short. Now you must listen. Will you do that much?"

She nodded.

He closed his eyes and began to sway—a slow, rhythmic movement. "We begin at the birth of the Blue Planet at the time when our Young Brothers wandered the forests in the cold of the winter and climbed the mountains in the heat of the summer. One day, when the young bear cub could climb and wander no longer, he lifted his eyes to the heavens. 'Oh, Great Creator, we must have pure water to renew our spirit.'

"'I cannot help you,' the Great Creator said. 'You must seek Meren of the Waterfall to renew your spirit.'

"'I will go,' the old Wolverine said.

"'You are too old,' the red fox said. 'The bear will go.'

"The following day, the bear set off into the forest, only to return tired and thirsty when the sun dropped behind the mountains. 'I failed,' the bear said. 'What shall we do now? Without Merenale we will perish.'

"'I will go,' the fox said. 'And I will not fail.' A week went by without a sign of the fox and without a drop of water to renew their spirits. On the following day, the fox stepped from the forest empty-handed. Another week went by, then a fortnight.

"The bear approached the old Wolverine. 'You are our last hope.'

"The night before she was to leave, the old Wolverine had a good dream. The following morning, she waved to her friends and vanished among the trees. Long days passed without a drop of Merenale finding its way into the valley. Days grew into weeks, then months, until one evening the crunch of a footfall fell on their ears, and the old Wolverine lumbered out of the trees, the handle of an earthen pot grasped between her razor-sharp teeth, turquoise water spilling over its earthen walls. When she reached the others, she set the pot on the ground, and her friends hugged her.

"The Great Creator made our streams, rivers, lakes, and oceans from this water." His eyes snapped open. "Do you understand?"

She shook her head.

"You are his Merenale, as he is yours. One will perish without the other. That is why you were both taken."

LOGAN SAT WITH her teammates at dinner that night. She loaded her plate with diced fruit, as well as tomato, cucumber, sweet onion, and herbed feta salad dripping in basil dressing, creamy pasta primavera, and crunchy bread rounds. Reilly sat beside her, gulping down chocolate milk.

As the night drew on, Logan worked her way slowly through each entree, fearful that if she didn't keep her mouth filled, she'd let her excitement about the lanky stranger and the old Blackfoot override her common sense and blab every crazy detail to her friend. She'd never confided in anyone about her love life—or lack thereof—especially Reilly, whose own romantic escapades paralleled the on-again, off-again affairs depicted in soap opera. Even if she did, what would she say? That she'd never felt the thrill of a man's mouth on hers? Never shared his bed? That she'd finally met a man who didn't leave her sick to her stomach? Telling anyone you harbored a rabid fear of a celestial body would buy you a one-way ticket to the loony bin.

With their serious training behind them, the week before a race was more like a paid holiday than a hard grind—rest and recovery in the form of easy cycling, overeating, and frequent napping made up the bulk of her workouts leading up to Saturday's race. Keeping her mind focused on something other than racing was her singular most-difficult challenge. Many of her fellow cyclists played musical beds to pass the idle time and burn off nervous excitement. Perhaps the stranger's case of mistaken identity, as well as the old Blackfoot's tale of a buried heart and shared memories, was the diversion she needed to see her through to the weekend.

Reilly set down her empty glass. "Earth to Logan."

She laughed. "Yes, ground control?"

"You got any chocolate? Cuz Grant is about to do his Grant thing, and between Black Bart's smarmy howdy-do and the pilot's resolution to hit every air pocket between Las Vegas and Kalispell, my mojo has hit rock bottom."

Logan reached into the pocket of her jeans for the Cadbury bar she carried whenever she left her cottage. "Here." She slapped it into Reilly's outstretched hand. "Chomp softly."

Their coach signaled for their attention. Grant hailed from the United Kingdom and had been an awesome cyclist in his own day, particularly suited to mounting winning breakaways during the long stages of grand tours.

"Ladies and gents—treat this week like you did before Moriarty. Easy pedal tomorrow, full-out Thursday, recovery ride Friday, and get as many calories inside of you as you can stomach. Any questions?"

Reilly raised an enthusiastic hand. "Why did the Federation banish us to this back of beyond to race nationals this year?"

"Remember last year's championship?"

"When the cement truck took out the cyclist because the traffic guard chose her romance novel over rider safety—those nationals?"

"The very same. That incident prompted the Federation to reconsider the wisdom of holding its events on open roads, effectively eliminating any city or town with a major thoroughfare. My sources told me the Federation sought out the Diamond Dust specifically for its isolated location and because it was one of a very few venues big enough to host our twenty-five-mile individual event and the sixty-mile team time trial. Rumor is it had a hard time convincing Jake to take us on, but somehow the Federation made it worth his bother, and here we are."

When he moved on to the weather report, Logan homed in on the neighboring table where a handful of Julie's teammates gathered. Her friend Allison Walker sat to the left of a stocky man she didn't recognize. Underneath the bright lighting, his clean-shaven head and diamond-stud earring sparkled. Tim sat to Allison's left, opposite a ridiculously handsome man. The man's white T-shirt stretched across his Herculean back but didn't obscure the faint outline of a tattoo peeking through the flimsy cotton fabric. Glossy black hair framed his oval face, and his turquoise eyes zeroed in on Reilly, who only had eyes for her pasta primavera. The man's only flaw was a handful of bandaged fingers beating out a drum roll on the table.

Julie sat on the fireplace hearth and wore a sloppy sweatshirt and sequined shorts. She'd spiked up her sun-bleached hair and blackened her gray eyes. Gold bangles on her arm jingled and jangled as she waggled her finger at her scrawny teammate, Fay White. Fay swatted angrily at the finger and stalked off. Sydney Long, the youngest member of Team Continental, darted in from the courtyard, slipped into Fay's empty chair, and let out a string of yawns. A film of perspiration stippled her hairline, and angry welts blossomed in the soft indentation of her elbow. Taylor, sitting to Rachel's right, stabbed at the keypad of a cell phone and frowned.

"I wouldn't spend too much time worrying about Miss Clydesdale," Reilly whispered.

"Why not? Julie is the reigning national champion."

"*Was,* past tense. We're way-more-trained-up now. One of us is due." Reilly pointed toward the fire where Jake had joined Julie on the hearth. "Hey, will you look at that? Black Bart has finally found the perfect vessel for his testosterone." She piled up her dirty dishes. "Come on. Let's get out of here while the getting is good—and by good I mean before Simon opens his garrulous mouth."

Logan scrambled to button up her pants. "What's your hurry?"

"Grant and I are strategizing tonight."

"Is that what you're calling it now?"

"Shame on you. You know I'm an engaged woman."

"For today."

She followed Reilly to a side cart, deposited her own dirty dishes, and refilled her coffee cup at the buffet.

"Holy cow!" Reilly elbowed Logan aside to get to the open gun cabinet on the wall where she lifted out a rifle from an assortment nestled on notched crossbars. "A modified German Jaeger. This baby has a grooved barrel so the lead ball twists prior to ejection—improves accuracy." She pointed the barrel toward a mountain of a man standing outside the kitchen and gave the grip stock a loving caress. "Locked and loaded, I could take down that Magic Chef from where we're standing."

"His name is Griffin."

"Griffin what?"

She shrugged. "Just Griffin, like just Cher."

"How do you know that?"

She scratched her head. "I don't know... I just do."

"You must've overheard somebody—Black Bart, most likely—drop his name. That man's mouth motors on like a marching band hopped up on Red Bull." Reilly nestled the antique weapon back into its nest. "Wow! This one is a Winchester Springfield thirty-aught-six like my dad's." She tugged back the bolt. "Chamber's loaded."

"Lemme see." Logan poked her nose into the opening. "Only one bullet. That can't be right, can it?"

"One bullet is enough for some of us."

Reilly placed the Winchester in its cradle as the long-limbed stranger burst through the door. Logan pinned herself against the wall to give him ample room to pass.

Fat lot of good it did. He came to a stop in front of her and touched his lips to her ear. "Do not fear me." Again, his face buckled with pain.

She stared up at her excited flush in his mirrored lenses. "Fear is not what I feel when you are near me."

———————

ORANGE STREAKS SWIRLED through a purple sky as she and Reilly stepped outside. The dogs no longer garnished the porch. Reilly lowered herself onto the top step, leaving the wrought-iron bench for Logan. They spent some time listening to mice burrow and swallows swoop, until Reilly joined her on the bench.

"What's going on between you and that slinky stranger?"

Her hand jerked up, splashing coffee onto her jeans. She slapped at the scalding liquid as it seeped into the thin denim. "Who told you something was going on between him and me?"

"I got eyes."

"Well, put some drops in them because nothing is going on. He confused me with another woman—not flattering."

———————

LOGAN'S HABITUAL ALOOFNESS toward men puzzled her. In the eight years they'd known each other, her training partner had never mentioned going on a date, let alone a boyfriend, lover, or partner—and, although Reilly liked her own men tall, dark, and mute, not gassy like

Black Bart—she wasn't sure what type Logan liked. Still, she'd bet a year's worth of dark chocolate something had passed between her friend and that sultry stranger, and whatever that something was had finally punctured Logan's icy armor.

As the fiery sun dropped behind the mountains, the crickets began their nocturnal symphony, and Logan's usual trepidation with nighttime bubbled up. When the savage cries of marauding coyotes joined in, her unease crescendoed.

She nudged Reilly's knee. "It's after nine. I'm heading back to my cabin and my date with the sandman. Coming?"

"Not just yet."

She'd taken her first step down the staircase when the dogs shot out of the shadows and collapsed onto her sneakers. A Doberman pup followed, nosing her muzzle underneath Reilly's open hand. When Logan backed up onto the bench, the snow-dog played tag with her boots. The women spent the better part of nightfall wallowing in puppy love and sipping coffee so weighty with caffeine even Logan's well-conditioned heart had trouble keeping up.

The ring of Reilly's phone brought out her frown, and she squinted at the display. "Grant cancelled our meeting."

When the ginger hound began to tremble, Logan urged her closer. The dog jumped into her lap, made a few nesting circles, and then settled down. "Sydney looked beat tonight, and she barely touched her food."

Reilly let out a well-timed yawn. "Fatigue comes with the job, but you're right. Tonight she looked utterly exhausted."

Logan stroked the hound's head. "She needs to be seen by a doctor."

Reilly popped a peanut butter cup into her mouth and made happy sounds. "You think?"

"You don't?"

"All she needs is a new mechanic."

"Allison told me that handsome bloke with the tattoo splashed across his back *is* Continental's new mechanic."

"My point exactly. If Grant had hired that sexy Romeo as our mechanic just days before nationals, I'd be utterly exhausted too."

Their laughter sent the dogs scampering back into the woods. With the owls heckling in the background, they made their way to the kitchen to return their coffee mugs.

Logan crossed the threshold first, recoiled, and landed on Reilly's sneakers.

"Hey, do you mind? My feet are attached to both my paychecks."

"Sorry." She plunged inside and leaned against the butcher-block countertop where Royal Dalton, Lady Godiva, and Hamilton Beach frolicked with Mister Coffee, Aunt Jemima, and Uncle Ben.

"Hey look!" Reilly pointed to a fudge cake in the corner. "A cake in detention."

Canvas bags of flour and sugar lounged on the floor, and a bank of refrigerators stared across at cabinets with faulty hinges.

Logan ran her finger through a puddle of flour on the countertop as the bottom half of a man wiggled out from underneath the nearest refrigerator. His upper half followed.

"Ladies!" He groaned himself upright and placed a honey pot among the appliances.

Reilly inched inside and dropped their mugs into the land of confusion. "I'm Reilly. She's Logan."

"Griffin."

"Like Cher?"

"Like Griffin. Would you care for a slice of my *special* fudge cake, ladies?" Without waiting for their answer, he seized up a knife and cut the dessert into four quarters. "Here." He lifted the platter and pushed it at Reilly.

She grabbed up her share of empty calories. "Thanks. I'll go share this with the sandman. Nighty night, y'all." She yanked open the screen door and fled into the night, leaving Logan stranded with a 1,000-plus calories of sugar, a horribly blackened sink, and a man wielding a three-inch blade.

Knife in one hand, platter in the other, he used his hip to nudge a knob on the stove and coerce a blue-edged flame into action. "Would you care for a cup of my special tea, my dear?"

"I would, thank you."

Three minutes later, the pungent aroma of ginger, cloves, and rose hips tickled her senses, and a cup filled with an amber-colored liquid sat in front of her on the countertop.

"Please, taste it," he said. "It's my new blend. Tell me what you think."

The acerbic sting of ginger burnt her tongue on her first sip. She'd lifted the honey pot to sweeten it when he slapped it from her grasp. It sailed through the air and slammed against the refrigerator, dripping sticky honey and ceramic shards onto the floor.

She ran to the sink and grabbed a sponge. "Why did you do that?"

"It's spoiled, moldy. It could make you sick, sick enough to stop you from racing this weekend. I could never forgive myself. Now, it's your turn to explain. Something is wrong with my tea?"

She dropped to her knees and scrubbed honey off the floor, bringing up other nefarious bits in the process. "Too much ginger for my taste."

"Perhaps a few sweet dates will take out the sting. Do you like dates?"

"Love them. I also love bad coffee over gourmet tea."

His hands came together. "Ah, so now we come to the heart of your disapproval. No matter. We have plenty of night left to drink my special brew. What is it you cyclists like—Blue Jamaican?" His dark eyes clouded with confusion. "Or is it Jamaican Blue?"

She scrubbed the refrigerator door, then ran the sticky sponge underneath the streaming water and tossed it into the sink. "Either. Bargain coffee works too."

For a big-boned man, he was as agile as a cat, scampering into the pantry with ease and returning just as quickly with an old-fashioned percolator in hand. While he scooped coffee into the basket, she flipped back pages of a cookbook lying open beside the stove, stopping when she came to a colorful arrangement of sugary quick breads and savory muffins flanked by luscious jams and jellies. Despite the naughty cake awaiting their approval, her taste buds begged shamelessly.

He moved soundlessly about the kitchen as he set out a bowl of sugar and a pitcher of cream. "I will make Anna's favorite tomorrow—cinnamon vanilla French toast. Would you like that?"

"I'm sure I will. Is Anna your wife?"

"No, my sister. Anna liked to ride her bike as you do. She had no talent in the kitchen, other than tasting, which I admit can be useful, not like that Julie Easton creature. Bah! That one has no palate."

She wondered how he knew Julie, but with the set of knives still within easy reach and his easily inflamed disposition, she pushed her nosiness aside. "Does Anna still ride?"

"My Anna is gone."

"She died? Oh, Griffin… I'm so sorry. Was it an accident?"

"Yes, but I have come to grips with it." He slammed the cookbook shut, opened a drawer, and passed her a fork. "Now, tell me. How did you like my basil dressing?"

"It was perfect. Don't change a thing."

He grabbed up a Post-It. "I shall write out my recipe for you."

She dug into his naughty cake.

Logan made her way back around to the front porch where Reilly sat on the bench with the Doberman puppy asleep in her lap. She lowered herself down and told her about the tea party, bad honey, and Anna.

"How did his sister die?"

"I didn't go there. His grief was still raw."

"Maybe it was recent."

"Maybe." She pulled out the Post-It. "He gave me his recipe for basil dressing."

"What good does that do us? Neither of us cook."

"Someday we might."

"Yeah, like Oz really lives in Kansas."

Logan burst out laughing. "I like people who live in technicolor." The reverse side of the pink square held a recipe for Griffin's special baklava. She returned it to her pocket. "How 'bout a walkabout to stretch our legs?"

Reilly placed the pup gently onto the porch. It didn't budge. "Fifteen minutes ago you wanted to fly off with the sandman."

"Ten minutes ago you did too. Besides, that was before we both had a bazillion molecules of sugar tap-dancing on our pancreases."

Reilly yawned herself off the bench. "You go. I'll let the sandman know you're coming. Come get me in the morning—five fifteen."

"Ouch!"

THE MOON HAD slipped behind the storm clouds when Logan circled the dining hall, then veered off onto the dirt road. A foreboding gorge flanked it on one side and a forest of quaking aspens on the other. She kept to the shadows until she came upon a cabin hidden among the trees. As she passed, a light inside the cabin flashed *on* then *off*. She bolted among the trees, crouching underneath a tangle of low-reaching limbs as a parade of ants goose-stepped across her sneakers. She counted down from twenty, crawled out from underneath the boughs on twenty-two, and walked back to the road. A moment later, the cabin door swung open, and a Golem ran out clutching a bag. It fled into the night, its diamond stud winking back at the stars.

Hemmed in on both sides, she dashed down the road as a deluge of rain fell out of the clouds. Soaked and shivering, she ran blindly through the open doors and into her stranger's outstretched arms. Once again, he withered in pain. She backed away.

She was halfway to the opening when a boom of thunder shook the walls. Out in the corral, the horses scattered, whinnying nervously as the lights flickered, then died. She dared not move, afraid if she did, she'd bump into him again and send him back into his abyss of torment.

When his arms snaked around her waist, she struggled to get free—for his sake.

"Please do not go," he whispered.

"If you let go of me, I'll stay—but you must keep your distance."

As the lights flickered back on, his grip slackened. She moved to a hay bale. He leaned against a ladder climbing up between an electric clock carved in the shape of two crayons and a hook filled with ropes of varying sizes. Each crayon on the clock was the size of a baseball bat, one painted bright green, the other canary yellow. She checked her own watch against it. The clock had skipped ahead more than an hour.

"I don't understand any of this," she said. "Why my touch causes you pain, why my heart aches when you are not close to me."

"Jeremy did not explain?"

"Not in any way that made sense."

"Do not blame yourself for the evil forced on us, *Nuttah*. It was the sun and the moon—together with the Old Man and Old Woman—that conspired against us. The moon sealed your heart in ice so that you could love no man but me. The sun spun a web of pain around mine to warn me you are forbidden. The Old Man and the Old Woman did not sanction our joining. Now the Great Creator has granted us another lifetime. If you choose to stay, your homecoming will undo that which has been done to us."

———

SHE WAITED UNTIL he'd faded behind the curtain of rain before she ventured out into the darkness and dashed between the puddles to reach her cabin. By the time she'd barricaded herself behind its sturdy walls where the moon could not trespass, the sky was awash with a trillion distant suns.

———

HE BRUSHED A gloved finger over her cheek. Her icy soul was as foreign to him as the woman lying beneath him, yet somehow she'd kept her promise and found her way back to him. She stirred, arced toward him, and slid the sunglasses from his face. The movement lifted her shirt to reveal her heart kicking like an unbroken mustang. His flaming eyes, filled with passion and desire, blazed down on her.

"Who are you to me?" she asked.

"I am the man who has waited a thousand years to kiss you."

CHAPTER 3

LOGAN AWOKE AT 0-dark-hundred, buried the alarm clock underneath the pillow, and slammed down her first Diet Coke of the day. By the time she'd emptied a second can, her headache was gone, and she could open her eyes without cringing.

She crawled back into bed and reflected on his visit. No use denying he hadn't gotten underneath her skin. His presence in her cabin hadn't upset her—far from it. Not only had she grown used to his mysterious comings and goings, she yearned for them. When he was with her, she felt calm and excited at the same time like a weary warrior returning from a victorious battle.

She dragged herself underneath a cold shower, then dressed in a serviceable jersey and black cycling shorts. Today's easy ride would require her only to persevere not perform—thank God.

REILLY STOOD OUTSIDE her cabin with cups of steaming coffee in both hands.

"For me?"

Reilly shook her head. "Simon—if we want our bikes adjusted with minimal orneriness."

Logan loaded Reilly's gear into the back of her Jeep, then hopped into the driver's seat as Reilly slid into the passenger seat. Firing up the engine, she drove them to the front entrance of the ranch. Both team vans sat at the edge of a small meadow northeast of the entrance, less than one hundred yards from the Craftsman.

A scratchy moan answered her rap on Simon's door. She pushed it open, then let Reilly slip in ahead of her. Their mechanic Simon Walsh snored fitfully inside a sleeping bag. While Reilly tried to roust him with the intoxicating aroma of burnt coffee, Logan backtracked to the Jeep for their bikes, leaned them against the front of Simon's van, then returned inside.

Nothing had changed since her last visit a month ago. A chipped microwave and a grimy sink still flanked his cluttered workbench. His meager supply of clothes still lived beneath the workbench. A filing cabinet sat beside the door, and spare parts and ledgers filled most of the nooks and crannies. Over her head, hooks filled with tires hung down from the ceiling. She batted one away as she moved behind the door. Simon crawled out of the sleeping bag wearing only his skivvies, snatched both coffees from Reilly's grasp, slammed one onto his workbench, and drank greedily from the other.

Reilly helped herself to a stale cookie left out on the workbench. "Rise and shine, Simon."

"Whatchawant?"

"I need a fifty-four."

His bloodshot eyes slid over Reilly's slender form, then moved to Logan's muscular legs. "You want the same?"

"Please."

"What for?"

"We need to average at least thirty mph if we want to beat Julie." Reilly backhanded crumbs from her lips. "At ninety-four rpm, the math works out to a fifty-four front chain ring and a thirteen in the rear cog."

He snorted. "That's a tall order, even for the likes of her"—he jerked his thumb at Logan—"but I'll do what I can with what I've got. Come back in an hour."

Reilly pecked his whiskery cheek. "Thanks. You're a sweetie."

"Yeah, thanks." Logan edged toward the door and tugged Reilly by the sleeve of her jacket back to the Jeep. "What now?"

"A nap?"

"Perfect."

They hopped back into their seats and fell instantly asleep. Sometime later, the cooing of doves stirred Logan awake. She opened her eyes to a hazy sunrise of gray-blues and streaky oranges.

"Holy cow—WAKE UP!" She shook Reilly's shoulder. "Grant will skin us alive if we miss breakfast."

She turned the key in the ignition, gunned the engine, and spun them back onto the gravel driveway, heading northwest toward the parking lot closer to the dining hall, but as she pulled in, Grant and Taylor stood shoulder to shoulder beside a dark bike propped against the cargo door of Julie's SUV. Julie was nowhere in sight.

THEY CAUGHT UP with their Russian teammates Katy Demenok and Sabrina Vuronov at the buffet in the dining hall. In the dawn's early light, the room smelled like wood smoke and burnt coffee with a dash of cinnamon. While her teammates giggled about the upcoming dance, Logan helped herself to French toast, hash browns, a buttery omelet, and a bran muffin, then carried her tray to a table overlooking the courtyard. Outside, streaks of anemic gray night hemmed in the orange sphere as fog billowed in from Flathead Lake and elk breakfasted on the grasses in the meadow.

She unloaded her tray with a restless heart. Try as she might, she couldn't stop herself from traveling back a thousand years to her *other* self—the one her stranger had kissed.

Reilly's sharp jab jerked her awake. She blinked and poured maple syrup over the French toast on her plate, while Reilly dumped cottage cheese onto Anna's favorite breakfast.

"How was the drive over from Michigan?" Reilly asked.

Sabrina took the huckleberry syrup to her French toast. "Not bad."

"Sabrina pulls your boot," Katy said. "We took Amtrak train. Dark horseman come for us."

Logan spread butter on the bran muffin. "Jake met you at the train station in Two Medicine?"

Sabrina giggled. "He is very—how do Americans say it—*hands on*."

Reilly scowled. "Jake Erde is not a broncobuster you want to mess with."

Sabrina's frown reached across the table. "We no mess with dark horseman. We dance with him."

Logan had chewed the muffin to pulp by the time Griffin stepped from his kitchen into the dining hall with a bowl of fresh fruit. Abandoning the remains of her breakfast, she joined the stampede at the buffet, almost colliding with Julie and Taylor at the end of the line. Julie had traded in last night's sparkles for a white skin-suit. Taylor had dressed tastefully in her blue, silver, and black Continental team kit.

"Better slow down on the eats, *sha*," Taylor said. "Another inch of suet on your waistline, and your contract with Continental will be in jeopardy, too. Then, you can kiss any whisper of that SR modeling gig goodbye."

"Like you even have a chance, *sha*," Julie mocked. "You're a *domestique*. Sapphire Rose will never sign a grunt." She grabbed up a banana, dashed across the room, and joined Jake, sipping coffee at a table by the door.

Logan filled a bowl with fresh pineapple, papaya, and mango and rejoined her teammates.

"Back home, we no dance in open," Katy said.

Sabrina took the bottle of hot sauce to her scrambled eggs. "Yes, but tonight we celebrate U.S.A style."

Reilly's hazel eyes circled the room. "The Diamond Dust is crawling with love-starved cowpunchers other than Jake."

Katy twisted around in her seat. "Where are these lovely animal fighters you speak of?"

"Yes, where?" Sabrina jabbed the air with her fork. "I see only rough men who ride horses and skinny men who ride bicycles."

Logan grinned at the tangled confusion Reilly had set in motion. "Let's see you talk your way out of this one."

Movement near the door brought the man with the diamond stud into the room. He cast stormy eyes at Julie, filled up a tray, and joined Allison near the fireplace. Jake pushed aside the sliding doors and strolled outside as Romeo strolled inside and joined Julie. She learned across the table and opened her mouth. He jumped from the chair. It tipped backward and crashed to the floor. Julie pushed back her chair and lumbered slowly onto her feet.

"I can do nothing more to your fancy machine that will make up for your faulty engine," he said.

The slap Julie landed on his cheek registered like a gunshot. Reilly unzipped her jacket to expose her lethal playmate and bridged the gap to the feuding couple in half a dozen strides.

"You"—REILLY POKED Julie—"sit." She crooked her finger at the handsome mechanic. "You—put those fists away. If you're as good at fixing things as Tim says you are, you can try your skills on my broken heart."

His rakish smile made her doodads tingle.

WHEN REILLY SKATED toward the buffet with her *stallion de joie* in tow, Rachel slipped in from the courtyard and led a miffed Julie outside, while Grant flopped down on the chair next to Katy. "Can I tag along on your ride this morning?"

Katy treated him to a coy smile. "If you promise me things."

"A spot of blackmail? Jolly cheek of you."

"No, no. Nothing like that. Tell us secret of daredevil breakaway."

"That's easy. Commit to your break, then pedal like the hounds of hell are after you. It's pure luck if it works. Now eat up. We need to get our ride in before the cold front drops in from Canada."

After they'd gone, Logan returned to the buffet for a coffee refill. She'd taken her seat when Reilly came out from behind a potted ficus, waving her arms frantically.

"Beelzebub! Get out—now!"

Then she, too, was gone.

A blink later, Jake eased himself down into Reilly's abandoned chair. "Are you enjoying the food?"

She pushed out her stomach. "Maybe too much. Where'd you find Griffin?"

"*Tilopiki* luck brought him to us. Once blessed, good fortune follows."

"Who does the blessing?"

"The *Tilopiki*. It's a society for Blackfoot women. I wasn't even looking for a cook when he turned up on Dad's porch one freezing morning last January. I warmed him up and offered him a job. He seemed to need it. I'm sure he has a past somewhere." He shrugged.

"Didn't you run a background check on him?"

"Ain't right prying into a man's private life."

"Isn't that risky?"

His unhurried smile slipped out. "Did you taste his French toast?"

She laughed. "Good point, and the ranch?"

"That was the Old Man's luck."

"Jeremy?"

"Not my old man—*the* Old Man. He and the Old Woman were the first humans on the Blue Planet."

"Are you telling me the Diamond Dust ranch is the original Garden of Eden?"

"No, ma'am. Our lands came to us through the Princess Warrior. The legend claims the child Running Eagle rescued a Piegan Chieftain—the youngest son of the Old Man and Old Woman—when a rival tribe shot his horse and then hunted him down. She restored him to health. He rewarded her with these lands and made her a princess. Later, when her husband left, she gave up her royal status to fight as a warrior, and the lands reverted back to the four remaining sons. Course, I wouldn't take that as gospel. When an elder dies, parts of our heritage go missing."

"How sad. To lose your roots."

"Living in the past is Slade's turn-on."

"Slade?"

"My brother. He hates your kind."

"Women?"

"No, incomers. He says they invade the ranch, pry into things, and upset nature's balance. If you've spent any time at our stable, you've probably seen him. He tends to our horses."

"I've crossed paths with a lot of people since I got here. What about the horses… any romantic Blackfoot tales associated with them?"

"Only one. The gift of a horse symbolizes the love of a warrior for his maiden. My father gave my mother forty ponies on the night of their engagement. My brother built our present herd from those love horses."

She pushed back her chair. "Well, Jake—I'd like to hear more about your family sometime, but right now I need to find Reilly before she self-destructs."

"How about lunch?"

"Today?"

"Tomorrow and every day after that."

She laughed. "Maybe we can fix something up after Saturday's race."

REILLY WAITED ON the porch, twirling her sapphire-and-diamond engagement ring around on her finger. At Logan's approach, she yanked it off and dropped it into the pocket of her shirt. "Ready?"

"Beelzebub—Jake's not that bad, is he?"

"Make me a promise. If you're done loathing the slinky stranger, marry the Magic Chef—not the jabbering fool. That way, you'll never starve."

"You mean *we'll* never starve."

"That, too. Come on. Bikes first, men later."

———————

THEY MADE THEIR way back to the main entrance where Simon sat on the porch of the Craftsman. A black bike—sans handlebars—lay beside him, a puddle of ball bearings swimming between his outstretched legs.

Reilly pointed to the blackened rag in his hand. "Whatcha doing?"

"What does it look like I'm doing? I'm fixin' Miss Julie's bike."

"Traitor," Logan whispered.

He cast her a black look. "You think I'm deaf?"

"What Logan wants to know is why are you fixing our rival's bike? What happened to Tom Drake?"

"He up and quit."

"Quit? So that gorgeous hunk of prime manhood is Drake's permanent replacement?"

"Aye, he is that now."

"When did this happen?"

"Right after Moriarty. Drake cashed in his winnings from Miss Julie's victory and took off for parts unknown. As for her coming to me instead of taking her troubles to pretty boy, how the hells do I know what's running around in that she-woman's head? Do I look like her con-fee-dant? All I knows is she come whining to me about how her shifters don't shift and how pretty boy just up and vanished during her hour of need. So I goes to Grant, and he gives me the nod to fix 'em, and when I opens up the dang things, I find a pack of black flies humping the bearings."

"Geez Louise. I'm sorry I asked. What about our bikes?"

He thrashed the rag onto the floor. "You can pick 'em up at the van. I lengthened your crank arms too. That should give you a stronger down-stroke, as long as you can push it."

Reilly dropped a kiss on his forehead. "You're a peach, Simon Says—a wormy one, but still a peach."

"Yeah, thanks," Logan said.

He snorted. "The only thanks I need from either of you women is a winning time Saturday. Dang blast it! Mark my words... you send me to the poorhouse again, and you can fix your own damn bikes from now on."

THEY SPENT THE morning crisscrossing the ranch, passing scrub-infested grasslands and pine-studded forests set between towering cliffs. An hour into the ride, a lone cyclist wearing Continental team colors pedaled past. A half-hour later a small peloton sped by. Grant pedaled up front, Katy and Sabrina followed in the sweet spot, and Tim brought up the rear.

A quarter-hour later, they came upon another Continental cyclist stranded alongside the roadway. Picking up their speed, they quickly bridged the gap.

"Logan. Reilly." Julie swung her foot over her bike and onto the tarmac, carelessly crushing a dung beetle whose only crime was jaywalking.

Logan pointed to the top tube of Julie's bike. Instead of running straight, it curved downward. "New bike?"

Julie poked a finger at the deflated front tire. "Yeah, and for all the money I dished out, it should be bulletproof."

"No spare tube?"

"I used my only spare on the rear flat I got practicing the course. Jake better sweep the road before Saturday, or I'm lodging a protest. Don't you carry spares?"

Logan plucked a spare tube from the pocket of her jersey and dropped it down to Reilly, already on the pavement wrestling the wheel from the bike's front axial.

She returned to Julie. "Where's Allison?"

"I unloaded her."

"She's out here riding alone too?"

"No, silly. I don't know where she is. I told her I didn't need her—ever. Tim paired me with Rachel this week, and Allison paired up with Taylor. Fat lot of good Rachel is—her with her nose stuck in a book twenty-four-seven. This morning she had the nerve to tell me she had better things to do with her time than turn herself inside out training for a race she had no chance of winning." Her eyes flickered down to Reilly, now ripping the inner tube from the outer tire. "Can't you hurry it up down there? I got a lunch date I don't want to miss."

Reilly flashed her a filthy look.

Logan crouched beside Reilly. "Need a hand?"

"I got this. You get back up there and snoop."

"Roger that." She straightened. "I don't see a brand on your bike, Julie."

"It's a one-off. I designed it, and Continental built it. I'm submitting a patent after nationals."

Logan slid her fingers over the flashy blue metal that made up the wheel rim. Although the frame was primarily black, luminescent flecks rippled throughout its textured surface, and the bike components came in an uncommon shade of lavender. "It's beautiful. Carbon fiber?"

"How should I know? I'm no chemist. What I do know is it doesn't contain any iron, so it will never rust, not even the chain. Won't crack either. The frame could have carbon in it or not."

Beneath them, Reilly had the tire in her lap. Her fingers skimmed the inside surface, coming away empty-handed. "No thorns or nails. You might've picked up a goat-head or not."

"Or our worthless new mechanic pinched the tube."

"What's the story on your worthless old mechanic Tom Drake?" Logan asked.

"He opened a bike shop in Portland. Tim plucked the new guy off Continental's assembly line, but if you want my opinion, he can't tell a cassette lock-ring from a pedal wrench."

"Can you?" Reilly raised her hand. "I'm ready for *your* CO_2 cartridge, Julie."

Julie shrugged off her blue backpack, wiggled out of her yellow jacket, and turned out the pocket—a wad of ABC gum and some paltry scraps of Kleenex encrusted with glitter fell out. "Oops, my bad." She scooped up the backpack and dug around until her hand was filled with finger-sized gold canisters. "Here." She tossed one into Reilly's lap.

While Reilly shot the CO_2 into the new tube, Logan folded up the discarded tube and then searched the ground for the abandoned fastener. "Where'd you drop the twist tie?"

"Back wheel," Reilly said.

It had fallen between two of the ten gears splined to the rear axial. Logan plucked it out, wrapped it around the punctured tube, and brought herself eye level with Julie. "Your rear cog has a boatload of gears. Is that new too?"

"Yep. It's an eleven twenty-three, one gear more than I used at Moriarty. Coupled with the front sixty I run, this race won't come down to the wire." Julie lowered her head. "Hey, are you finished yet because I'm kind of in a hurry."

Reilly pocketed the empty cartridge, then straightened and jammed the inflated wheel into Julie's gut. "Put it on yourself." Then, she walked down the road, the cleats on her cycling shoes tapping out her annoyance.

Logan ran to catch up. "Hey, wait for me."

"God, she's rude," Reilly said as Logan moved in alongside her. "She didn't even thank us."

"Look." She pinched Reilly's shoulder, turned them around, and pointed to a speck moving west along the road. "If Julie is so concerned she'll be late for her lunch date, why is she riding away from the ranch?"

"And why did she lie to us?"

"She lied to us?"

"Who eats lunch at nine thirty in the morning?"

The outback was as still as a cemetery. Mid-morning, a few clouds rolled over, and a soft breeze stirred the ponytail that fell to Logan's waist. Basins of sand and rock gave way to forests of pine and larch, where deer and elk napped in the cool grasses. On several occasions, they sat on smooth boulders and sipped water. On one such break, Logan picked up a flat rock, yelped in pain, and flung the rock into the heavens. No less than half a dozen paper wasps had driven their stingers into her wrist, blistering her skin. After that, she stopped picking up the landscape.

She was inspecting her welts when Reilly offered her a consolatory chocolate bar. "You do know this stuff can ward off evil juju, right?"

"Yeah, but can it make me ride faster on Saturday? 'Cause if it can't, I say we go practice the course."

They continued to ride side by side until they came to a bend in the road, where Reilly pointed out a river winding its way through the rocks to the north. "Jake's map indicates the turnaround is near a river. That could be it. Let's go look."

"Fine by me, but you'd better take the lead. You know I'm hopeless when it comes to getting from here to there."

Back on the road, they pedaled their bikes at a snail's pace until Reilly spotted a fork in the road. Two hundred feet later, she turned right and sailed down a steep descent. Logan launched her bike likewise, joining Reilly at the bottom of the hill, where they soft-pedaled toward the turnaround, designated by an orange traffic cone.

Logan twisted around in the saddle and pointed back at the hill they'd plunged down only moments ago. "If this is the turnaround, we're going to have to climb that hill on the return leg. Doesn't that negate the hundred-foot elevation gain limiter for a record course?"

"It's less than sixty feet. More importantly, if we have to climb it, so does fat Julie. Let's ditch our bikes for a while and do some exploring on foot."

They pulled off the road, braked to a stop, and dismounted.

Reilly laid her bike behind a mesquite bush north of the orange cone. "We'll leave our bikes and helmets here so we can find them easily."

They picked up their water bottles and set off across a landscape of sand, shrubs, and rocks.

They'd walked a good quarter-mile when Reilly stopped. "Let's try and find the old stagecoach route."

"Did Jake give you that speech, too?"

"He tried to when he picked me up at the airport, but I started snoring. Nothing turns a guy off quicker than a woman who snores, and Black Bart is the kind of guy who needs a lot of turning off. What did I miss?"

"Wooden tracks, steel tracks, and a woman named Betsy in a place called Two Medicine." Logan pointed to the basin below them. "That valley is pretty open, an easy spot to lay down tracks. Let's find a way down."

They soon came upon a footpath that twisted through the rocks.

Logan shielded her eyes from the brilliant sunlight. "This path looks promising."

"My God, these rocks go on for miles. Why would a lonesome cowboy put down roots in such a remote spot?"

"Not cowboys, Native Americans. Jake and his family are Blackfoot. They pretty much came with the land."

"Maybe that's why they don't put locks on their doors. They don't like to be hemmed in."

"Maybe. Those rocks up yonder are the Canadian Rockies."

"Why does the Diamond Dust call itself a ranch? I've yet to see even one measly cow."

"And you probably never will."

"Why not?"

"Because the Erdes train cutting horses."

"What's a cutting horse?"

"Cutters are horses that like to work cattle."

"Work 'em how?"

"Round 'em up. Move' em out. Like people, a horse has its own likes and dislikes. If one shows a natural tendency to chase cattle, it's taught to separate a cow from its herd."

"How you gonna work 'em if you don't have any cattle to work?"

"Maybe they take them to the neighboring ranches for their final exams."

"How do you know so much about horses?"

"I spent my summers at my aunt's house in Colorado. She was an expert horsewoman, and I am too."

"Why do you ride a bike?"

"I prefer my own motor."

Reilly plopped down on the sand, pulled out a banana, broke it into halves, and tossed a piece at Logan. "What'd you do last night?"

"How do you know I did anything?"

"Because I walked over to your cabin to steal some peanut butter cups, and you were gone."

Logan had hoped to take her secrets to a lonely grave, but her arrival on the ranch had changed all that—changed her—and although she could hardly explain to Reilly what she didn't understand herself, it was long-past time to let her in—a little.

"I walked down to the stable and bumped into that tall stranger."

"Are you interested?"

"Yes, no… maybe… it's confusing… he's confusing. I'm not like you. Whether you care to admit it or not, you're settled in—cop, cyclist, fiancée. Some of us aren't so… well… so organized. In fact, some of us are a hot mess. Between cycling and figuring out what I want to do with the rest of my life when my racing career is over, I don't have any time leftover to bed-hop with any man—Mister Right or Mister Wrong."

"Is that why you're so aloof when any man shows an interest?"

"Partly."

"What's the other part?"

"Staying in one place scares me. Maybe that's why I chose this life."

"Want in on a secret?"

She nodded.

"It scares me too. Still, keep me posted on Mister Right."

THEY TOOK THE footpath that wound them down to the valley floor but uncovered no tracks—wooden or otherwise.

"We'll skirt the foothills so we don't get lost," Reilly said.

They ambled lazily along in a westerly direction until Reilly pointed toward a pinnacle in the distance. "Look! Doesn't that look like a staircase chiseled into those rocks? If we climb it, I bet we can see for miles."

They were within thirty feet of the staircase when Logan stumbled over a piece of wood half-buried in the sand. She went down on a knee and brushed away the sand to reveal a pine-tar-infused plank. "Hey, I found the old wooden railroad tracks. The Great Northern steel tracks can't be too far away. I'll keep going north. You check behind us."

It took Logan only six of them to locate the opening in a rock roughly fifty feet north of where they'd parted. She strolled inside, expecting darkness, but finding light and a set of scratched metal rails that wound east. Returning outside, she met up with Reilly.

"I found some steel tracks inside that rock."

"Show me."

"Oh, boy!" Reilly said when they stood outside the opening. "I love tunnels." She plunged inside.

Logan followed at a snail's pace.

Noticing Logan's discomfort, Reilly stopped and motioned her closer. "What's wrong?"

"This place stinks. Like a bazillion animals came in here to die."

"So? They're dead."

"What if some of them aren't quite there yet?"

"Then somebody is going to be somebody else's last supper."

Reilly vanished around a shadowy bend, leaving Logan running to catch up. When she did, Reilly reached into the pocket cut across the back of her jersey and brought out her holstered gun.

Logan filed in behind her. "What's that for?"

"I don't want to be anyone's last supper. Did Black Bart mention this tunnel?"

"He could've."

"I need more than that."

"That's something you should've considered before the faux-snoring."

A few twists and turns later, the tunnel widened, and the dim lighting that had accompanied them earlier yielded to brighter white light from overhead lamps. The polished white brick that lined this section of the tunnel intensified the effect to create a false daylight. The odor of decay grew stronger as a cooler breeze from deeper inside the tunnel rushed past them. Reilly plunged around the next corner, leaving Logan traipsing after her. Another fifty feet brought Reilly back into her view. Her friend stood off to one side, staring down at the ground. Logan crept forward, glancing from side to side until she slammed into Reilly's legs.

"What are you...?"

A blue metal rim jumped out from the white brick wall.

"Is that?"

Reilly nodded.

"Crap."

Reilly crept forward with Logan on her heels. A second wheel nosed up out of the gravel.

Reilly unholstered her gun, returned the leather case to her pocket, then took the grip stock in both hands. "Don't move."

She pressed herself against the wall. In front of her, Reilly recoiled in horror.

Logan sucked in a lungful of the foul air. "What is it?"

"Bad news."

She moved behind Reilly. "Oh, my God!"

Sticky pools of blood sullied the pebbles. More blood in the form of dribbles and dots sprayed the brick veneer. Still more had dyed Julie's white skin-suit a deep merlot.

While Reilly knelt down and checked for a pulse, Logan doubled over and vomited.

Reilly jerked Logan's arm and pointed toward the corner. "Take it over there. You're messing up somebody's crime scene."

She moved away as Reilly brought out a small notebook and began scribbling.

Reilly had been right. She'd wasted her time worrying about losing the championship to Julie. Somebody had already stolen that victory from their rival when he'd staked her Brobdingnagian thighs to a pair of discarded railroad ties.

CHAPTER 4

R EILLY RETURNED HER phone to her jersey. "Not enough bars. You stay here. I'll go back to our bikes and see if I can get cell service." "No way. You're the cop. You stay. I'll go."

"A cop out of her jurisdiction. We'll both go."

"What about Julie?"

"She's not going anywhere."

They were back at the turnaround before Reilly punched in her 911 call. Afterward, she collapsed beside Logan.

Logan took a deep breath, then another, as she tried to expunge the image of Julie's mutilated body from her memory, but every blink brought it back grislier than before. She threw herself backward, melting into the hot sand. "Who would do such a thing?"

Reilly shook her head. "And in such savage fashion. Sure, Julie-the-racer was petty, mean, and selfish, but what could Julie-the-person have done to warrant such a grisly ending?"

"We don't know anything about her life when she wasn't riding her bike. Where did she live? Did she live alone? Did she have a second job too?"

"True, but what little we do know suggests she was no angel in civvies either. By all counts, she was the face of the All-About-Me Foundation."

Logan dug around in the pocket of her jersey until she found a stale bag of Jelly Belly Sports Beans. She pulled it out, helped herself to a handful, and then passed the bag to Reilly. "They're leftover from Moriarty, but sugar and electrolytes never go bad, right?"

"If they do, I don't care. My head is swimming."

They munched in silence, passing Reilly's water bottle between them to wash down the sweet grit.

A quarter of a hour later, Logan shoved the empty bag back down into her pocket. "Did your eagle eye discern anything odd about the crime scene?"

"Julie's killer drove the spikes in at an angle, suggesting he stood directly over her."

Despite the heat of the midday sun, Logan shivered. "Yuck! Too much information. Do you think Jake will call off the race?"

Reilly shrugged. "Only the Cycling Federation can do that, and it's doubtful. Riders have died during a grand tour and still the race went on. Remember last year's Vuelta? The race organizers must have been high on sangria when they sent the riders out at night without lights in the pouring rain for a team time trial on the streets of Barcelona. If that's not an example of the show-must-go-on, I don't know what is."

"I remember. It's a miracle nobody got hurt. The race organizers dodged a cannon there. So what do we do now?"

"Wait."

The sun was high in the sky when Jake's dark truck crested the hill. Expecting someone more official, they didn't hide their surprise when he charged at them. "Where is she?"

Reilly pointed toward the cliffs. "In the tunnel where the tracks run. What are you doing here?"

"The sheriff's my cousin. He asked me to see to the witnes... you women." He glanced at the notebook Reilly pulled from her pocket. "What's that?"

"A few things I jotted down—when we found her, my impressions of the crime scene. Here." She passed it to him.

"When did you have time to do that?" Logan whispered.

"When you were donating your breakfast to the somethings."

Jake read through Reilly's scribbles, closed the notebook, and set it in the sand. "Did you…."

Reilly nodded. "I did. No signs of life. When you see her, you'll get it."

"My cousin is driving in from Two Medicine with the medical examiner, so it'll be a while before we can move her. I'll run you both back to main site now. By the time I get back, the ambulance should be here, and I can be on site to lend a hand."

Reilly picked up her helmet. "Won't your lawman want our statements?"

"In due time. Right now, we all could use a little downtime."

When Reilly claimed the back seat of the rear cab, Logan helped Jake secure their bikes inside the bed of his truck.

He gave the orange safety strap a vicious tug. "When I signed on to host this race, I never imagined anything like this would happen."

"I bet Julie didn't either."

As he fired up the engine, she set their helmets and shoes on the dash, buckled herself into a passenger seat that smelled of metallic fumes and his spicy aftershave, closed her eyes, and let the hum of the motor serenade her to sleep.

IT WAS AFTER noon by the time she and Reilly walked into the dining hall. Romeo sat at a table near the window. A gelid Rachel sat beside him, a thick book in her hand. She and Reilly joined Grant at a table near the buffet, leaving the chair to Logan's left empty. Allison thumbed through a glossy magazine at a side table, sipping from a bottle of Gatorade. The rest of Team Continental had gathered near the fire. Taylor sat on the hearth polishing her fingernails. Tim sat beside her, writing in a notebook. Fay stood by a window sipping coffee. A yawning Sydney had spread herself across the window seat. Jake hadn't returned yet.

Another quarter of an hour passed before a man in his early thirties strode past the gun cabinet and joined them in the main room. His tan uniform was spotless and fit snuggly across his lean form. A holstered Colt-45 six-shooter lolled on his thigh. He was tall like Jake, but where Jake's skin and eyes were dark, his cousin's were the color of a newborn fawn and his eyes rimmed in silver. He headed for the table where Allison sat and released a shiny iPad from a battered briefcase.

"I'm Chief Byrd," he said, his manner somber. "I'm very sorry for your loss, folks."

His commanding, yet compassionate, tone pinged a warm memory buried deep inside Logan. *"Friend, not adversary,"* her soul whispered. She held her breath and waited for something more to reveal itself. *A monochrome image of five grainy figures in diffuse shades of gray—from light ash to dark charcoal—galloped through the grasslands, unaware of her presence. She blinked, losing them in the harsh sunlight.*

He scrolled through a series of digital screens. "Here's what we've learned about your friend's death so far. Our medical examiner, Doctor Alexander, determined Miss Easton died from femoral-artery bleed out between ten and eleven thirty—give or take—given that she died in a cold, dank tunnel."

Reilly raised a hand.

"Yes, Officer Dawson?"

"How did you... uh, know...?"

Logan had never seen her friend so tongue-tied around a man before.

He threw Reilly a wink. "I do my homework too."

"You should know Logan and I fixed a flat tire on Julie's fancy bike sometime after nine, yet we didn't find her... er, find her body until eleven twenty-three."

"Did you remove her bike?"

"Are you accusing us of messing with your crime scene? Shame on you, Sheriff."

"Thank you, Officer Dawson." He scrolled to the next screen on the iPad. "To allay any rumors you may hear, Miss Easton's death wasn't accidental. It was cold-blooded murder. Her killer came prepared. He impaled her to the railroad ties, driving the spikes in at an angle so her arteries didn't close off. We found no prints on the spikes and no driving hammer in the tunnel, although our search is far from over. Doctor Alexander believes Miss Easton would've lost consciousness in thirty seconds, and she probably died within three minutes—a small mercy. Official cause of death is exsanguination—loss of blood."

The sound of a chair hitting the floor made heads swivel as Allison thrashed her way outside. When Slade slipped out of the shadows and went after her, Logan's heart went into its usual tizzy. They reappeared within minutes beside the gun cabinet. He guided Allison back to her seat, then lowered himself into the empty chair beside Logan. His closeness felt like a soothing balm on a festering sore.

"In addition to your own whereabouts this morning, I'm going to ask each of you to give me a snapshot of Miss Easton's life—her friends, enemies, interests outside of cycling. I'll take you one at a time in Griffin's office." He pointed to a room catty-corner to the buffet. "Officer Dawson?"

Reilly stood at attention. "Yes?"

"If you can spare the time, I could use another pair of trained ears."

His long strides made short work of the space between the buffet and the door to the office. Reilly followed him inside.

A short time later, Reilly reappeared and ushered a pale Allison into the office first. Julie's teammate was in and out in under fifteen minutes. As the afternoon drew on, and the buffet table remained empty, Logan pulled out her phone and scrolled around for a pizza joint in Two Medicine. Since she'd heard nothing about the status of the race, she assumed it was still on. For her and the other racers, it was business as usual. She'd already forfeited her breakfast. She couldn't afford to give up her lunch.

She was still scrolling when Griffin came out of the kitchen and set out a buffet of soup and sandwiches. As the rest of the cyclists returned from their morning rides, they poured inside the spacious room to claim tables and chairs. Logan hurried over to the buffet and filled a bowl with ham and cheddar soup, helped herself to a club sandwich, then settled in at a table alongside the fireplace. She'd scraped the bowl clean when Tim walked over with a slice of apple pie and a cup of black coffee in hand and took the seat opposite her.

He set the plate between them. "Care for some pie?"

She shook her head. "No, but I'd kill for that coffee."

He pushed the mug alongside her empty bowl.

"Thanks." She reached for the creamer and poured in a dollop.

"So, you and Reilly found Julie. Was she—"

She shifted uneasily in the chair. "Yes. It was awful. Poor Julie."

"Do you have any idea why she was in that tunnel?"

"Not a clue, unless she…." She seized up a spoon and plunged it into the coffee. "No, that's ridiculous. If only she hadn't been alone… then maybe…."

"Julie was alone because her lies, threats, and bullying had alienated her teammates. They flat out refused to have anything to do with her."

"Why did you let her get away with it?"

"Julie was our winner. Without her, we had no sponsor—no sponsor, no team. The other women's jobs were at stake, too." He cradled his head. "God, what a mess!" He lifted his eyes and stared into the dying embers. "You might think this callous of me, but you really have no idea what happened to her bike?"

She shook her head. "Of course not. Why would I?"

"Wishful thinking on my part."

"Is it that important?"

"Continental forked out upward of twenty-five grand to finish that prototype in time for Julie to ride at nationals. Now, they're breathing down my neck to get it back."

"Twenty-five thousand dollars? Is that because of its metal alloy?"

"Julie told you about that?"

"She didn't go into specifics."

"It's an al-you-min-ee-um titanium alloy."

"Doesn't Litespeed own the patent on Al-Ti alloys?"

"Owned—past tense."

"Is it true she designed it?"

"She told you that, too?"

"Bragged is a better modifier."

"I assumed its design was a collaborative effort, but I really don't know."

She gave her coffee a lazy stir. "Sorry, but I can't help you. I only saw the wheels before we… before Julie, and then… well, you understand why we were anxious to get out of that tunnel and call nine-one-one."

"Of course. Jake picked up the wheels for us, but it's the frame that's the real loss. It's not just the initial cash outlay that's worrying Continental. It's the future revenue the company expected to rake in. If Julie had won Saturday, Continental would've had exclusive rights to its design and fabrication. If the frame gets into the hands of another bike manufacturer, that revenue is lost. Promise me you'll come get me if you—or Reilly—find it lying around, okay?"

She assured him they would.

After he'd gone, she sat alone with his untouched apple pie and her uneaten sandwich until Reilly slipped into his empty chair.

"Apple pie!" She picked up the fork. "Yum. May I?"

Logan nudged the plate closer to the fork. "How's it going?"

"It's going. You're next."

She pushed back her chair. "You coming?"

"No, I'll sit this one out. I already know what you know. Besides, a girl has to eat."

"Help yourself to that sandwich too." She took a last fortifying swig of coffee and returned the cup to the table. "So?"

"So what?"

"Is he okay?"

"The sheriff? Oh, he's more than okay."

"How much did you tell him?"

"I'm a sworn officer of the law. I spilled my guts."

"How much do I have to spill?"

"If I tell you, that's cheating. I will say you're under no obligation to volunteer anything extra. Just answer his questions and keep in mind words like *yes* and *no* are perfectly acceptable. Tim paid you a visit. Anything there?"

"Not anything we don't already know. Julie's teammates pretty much hated her, and her fancy bike is still MIA—a fact that has Tim rattled."

CHAPTER 5

LOGAN RETURNED TO her cabin following her session with Chief Byrd. Slade waited on the bed.

She lowered herself onto the laundry hamper sitting to the left of the screen door. "Who is this woman to you? The one you think I am."

"You are my honored consort."

"Your wife? What happened to us... I mean to her... when we... before I came home damaged?"

"We were taken."

"Kidnapped?"

He nodded. "The sun enslaved me, and the moon...."

As her ordinary world began to unravel, she ran blindly out the door.

———

LOGAN HAD REACHED the end of the road when she caromed into Jake, coming out of the stable.

His arm lashed out and caught her around the waist. "Hey, beautiful." His hands moved to her arms. "Whoa... what's going on?"

She twisted sideways, broke free, fell across a bush, and gave up her soup. He reached for her, but again she wrenched free and crumpled to the ground.

He sunk to his knees, locking his arms at his sides. "Please, tell me what's going on with you... and why—"

She dragged herself farther into the bushes, vomited again, and then collapsed onto the dirt. She raised her head to a different world. *She'd stalked them for miles—he among them—from their lodge, through the woodlands, to the meadow of sunflowers, and now into the beargrass. They were three among many that had trespassed into her world—one destined not to return.*

She waited until her breathes came easy again before she walked back to the road. Jake stood where she'd left him. She fought down the nausea his closeness brought on. "I'm sorry. You were right—the stress of traveling... finding Julie. It was awful. I'm still a bit ragged."

"I can't imagine. Yours is not an easy life."

"It is, really. I live on my own terms, make my own schedule, spend my days outdoors. As long as I do what Grant tells me to do and win some races, the people who sign my paychecks stay off my back. How many account executives can say that?"

"We've a lot in common, coming from different worlds and all." He brushed a handful of stray hairs from her cheek. "Feeling better?"

She flinched and grit her teeth. "I'm getting there. Mind if I wander around?"

"Knock yourself out. If you turn right at the fork down yonder, you'll run into our greenhouse and apiary. It's presses up against the mountains. Will I see you at the dance tonight?"

"Is it still on?"

"Is that wrong?"

"I assumed the Federation would cancel the race, and you'd cancel everything else, but Reilly told me the Federation rarely cancels an event."

"I was able to convince them Julie's death had nothing to with their championship or my ranch. Besides, we've got a contract, and they're bound to honor it."

LOGAN SLIPPED INSIDE the barn. Her rubber-soled sneakers made no sound on the hard concrete. Since her last visit, someone had tacked brightly colored *parfleches* onto each stall door, freshened the hay on the floor, and placed a well-oiled saddle on the bench.

She moved back outside and walked across a treeless meadow, working her way over decaying stumps and lumps of granite to a babbling river. The slate-blue waters sparkled in the bright sunshine. A rocky shoreline mapped its tumultuous passage, and centuries of turbulence had honed the boulders smooth. She crawled up onto one of them, stretched out, and fell instantly asleep.

THE HISS OF the waters banished her carnal dreams, and she shook herself awake. Tugging off her shoes and socks, she waded into the river. The water was freezing, and she lost her footing. She threw out her hand to keep from going under. As she pushed herself back up, her fingers closed around something flat and smooth.

The piece of metal looked like half a brake pad from a bike. A silvery substance coated the edge. She crouched down and ran her fingers through the silky loam. They came back covered in a silvery dust. She pocketed the pad, wiped her hands on the soft denim of her jeans, and made her way back across the meadow with a strong wind at her back and billowy clouds circling overhead. She'd covered half the distance when Slade grew up in front of her. The sun's sudden disappearance left her shivering in her wet clothes. He removed his *capote* and wrapped it around her shoulders.

She smiled up at him. "For all my life, the moon has terrified me."

"Your escape has angered the Old Woman. She still hunts you."

"Maybe we could stop skipping the first chapter. Tell me about us... you and your wife."

"I will show you where we began."

She held out his coat. "Your *capote?*"

"Keep it. I have no need for it now. You are with me."

She had a difficult time matching his furious pace. When he lead her through a maze of boulders, the tip of her sneaker jammed into a bough half-buried in the rocks. As the river rushed toward her, she braced herself for another icy plunge, but he reeled her in and twisted her around until their faces were only inches apart. Foolishly, she reached up and touched his cheek. Once again, his face buckled with pain.

She pushed herself away and scrambled into the nearby grasses. "My God, I'm sorry. Are you okay?"

"It will pass." He sank beside her.

She fell back and gazed at the clouds. "You are the only man whose touch does not sicken me, yet ironically I'm the woman who causes you pain."

"You have escaped the moon, but the sun still claims me."

"Claims you—in what way?"

"In all but one. Come."

He led her to a field filled with sunflowers bending in the wind. "This meadow is where you chose me."

"We met here?"

"No, over there." He pointed toward the forest. "You brought me back to life."

Pole trees—standing stiff and tall like wary sentinels—blanketed the edge. *She'd left the safety of the forest to patrol its edges, to hunt where many of their kind often wandered—some too ignorant to realize the danger, others too arrogant to acknowledge it. Hunting had been difficult at first. Her innocence had made her an easy target, had forced her to bend to their will—until the end came. Only then did they realize too late she was the hunter and they the prey. The difficult had become easy. The thrill had faded to the point where she now took only enough souls to sustain life in the forest, nothing more. As she studied the warrior with his markings of strength and courage, she felt a soul on fire—a soul like her own. She would have him, not for one night, but for all eternity.*

His fiery eyes explored her icy ones. "You once told me you could not take me against my will. Only after the passing of many centuries do I understand your words. Now, I must wait, and you must choose."

"Choose a man? But I can't... I don't want... I'm not even sure I'll ever...."

"Your otherworldly logic is of no use to you here, *Nuttah*. You are a child of this land. Do you not hear the soothing whispers of the wind? Feel the strength of the granite seeping into you? You are also its guardian, the daughter of the Enchantress and her guardian, the Blood Warrior. The responsibilities of that guardianship fell to you when your mother perished, only to be suspended when the Old Woman conspired with the moon to steal you from your homeland. Now, the shamanic power of the land is melting the ice that has imprisoned your heart for centuries. The balance... our timeline must be restored. As you revert to your true self, your allure will heighten, drawing men of strength to you. When your need to mate overrides your desire for solitude, you will choose."

"And if I don't mate?"

"Do not waste what little time remains arguing something you can't stop. Your preparedness is of no consequence. When the need consumes you, you will not resist, nor will he."

As the sun slid out from beneath the clouds, his face froze. "Go. She must not know of us." Turning on his heel, he darted into the forest.

When the pines had claimed the last of him, she made her way up the road, trying to forget about the man with the golden eyes and the lost world he lived in.

She almost succeeded.

LOGAN SAT ON the bench in the courtyard keenly aware Saturday's race had fallen off her radar.

"Mind if I join you, *sha*?" Taylor lowered herself on the opposite end. "I'm expecting an important call. I'd be lying if I said I didn't need to get away from my weepy teammates. The manner in which Julie died is awful, not the fact she died."

Jake's sudden appearance at the fire pit made Logan bristle. As he knelt to stack his kindling, he raised his head, and their eyes locked. His indolent smile rolled out, but as his dark eyes lit on his brother's capote, his smile vanished.

Taylor squinted at the display on her phone. "I'm sorry you had to be the one to find her."

"I'm sorry, too, but I imagine it's worse for you—the uncertainty of what happens next."

"Are you kidding? Julie's death is the best thing that could've happened to us as a team. Her arrogant stupidity had torn us apart. She couldn't get it through her skull cycling is a team sport—and oh, my Lord—you have never met a more overbearing woman."

"Wasn't that part of her job as captain?"

"Maybe, but did she have to bully us? Reilly doesn't ride gunshot over you."

"You expect me to believe you and the others were sacrificial victims to the cycling goddess Julie Easton? What could Julie have done if you'd refused her?"

"Ruined my career, the same as she did to poor Allison."

"Ruined Allison's career... how?"

"She threatened to tell Tim that Allison had doped. That's the kind of shenanigans Julie pulled when she didn't get her way."

"That's not bullying, that's blackmail. What did Allison have that Julie wanted?"

"Winning time trials wasn't enough for Julie. She wanted to be queen of the road races too."

"How did her teammates feel about that?"

"We were against it. When it comes to strategy, nobody is better in the longer races than Allison. She has the uncanny knack of knowing when to go solo and when to let the peloton do the work. Moreover, she has all the skills necessary to pull it off.

"Did Julie have actual proof Allison had doped?"

"She didn't need any proof. Once she'd made up her mind to get rid of someone, she'd plant the seed in Tim's mind, then stand back, and watch it grow. Tim's terminating Allison's contract at the end of the season."

"Julie followed through with her threat?"

The lyrics to "Pretty Woman" jumped out of the phone. Taylor lunged for it. "Hello. Yes. Hang on a sec, okay?" She turned to Logan. "Do you mind? It's the call I've been waiting for. I'm pretty sure they're going to offer me a contract to model for Sapphire Rose."

"Really?"

"You disapprove?"

"My opinion doesn't matter. I'm just wondering why an athletic clothing mogul would offer a major endorsement to a relative unknown. You've never come close to winning a race, let alone an important one like nationals. In the world of product endorsement, women have always taken a backseat to men, and sports like ours—cycling, skiing, swimming, even skating—have traditionally taken a backseat to mainstream sports like golf, basketball, and tennis. Look no further than Mikalea Shiffrin. She's won gold cups for years, yet it wasn't until she'd elevated herself to GOAT status that she finally won a long-overdue Espy. Maybe if you win nationals…."

Taylor stalked off, her phone thrust out like a dagger.

Logan picked up the *capote* and strode off, stopping at Reilly's cabin on her way back. Her friend was in bed, tapping on her laptop.

She set the brake pad on the nightstand. "I found this by the river. Maybe it's from Julie's bike."

"By the river?"

"Okay, in the river."

"I'll get it over to the sheriff after I finish these background checks."

"Whose lives are you snooping into today?"

"Everyone's."

By the time Logan had stepped into her cabin, the sky had darkened to deep amethyst. Collapsing onto the bed, she picked up a brochure Jake had left behind on the nightstand. The rainbow-shaped bookmark claimed the library in Two Medicine stayed open late weeknights. She performed her nightly ritual of switching on every lamp in her cabin, traded in her soiled blouse for a clean T-shirt, shucked off her sneakers, and curled into the warm bed, hating her stranger for disrupting her solitary world.

THE FRAGRANCE OF fresh rain mingled with that of his smoky scent. She opened her eyes. He sat on the edge of the bed. Once again, thick gloves protected him from her touch. His closeness made her heart ache.

"You will choose tonight."

"Tonight, but the moon… I can't… it's too dangerous…."

He set his hand on hers. "On the dark side of midnight, the north celestial pole touches Polaris, pushing the sun and moon to their greatest limits. The moon will be too far away to claim you. You may enter this night without apprehension and form the immortal bond with the man of your choosing."

She looked away. "How do I find you?"

"Your heart will find mine."

"What about the sun's claim on you?"

"Come to me when she sleeps. When she awakens tomorrow, it will be too late."

Twenty minutes later she hopped behind the wheel of her Jeep and began the long, solitary journey to discover a mother, father, and husband she couldn't remember and wasn't sure she wanted to find.

CHAPTER 6

THE VILLAGE OF Two Medicine incorporated a sizable main street and a few truncated side roads. A hydroelectric dam sat on its southern boundary. An inland lake on its northern side led to the mountains. Main Street came with a hodgepodge of nineteenth-century New England clapboards, twentieth-century Victorian charmers, and twenty-first-century glass boxes catering to tourists—an ice cream shop, an over-the-top kitchen shop, and a huckleberries-R-us shop, which offered everything from huckleberry-flavored jerky to huckleberry-spotted teapots. Logan squeezed the Jeep into a parking spot underneath a streetlamp and made a quick pass over the weathered planks linking storefront to storefront and ending at the covered bridge overlooking the dam waters. Slipping a penny from her pocket, she closed her eyes, made a wish, and tossed it into the swirling stream. It wasn't the Fountain of Trevi, but it would have to do.

PETER PAN ALL-GROWN-UP sat behind the librarian's desk squinting at a computer monitor. A few coquettish ringlets of blond hair flirted with his graying sideburns, while the scowl on his face pursed his pink lips like a tulip unwilling to bloom. The nameplate on the desk read Peter Panama.

Her approach sent the scowl packing. "May I help you, ma'am?"

"Yes, I'm interested in the culture and traditions of the Blackfoot."

"Here to find your roots?"

"How did you know?"

"The sadness in your smile, the wariness in your eyes, the longing in your face—seen it in the pictures of your ancestors. Sometimes knowing helps folks feel grounded. Some even stay."

"And the ones who know but can't feel?"

"They run. Belonging comes with much responsibility." He crooked a finger at her. "Come with me, and we'll see what we can do about it."

He set off through a maze of shelving. She followed behind him, trying not to step on his heels when he stopped. He slid a book from a shelf and pushed it her way.

When the stack in her arms reached her chin, she tapped his shoulder. "We can stop now—thanks."

From the depths of a cushy chair by the fire, she switched on a reading lamp and lifted the top book. Tales of past centuries filled its pages in prose too cryptic for her to unravel. The second book dealt with killing buffaloes and warring tribes. The third described the dreams of tribal leaders the night before they went to battle.

A thin yellow paperback stuck out from the bottom of the pile. An inked sketch of a chieftain in full feather illustrated its cover. The preface suggested it was a primer for children of the tribal lodge. The author had organized the lessons chronologically in a manner similar to the Old Testament with each one encapsulating a moral code. The first lesson told of the Old Man and Old Woman sent to the Blue Planet to establish the *Order of Life and Death*. In a partnership, the husband had the first word, his wife the last. The Blackfoot called this *first* and *second say*. The explanation of the *Order of Death* was more complicated, covering in a few pages what she summed up in one sentence—death was necessary for compassion to exist in the world.

The Old Man and Old Woman had begot five sons. As a reward for their good deeds, the Great Creator had given them eternal life, ironically sparing them from the *Order of Death* they'd designed for their kinsman. When the Old Man's days on the Blue Planet were over, he joined with the sun. When it was her time, the Old Woman joined with the moon.

The caption "Lynx Woman" headed up the second legend. Logan read through the narrative once, then combed through it again, digesting every word. The Lynx Woman was an enchantress who'd lived on the lands now known as the Diamond Dust ranch. She appeared as either a beautiful woman or handsome man hunting for the souls of young warriors and maidens. Why she needed—or wanted—souls was anyone's guess, as no mortal had ever returned to the lodge to tell the tale. The message of the parable was simple—*stay out of the woods after dark.* The story didn't reveal the fate of this enchantress, nor did it mention a Blood Warrior husband or a daughter with an immortal soul.

She scooped up the books and made her way back to the front desk and Peter. "Would you look something up for me?"

"That depends. Look it up where?"

She pointed to the computer. "A Blackfoot word."

"Sure thing." He flexed his knuckles, manned the mouse, and pointed and clicked, then clicked and pointed, as he waited for the worldwide web to unclog. "Okay, ready when you are."

"*Nuttah.*"

"Shucks, don't need to fire up nothing for that. Means *my heart.*"

BACK IN THE cabin, Logan took her umpteenth shower of the week, wrapped herself in towels, and returned to the bedroom, stopping short at the sight of Slade sprawled across her bed. Unwinding the towel from her head, she released her dark hair to fall untamed to her waist, while she skipped her chilly eyes along his sultry form. His overbearing magnetism left her little room to breathe let alone think. She gave him a wide berth and perched on the hamper.

"If you choose me, our lands will be your world, not the one through which you move now. My life shall continue along the path destiny chose for me, and I will return to my status as your guardian, but in order for the Great Creator to grant us a second timeline together, you must believe. If you do not believe, yet choose me for your own reasons, the consequences will be dire."

"If I believe but choose someone else?"

He rose from the bed and moved beside her. Despite the heat he brought with him, cold shivers racked through her.

"I can't predict your fate with another man, other than my brother. Jake has ties to both your present world and our past world and your current time and our past time. If you do not wish to forfeit that which you have worked so hard to achieve, you would be wise to choose him."

As he slipped through the door, she felt a pain in her chest so sharp she thought he'd driven a knife into her heart.

Just before six o'clock, Logan walked into Reilly's cabin.

"Right. Yep. Sure." Reilly signaled her to sit then returned to her caller. "You'll let me know? I'll be there soon. Yes, until Sunday. My plane leaves Glacier at eleven. Yes, she is. Yes, I've got your number. I'll call if I learn anything. All right. You, too. We'll talk tonight. Bye."

"So?"

Reilly punched the end-call button.

"Was it Julie's brake pad?"

"With her bike still missing, we don't know. The sheriff sent it to the police lab in Missoula for analysis. He expects the results back tonight." She shrugged. "Maybe we'll get lucky, and they'll find something."

Logan pushed aside a pile of towels and stretched across the bed. "We?"

"The sheriff deputized me."

"You're kidding!"

"I am, but I'm part of his investigation."

"A good part?"

Reilly laughed.

"What does he have you doing?"

"Background checks, informal interviews."

"How informal?"

"All right—he's got me snooping."

It was Logan's turn to laugh.

Reilly's expression grew sober. "Hey, you okay? You seem oddly happy and sad at the same time."

"I'm happy the championship is almost here. The fun of oversleeping and overeating day and night is wearing thin. Which reminds me, can I steal a Diet Coke?"

"My *casa* is *su casa,* besides you know that stuff tastes like blackwater swill to me."

She heaved herself from the bed, made a beeline for the refrigerator, tossed Reilly a Mountain Dew, and helped herself to a Diet Coke.

Reilly placed her unopened can on the nightstand. "Still feeling a bit rocky?"

"Julie was my first dead body. Yours?"

"A drunk—oops, an alcohol-challenged woman. One stormy night out by the old McCarron Airport, I came upon a wee lass passed out on the side of the road. She died in the ER an hour later from alcohol poisoning."

"Obviously you haven't forgotten."

"No, but I heard some people do."

"And those of us who don't?"

"Go to therapy."

She blew out some stale air, bounced off the bed, and returned with a second Diet Coke.

Reilly waggled a finger at the can. "Hey, go easy on that stuff. I need you lucid tonight."

"Why tonight?"

"How would you like to help us?"

"What can I do that you aren't already doing?"

"Listen. People open up to you. If you need any proof, look no further than Tim. In ten minutes, you learned more from him than either of us learned from the rumor mill in eight years."

"Does this mean we're both off the sheriff's naughty list? Because in the mysteries I've read, the good woman unlucky enough to stumble upon a bloody corpse is the first person the bad cop locks up."

"My credentials practically guaranteed me a pass, and you must've made a good impression because the sheriff gave you one, too."

"I suppose it wouldn't hurt me to listen. Am I listening for anything in particular?"

"I trust your judgment, but remember you're an information broker, not a detective. Don't ask too many questions, and for God's sake, don't seem too eager. If you rattle the wrong cage, more bad stuff could happen."

She tossed her empty cans into the wastebasket. "I ran into Taylor this afternoon. She went out of her way to tell me Julie accused Allison of doping."

Reilly's face flew apart. "That's absurd. Why would Allison do something stupid like that? She's closer to retirement than we are. Besides, only idiots dope, and Allison isn't an idiot."

"The way Taylor tells it, Julie tattled to Tim, and now he isn't renewing Allison's contract with Continental for next year. Talk to Allison before you go running to the sheriff with something that probably isn't true."

"I will, and if Allison tells me what I already know, that's the end of it." Reilly grabbed shampoo and soap from her cosmetic bag and moved toward the bathroom, stopping short to point at a stack of papers on the bookcase. "You're not running off, are you?"

"I wasn't planning on it. Besides, I've pretty much run off to everywhere there is to run off to on this ranch."

"Do me another favor and take a look at that background report I put together on Tim, then tell me what I don't know."

Logan waited until the sound of splashing water drifted in from the bathroom before she picked up the top sheet. According to Reilly, Julie's coach Tim Richard hadn't existed until December 2009. *And here's some more weirdness,* Reilly had penciled in. *Tim doesn't have a criminal record, driver's license, or voter-registration card in any state.*

"Hey, wake up—girlie."

Logan stretched herself awake.

Reilly tousled her damp hair. "So, what do you think about Tim?"

"There's only one thing to think."

"He's a fraud?"

"He's a ghost."

Reilly throw a pillow at her. "Thanks for nothing." She pulled a blue sheath from the makeshift closet.

Logan let loose with a wolfish whistle. "Too bad you're gonna waste that on Jake's cousin."

"Oh, he's not such a waste." Reilly dared to pick up her gun.

"Tell me you're not packing a pistol to a barbecue."

Reilly stuck out her tongue, shoved the gun underneath her dress, and checked her reflection in the mirror.

She returned the papers to the bookcase. "We know one thing about Tim."

"We do?"

"He was either raised in Europe or spent time in the U.K. He says aluminum like Grant does—*al-you-min-ee-um.*"

THEY MADE THEIR way to the dining hall in a companionable silence. Slade waited for her on the porch bench. Reilly gave him a long look and a pleasant smile before she vanished inside, leaving Logan alone with him.

"If I am not her—this woman you think I am—and I choose you, what will happen?"

"I will die."

She slipped in beside Reilly just as Grant reached them.

"Logan, Reilly—can I have some time with you tonight?"

Reilly smiled. "You can have Logan right now. I've got other plans."

Logan smiled up at Grant. "Let's go grab us a table, and you can tell me everything about life as an international coach."

As soon as they were out of sight, Reilly took the shortcut through the kitchen, out the back door, and onto the courtyard. The sheriff sat at a picnic table pushed close to the fire pit.

She sat across from him. "Any news?"

"Good evening to you too." He stood up, moved to her side of the table, and pulled her back up on her heels. "Plenty of night for talking. I've had one grueling day, and right now, I'm as hungry as a bear waking up from torpor."

They spent a happy ten minutes at the buffet dishing up grilled steak, roasted potatoes, spiced squash, baked fish, and buttered cabbage before they returned to the picnic table.

Reilly cut into a piece of steak as thick as a two by four. "I've been meaning to ask you, has anything like this ever happened up here before?"

"How much do you know about this place?"

"Other than what's on the brochure, not a thing."

"Jeremy doesn't own the Diamond Dust. It's tribal land. He and my cousins manage the ranch, as well as several other businesses, for the Blackfoot Confederacy, made up of Kainah, Piegan, and Siksika tribes. With that said, our lands and waters have sopped up their fair share of spilt blood but nothing unjustified like what happened today, if you don't count the wholesale slaughter of my ancestors."

"I'm sorry."

"So am I, but we can't change a past that didn't belong to us."

"Yet a loss like yours—one so horrific it weaves its way into your soul—still stings, even after all the time that has passed. The 'what-ifs' are gut-wrenching." She ran her fork through the puddle of mashed squash on her plate. "Julie's death was the polar opposite. You'll be hard-pressed to find anyone who felt that way about her or thought they didn't have a good reason for wishing her gone."

"I sensed as much this afternoon, along with a genuine feeling of relief."

"So, let's start somewhere else. What kind of strength does it take to drive a steel spike through flesh and into a railroad tie?"

"You looking to eliminate someone?"

"It would make your investigation easier."

"I'm comfortable with letting Sydney Long go but only because she's sick. I've seen itty things like her and her teammate Fay White haul tree trunks four times their size up mountains, shoot a bear with a bow and arrow from thirty yards, and paddle a canoe through whitewater. You ladies may be the fairer sex, but that weaker stuff is bullshit."

"You travel in interesting circles."

He laughed. "We also need to consider the possibility Julie's killer wasn't working alone."

"Well, don't that beat all. We've barely dipped our toes in, and you're already muddying up the waters."

Their plates were clean when the sheriff pulled a shaft of paper from his briefcase and set it between them. "That doodad Logan found is two plates that form one half of a cantilever brake. Take a gander at the second page."

She set aside the top sheet to expose a lab report. "The outer plate is carbon and vanadium, the inside plate Babbitt metal. I remember reading something about Babbitt metal in one of my gun books. It's used to reduce friction, right?"

"Mostly used in bearings. Lab boys said they've never run across anything like that carbon-vanadium blend before, nor could they find a company that made it."

"How did Julie's sponsor come by it?"

"We don't know it fell off her bike yet."

"Then try her mechanic. He might recognize it. What about these diamond crystals mixed with aluminum granules? Where did they turn up?"

"Around the edges. It could be road residue from the brake striking the wheel rim."

"Did you check the wheels?"

"They disappeared, too."

"They didn't disappear. Jake returned them to Tim. Your cousin is a real go-getter, isn't he?"

"A murder in his backyard isn't good for any of his businesses."

"How many does he oversee?"

"The cutters, some logging interests, Jeremy's artwork, some investments in Two Medicine, your race—which he'd hoped would be a stepping stone to bigger things—mining, of course."

"Don't tell me the Diamond Dust includes a diamond mine."

"No, aluminum. The ranch supplies the local plant with its raw materials, which in turn processes them. You visited the stable?"

"Haven't had the time."

"Jake cooked up some deal with the aluminum plant that stipulates they can take it off our lands in return for finished goods, like the load of aluminum-alloy cylinders they brought in to expand the corral. My uncle and cousin use diamond-bladed saws to cut them up. I suspect that's where the diamond crystals came from."

She was pouring out coffee when Jake stepped onto the flagstones. "Got a second, cuz?"

The sheriff lumbered to his feet. "Stick around. This won't take long."

JAKE HAD FADED into the dusky night, when the sheriff returned. "Finished?"

"Where's the lab report for the Kleenex?"

"What Kleenex?"

"In Julie's jacket."

"She wasn't wearing a jacket underneath all that blood. Didn't find one at the scene either. Jake and Joe scoured the tunnel."

"Joe?"

"My deputy Joe Amundsen."

"I don't see anything here about a blue backpack either."

"Hang on." He pulled his phone from his pocket and made a couple of punches and taps. "Joe, it's Reko. Round up some cowpunchers and go back to that tunnel. Yeah, a blue backpack... hang on...."

"Yellow—her windbreaker was banana yellow."

He returned to Joe. "A bright yellow windbreaker."

She licked butter from her fingers. "Reko, huh?"

"My father was a Norseman who never went home. Ready for dessert?"

"What'd you have in mind?"

"Hand-turned ice cream. My treat."

"It's about time you bought me a milkshake, shamus."

CHAPTER 7

L OGAN TOSSED HER dirty clothes underneath the nightstand and replenished the pocket of her windbreaker with spare tubes, CO_2 cartridges, and candy bars. Then, she flopped onto the bed and thumbed through a wildflower field guide until her vision blurred from the tiny print. Moving toward the door, she draped his *capote* over her arm and headed outdoors.

She skirted around the stable, stopping to admire the red, white, and orange blossoms that had turned the wall into a floral canvas, then continued her walk along the rocky shoreline next to the river, until she came upon an orchard of dwarf apple trees. The cold front Grant had warned them about had settled in. Its chilly nip had already bleached a few leaves yellow.

The orchard left off at a labyrinth of granite terraces filled with wild irises and glacier lilies. A staircase led to a glass house set into the side of a mountain. The simple architecture consisted of a vaulted rectangle with a kitchen on one side and a bedroom on the other. The walls were interlocking panes of glass and French doors.

She trespassed up the staircase and pressed her face against the glass. The room was a blur of pale woods and soft leathers in shades of green and honey. A staircase tucked away in the corner led to a suspended catwalk. She laid his coat on a lawn chair and fled back to her cabin.

She shed her casual jeans for an off-the shoulder party dress and slipped her feet into a pair of heeled boots. On her way out, she switched off every light in the cabin except the one on the nightstand. She took a circuitous route around to the courtyard, where she found him sitting alone on a bench waiting for the sun to die. She lowered herself beside him, then—for the first time in her life—watched the moon rise without fear.

"What did you mean if I don't believe the consequences will be dire?"

"You are lost to me forever."

"And if I believe but choose someone else?"

"Without purpose I will vanish from this timeline."

LATER, SHE SLID back the doors to the dining hall, crossed inside, and careened into Jake. As the familiar queasiness bubbled up, she extricated herself from his embrace. "Sorry."

"Save a dance for me?"

She shook her head. "Early night for me."

With a tip of his Stetson, he sauntered away. When he turned right at the hallway that lead to the kitchen, she skirted the dance floor and dashed out onto the front porch.

The dogs were waiting for her by the bench. She made good on her promise and stroked their soft fur until movement among the trees sent them bolting into the woods after some hapless prey. Brushing off her dress, she stepped toward the stairs as Sydney Long appeared around the corner. The girl's diaphanous salmon dress and unsteady gait gave the impression of an intoxicated Alice in Wonderland.

Logan leaned against the railing. As Sydney grew closer, the glow of the porch light fell on the angry red streaks that now ran the length of her arm and the dull eyes that stared listlessly into the darkness.

When Sydney tripped over the last step, Logan rushed forward, caught her around the waist, and guided her to the bench. "Are you all right?"

The girl didn't answer.

"Have you seen a doctor?"

"Tired." The girl's voice was as unsteady as her gait.

"Do your parents know you're sick?"

She shook her head. "Uncle Tom."

"Tom Drake is your uncle?"

"He didn't warn me. Forced out." Her head dropped to her chest.

"Sydney."

The girl surrendered a few ragged breaths.

She wrapped her arms around Sydney's sagging shoulders. "Come on. I'm driving you to the hospital."

"Uncle Tom should do."

"Give me his phone number, and I'll call him. He can meet us."

"He said he was sorry."

"Sorry for what?"

"She bullied me." Her head lolled sideways as she fell into a fitful sleep.

She gave Sydney's shoulder a gentle shake. "Wake up."

As the girl swayed forward, Logan swept her up and hurried inside.

JAKE DANCED WITH Allison on the far side of the room. When he caught sight of Logan cradling the unconscious Sydney, he ran over and gathered up the sick girl. Mercifully, somebody switched off the loud music, and a hush descended on the room.

"How long has she been like this?" he asked.

"Unconscious—minutes. Sick—days."

Rachel emerged from the crowd to join them. "Take her to my cabin."

"Take her to the hospital," Logan protested.

To her disappointment, Jake followed Rachel out onto the courtyard.

SHE STARED UP at the overhead beams in her cabin when his long shadow fell across her bed. Once again, her heart began its wild dance.

She took in the exotic angles and curves of his face. "Tell me what I need to know about you."

"I am the man who has searched for you in every woman's touch and has lain with no other woman since your skin first touched mine." Turning his back to her, he strode toward the door and gripped the knob until his fingers shook. To look at her for the last time was too much to bear. "I am sorry you do not feel the magic of us."

"But I do," she said when only his heat remained to torment her.

THE NIGHT HAD drawn down when she returned to the dining hall and looked out at the dancers—Jake wasn't among them. Perhaps his absence meant he'd reconsidered and taken Sydney to the hospital. When her head began to ache, she turned on her heel and all but ran toward the front door. She'd passed the gun cabinet when a man's voice floated past.

"We dance, please?"

She turned around. Romeo leaned against the buffet.

"Cortland Krause." He made a sweeping bow.

"Logan. I'm afraid...."

"Shh." He rushed over, lifted her hand, and planted a kiss on her palm.

The touch of his lips seared into her skin. She wrenched away and jumped out of his reach, watching the shock of her rejection undermine his confidence. *Drawing men of strength to you.*

"You are not pleased with me?"

"Not pleased with *the* Cortland Krause—the cyclist who still owns the record for both the individual and team time-trial events at the Pan Am Games?" She smiled at him. "In another place, at another time, I'd be thrilled at your attention—but right here and right now, Reilly will use me for target practice if she sees us together."

"Your Reilly has noticed me?"

She laughed. "Notice is an understatement. You'd stand out at a convention of male models."

His face brightened. "This is a good thing. Reilly is free—yah?"

"Reilly is never free. Available, now that's a possibility. If you're interested, I suggest you take it up with her."

He gestured her to the window seat across from the fire. "Please. We sit, and you tell me about this possibility."

She went with him but kept her distance, lowering herself onto the hearth as he sprawled across the seat.

His head cocked to one side. "How good is this possibility?"

"Pretty good. Reilly dumps men like a Labrador sheds—messily and continuously."

"She has recently shed someone?"

"I can't say for sure, but the signs are there."

"What do you advise?"

"Ignore her. It'll drive her right into your arms."

"I don't understand."

"Reilly fancies herself a modern-day Annie Oakley."

"Ah, she likes the shooting."

"She likes the romance."

"I am a patient man. I wait."

"Your self-control with Julie this morning was admirable."

"Many—I among them—are relieved she no longer perpetrates her wickedness on others, but her deeds, although vile, did not warrant such a cruel ending."

"I understand she claimed credit for your design," she lied.

"When I have the bike back in my possession, a wrong will be righted." He studied her legs with frank interest. "How do you feel about Saturday's race? I trust Julie's death will not disrupt your focus?"

"You trust right because, along with everything else, I put my focus on a holiday last Monday. It's part of my pre-race routine. Why?"

His lips parted into a sheepish grin.

"Did you bet on me?"

"A small wager. As you are aware, the mechanic for the winning team gets the lion's share of the prize money. Without Julie, I must look elsewhere for my money. Yet, even if Julie were alive to defend her title, I would still put my money on you. I have followed your times on the circuit. They are within two minutes, regardless of the course. You eat, but you do not overeat. You ride with purpose, but you do not let your emotions dictate how you ride. You are disciplined and methodical. Julie was not any of those things—not on her bike or in her life."

ROMEO HAD LEFT her to shake his booty with Taylor by the time Jake slipped in from the courtyard and joined her on the hearth.

"Hey, beautiful."

She managed a wooden smile. "How's Sydney?"

"Rachel put her into an ice bath to reduce her fever."

"Damnit! Those welts on her arms suggest Sydney may have a *staph* infection? Her life is at stake." When she jumped up, he did, too, blocking her escape.

He pointed to the window seat. "Sit down and let me explain."

She retreated to the hearth.

"Our hospital is in Plains—three hours south of the ranch through some very rugged terrain—not a journey for a woman alone. I gave Rachel and Tim a spare set of keys to the trucks. It's their mess. Let him handle it."

"Sydney is little more than a child, still in need of a guiding hand. How can Tim not see that?"

"It is a rare man who sees a woman the way another woman does— women being what they are. Most men are immune to suffering unless it's their own."

How could a man sound so insightful and so utterly chauvinistic at the same time?

"Well, thank you for trying to help." She pointed at the dance floor where Allison swayed in the arms of the man with the diamond stud. "Who's that man with Allison?"

"Davis Morgan. He works with my brother." His eyes slid sideways. "I saw you with Slade in the courtyard this evening. If you're thinking of making any kind of permanent arrangement with him, you might brush up on our tribal law. If he dies, his wife belongs to his brother in every way she belonged to him."

Belonged—suddenly that word terrified her.

SHE RAN A hand across her forehead. It came away damp, and although the heat of a thousand fires burned within her, she shivered. When she tried to stand, her legs slid out from underneath her. She crawled onto the window seat, hoping anyone who noticed would think she'd drunk too much of Griffin's hard lemonade. It was happening just as he had told her it would.

She managed to haul herself up on her next try. Using the wall as a crutch, she'd moved as far as the buffet when Grant hurried over and caught her around the waist. Nothing happened—nothing unpleasant.

"Blimey, are you okay?" His gray eyes flickered over her face. "My God, you're as pale as chalk. You didn't catch Sydney's bug, did you?"

"A temporary setback. I'll be ready to race on Saturday—guaranteed. Have you heard anything?"

"Tim, Rachel, and Sydney are on their way to hospital."

"That's a bloody relief. Did Tim call Tom Drake?"

"Why would he?"

"Drake is Sydney's uncle."

"Blimey! I had no idea."

"It seems to be a well-guarded secret. Do you know why he quit so unexpectedly?"

"This life is not for everyone."

"Yes, I'm beginning to understand that."

"Having second thoughts about coaching?"

"I've barely had first thoughts about it. Why did you stop racing? Was it because you lost your competitive edge?"

"Worse—because I almost lost my life. A car skipped lanes around a blind corner. I dumped my bike and hurled myself down the embankment. It was the best move I ever made off a bike. When you're sitting in a wheelchair with a titanium rod in each leg, you see the world for what it is, and then you see that maybe how you've fit yourself into it isn't your best option. Coaching let me keep the best parts of this life and jettison the worst. I still ride my bike most days, still travel the world, and still feel the thrill of victory whenever you or Reilly win a race, but I do it from the comfort of the roadside with a cup of Joe in my hand and—best of all—pain free."

"You never get lonely?"

"Of course I do, but it passes—and for all the beds I've slept in—I have yet to find my forever bed."

Suddenly exhausted, she let go of a yawn.

"Come on, gorgeous, off to bed with you."

She pulled out of his grasp. This wasn't right. He wasn't right.

"Tomorrow's time trial promises to be grueling."

She stopped, blinked, and whirled on him. "Time trial—what day is it?"

"You haven't heard?"

"Heard what?"

"Jake is having a go at a mock time trial in the morning. He's not leaving anything to chance. What's more, he seems more nervous about this race than the racers." He gathered her into a cozy embrace. "Hmm. Your scent is intoxicating."

Suddenly, she was wide awake. "We had planned on interval training tomorrow. I'd better go tell Reilly. See you in the morning—and thanks for everything, Grant."

She left him standing by the gun cabinet with a look of longing on his face.

SHE STUMBLED INTO Reilly's cabin and threw herself onto the bed, her heart racing, her thoughts jumbled. "Jake scheduled a mock time trial for tomorrow morning."

"Best news I've had all day. I'll take a race any day over anaerobic intervals—they hurt." Reilly stopped tapping on her laptop long enough to run a critical eye over Logan's everything. "Hey, what's wrong with you? You look like death warmed over. Did something happen tonight I should know about?"

"Nothing yet, but I'm running out of time, and I need you to listen to me."

Reilly set the device on the pillow. "Now you're scaring me."

She gave it to her word for word as Slade had given it to her.

Reilly eyes grew wider throughout her spiel. "Holy cow! You and the slinky stranger—a match made in heaven. Who'd have thunk it?"

"Destroyed there too."

"Geez Louise, and I thought my love life was complicated."

"Now you understand why I'm so uneasy around men and so circumspect with you. How could I explain what I didn't understand myself? I still don't, but I have no choice other than to believe him. Do you think I'm crazy?"

"My time at the academy taught me everyone is some kind of crazy— your kind I can work with. Let's cut to the chase. Do you love him?"

"My heart aches when he leaves the room."

"Close enough." A tear slipped down Reilly's cheek. "Is this goodbye for us?"

She gathered Reilly into a bear hug. "Heck no. My *casa* is always *su casa,* and I'll even throw in the Magic Chef. After tonight… well, I needed to warn you in case I'm different in the morning."

"If you aren't, I'll be disappointed. That's the power of love." Reilly made shooing motions. "Now get, girlie—before somebody turns into a pumpkin."

Four of the horsemen scattered into the wind, leaving her golden-eyed Warrior alone and vulnerable. She seized her chance and entered the meadow, running freely and openly toward him. The first arrow grazed his horse's withers. The second dug deep into her Warrior's leg. As he fell to the ground, a third arrow sunk into his shoulder. As she reached him, she fell upon him, covering him with her nakedness, willing the next arrow to take her too.

She awoke drenched in sweat.

A gentle rain fell out of the heavens as she stepped from the cabin. Overhead, the moon and stars had vanished altogether, rendering the night pitch-black. She ran down the road, past the horses, to the rocks along the river. When they started to whirl about like frenzied dancers, she squeezed her eyes shut to make them stop. The next time she opened them, she was clawing at the swirling waters trying to escape the invisible force sucking her into its deadly abyss. She awoke in a puddle on a bed of wet rocks consumed by an unbearable sense of emptiness. She couldn't go on breathing without him. She staggered to her feet and ran blindly into the forest.

She hesitated outside his bedroom and pressed her nose against the glass—drinking in the man she was destined to spend eternity with, watching the shadows of candlelight dance across his sleeping form and tint his coppery skin burnt sienna. Why had she ever doubted him?

Only a man truly in love would have sacrificed and endured as he had for a woman he'd barely known in one lifetime and didn't know at all in another. Yet, he was still willing—no scratch that—he was still eager to love and protect her on faith alone. The time had come for her to give him what he'd waited a millennium to possess, to give herself what she'd waited a lifetime to share.

She cracked open the door. He was asleep—his fiery eyes shut away, his dark hair splayed out over the pillow, his chest rising and falling in a gentle rhythm. Slipping noiselessly inside, she stripped off her dress and slid under the bedcovers, inching as close to him as she dared. The air hung heavy with his virile perfume.

Dizzy with desire, she freed her heart from its icy prison and reached for him. His eyes flickered before her image blurred.

A small band of Niitsitapi warriors painted in the black-and-yellow strips of his enemy flanked him—one on the edge of the forest, two in the meadow, one biding his time along the river. Whoosh! Snow Runner crumpled beneath him, falling out from underneath him. Pitching forward, he twisted sideways, hitting the bloodstained grass with a gut-wrenching jar. Whoosh! Whoosh! He scrambled up—whoosh! A sharp stab rendered his right leg useless. Still, he ran, dragging it into the tall grasses. Whoosh! The force of the arrow as it dug into his shoulder blade flipped him onto his back. As his world began to darken, then narrow to a blurry dot, he opened his eyes for the last time. Better to look into his enemy's eyes and die with honor than to slither away like a snake.

His eyes snapped open, then blazed as they swept over her naked form. He grabbed up her hands, clutching them tightly, imprisoning her in his bed. "I must warn you. If you do not truly love me, our immortal bond will not be restored, and we will both die."

She moved on top of him and touched her lips to his. "I am certain, dear husband—neither of us will die tonight."

He was powerless to stop his body from responding to her touch, from surrendering to her pulsing rhythm as it had done a millennium ago.

CHAPTER 8

GARISH SUNLIGHT AWOKE her from a dead sleep. She groaned herself out of bed, fished a Diet Coke from the refrigerator, and drank it standing by the window looking up at the heavens. The sun's bloody scowl was the only reassurance she needed—they'd triumphed. She drew the curtains shut to banish the hapless troublemaker and padded groggily into the shower, feeling like something the cat couldn't be bothered to drag in. Afterward, she tugged on his suede shirt and dared to look in the mirror. A radiant woman with eyes the color of Columbian emeralds and skin tanned to golden honey stared back at her.

"Who are you really?" she asked her other.

IT WAS AFTER six o'clock when she joined Reilly in the dining hall.

"If you're what bewitched looks like, I want some."

"Does it wear off?"

"Not if you're lucky." Reilly disappeared into the kitchen but returned shortly with a carafe of hot coffee and large earthenware mugs. "Today's race is practice, mostly for Jake and his crew. Grant will understand if you want to opt out."

Logan rubbed her throbbing temple. The pain grew stronger. "I've never missed a start, and I'm not going to mess that up now. When do we go off?"

"Me, eight thirty—you, eight thirty-six."

While they breakfasted on English muffins, cottage cheese, and honey, she told Reilly about Sydney's relationship to Tom Drake, as well as Jake's refusal to run a background check on Griffin.

"In this day and age that's a crime, even if it does involve your nearest and dearest. How'd you get from Magic-Chef-in-the-kitchen-with-a-naughty-cake to Julie-in-the-tunnel-impaled-on-a-railroad-tie?"

"You told me to listen. This is me listening."

Reilly brought out her notebook. "Anything else?"

"Sydney said her uncle was forced to quit."

"Forced?"

"Maybe... so, okay, I'm not really sure, but while she was fighting off the fever from hell, she let go of 'forced out,' 'uncle,' and 'he didn't warn me' almost back to back, and the only 'he' in all her gibberish was Tom Drake."

"You said she was hallucinating."

"I said she was feverish. You'll look into it?"

Reilly brought out her phone. "I'll send the sheriff a text right now."

Raised voices drowned out the tapping sound of her finger as it punched the keypad. Romeo and Tim stood at the buffet engaged in a very public argument. The flare-up died as quickly as it had started with Tim storming outside.

Logan clutched Reilly's arm. "Put that away. We've got company."

The sight of Romeo's muscular physique bearing down on them brought out Reilly's wicked grin. "Oh, my! Dibs on bad cop."

"Dibs on Invisible Woman."

He slid his tray onto the table without so much as a "howdy-do." "May I join you?"

Logan pulled out a chair. "Please do."

He turned his still-flushed face on Reilly. "I apologize for barging in on your private meal, but I must speak candidly with you."

Reilly had the decency to wait until he'd unloaded his plate of omelettes before she pushed her I-can-legally-poke-my-nose-into-your-beeswax badge in front of him. "To us."

His heavily lashed eyes fell to the badge. "Very well. It is about my friend Theo. You know him as Tim Richard."

"If you're going to tell us he's not Tim, we're already there."

"But do you know who he is?"

"No, we aren't that far."

"His German name is Theo Pritchendorf—P-r-i-t-c-h—"

Reilly held up her hand. "I don't mean to be rude, but Logan and I have a race to get to, so we'd appreciate it if you'd skip the spelling bee. Or, if you prefer, we can do this another time in my cabin."

"No, we will talk now, as Theo refuses to speak for himself—but before you and I exchange words—I must have your assurances the big sheriff will not prosecute Theo for something that happened more than a decade ago for a reason too many Americans take for granted."

"Which is?"

"The freedom of a man to choose his own future."

Reilly shook her head. "I'm not the big sheriff's mouthpiece. My job is to uphold the law—not make it—and certainly not interpret it. Neither he nor I have the authority to give anyone—particularly someone who had broken our laws—any guarantee or leniency. I can however promise I'll do my best to help your friend out of the mess he's gotten himself into, as long as his mess has nothing to do with Julie's murder."

"I will accept your terms." He drained half the orange juice from the glass still on his tray.

"You know I am from Germany, yah?"

"The notion had crossed my mind, yah."

"It is so. The year was 2007. I was barely out of gymnasium, a young pup on a bike. Theo was more seasoned with his certificate from *hochschule*. We meet at our national camp for athletes in Munich to exhibit our skills. The government selected us to the national cycling team. We were flattered. Our sponsors assigned us to the same living quarters. It is here Theo and I become good friends.

"Our time in the sport was not the era of independent thinking. German coaches designed for us a very regimented program—what we eat, when and how we train, even when we must sleep. Lights out at nine o'clock. Me—I questioned nothing. Theo—he questioned everything. We perform very well. Theo thinks too well. He convinced himself the medical staff had drugged us, either through our meals or injections."

"Drugged, as in given you performance-enhancing pharmaceuticals?"

"Theo believed so. As I said, it was a different era in cycling—in all sports. Late in 2009, we race in the Tour of California. We are excited to go to America—Theo excessively so. The night before we leave for America, he tells me he is not returning to Germany."

Reilly's hand shot up. "Stop right there. If you're going to tell me you helped him defect, I'm warning you to shut up. I don't relish the idea of arresting you for aiding and abetting a fugitive."

"If you view hiding a duffle bag a crime, then I plead guilty."

"That depends. What was in it?"

"I don't know. I didn't look."

"That's all you did—hide a getaway bag for him?"

"I cross my heart."

"I'll pretend I believe you. What happened next?"

"Theo told me little, and as a racer myself, I focused on my effort. Later I was to learn he'd done it on the final stage—a serpentine time trial down the Big Sur coastline. You know of it?"

"Only in a motorcar."

"It takes away the breath of the tourist, for sure—but the biker is aware only of its dangers—the sharp twists, hidden corners, treacherous drop-offs. The road—it is too narrow—and the crowds too heavy and pushy. I was high in the standings—third place—so I went off late. Theo's slight build rendered him a good climber, but the race of truth was his nemesis. He started a good forty-five minutes ahead of me. Somewhere after the second checkpoint, he disappeared."

"Off the course?"

"Out of existence. The police found his team bike in a consignment shop in Santa Monica the next day. Puff! Theo is gone. I did not look for him, as he did not wish to be found. I returned to Germany and served out my remaining year on the national team. Afterward, I rode for AlpzinerCorp in Europe for many years. I did not return to America until after I am through racing. Theo and I—we meet again at Continental—only this time, he uses the name Tim Richard. He, too, no longer races his bike. Instead, he makes the rubber tires and metal parts."

"How many years passed?"

"Too many to count."

"I'll rephrase it. Your immigration papers are dated 2015, your declaration papers for naturalization are dated 2 May 2020—which leaves a six-year window between your first crossing to America and your second. After that, Tim would presumably have no idea how to contact you. In these six years, did he ever get in touch with you?"

He grinned. "You catch me out. Yes, it is so. He sent for his notebooks."

"What notebooks?"

"The ones he left behind."

"You sent them?"

"Yes."

"Where?"

"I don't remember."

"He made no other attempts to contact you?"

"Attempts?" He shrugged. "This I cannot speak to—successful attempts, yah—only the one time."

"Never again?"

"I tell you *no*. You call me a liar?"

"We'll skip the name-calling. Then a month ago, Tom Drake quit his job, and you show up as his replacement."

"I see the vacancy for a mechanic, and I apply. They hire me because I am very good at what I do." He took a fork to his omelette. "I have nothing more to confess."

"Really? Because from this end of the table, your memory seems to be on the fritz. Could it be you forgot Tim told you Julie had uncovered his secret and was blackmailing him? Or perhaps it was more basic than that. He came to you to fix his problem, which you—as his loyal friend—did—permanently."

The corners of his mouth turned down. "Your accusations sadden me, but I can say nothing more other than your mistrust of my character is not an ideal beginning to our beautiful friendship, but for now it must be so."

"Why is that?"

"Because you and I, we hit a sticky patch in the road, and I must plead my American right to silence."

"STICKY, STICKY!" REILLY slapped her notebook on the table. "The nerve of that guy evoking his inalienable right to clam up when I associated Julie with the B-word!"

An awkward silence slipped between them as Romeo left with his plate of cold omelettes to join Grant and Simon, now seated at a table near the window seat.

"Oh, I don't know." Logan dumped cream into her coffee and then swirled it vigorously. "For a former cycling deity, he's done a pretty good job of masquerading as a mechanic."

"Masquerading?"

"How many pro-athletes do you know that have switched from racing bikes to fixing them?"

"What other skills does he have? There's nothing in his background to indicate he went to any university or trade school. Maybe fixing bikes is the only way he can earn a paycheck."

"What about the years he rode for AlpzinerCorp? He was a world-record holder—still is. A cyclist of his caliber must've signed a lucrative contact after the national team cut him loose."

"Two decades ago a cyclist's salary was half what it is now, if that. Or it could be he just likes the life, traveling for free…."

"Save it. Grant gave me that homily last night." Logan drained the last drop of coffee from her mug. "What are you going to do now?"

"Ride my bike. You coming?"

———

Trading sneakers for cycling shoes, they set off for an easy pedal along the main roads of the ranch. Three-quarters of an hour later, Logan unloaded one of two trainers she'd packed from home and tossed Reilly the keys to her Jeep. While Reilly drove off to set up the other trainer closer to the starting box, Logan remained behind and set her trainer up in front of Simon's van. She mounted the bike, pulled out Grant's warm-up script, and began working her way through his intervals, shifting gears and cadences to elevate her heart rate to target levels.

She'd barely worked up a sweat when Grant strolled out of his van and headed her way. "By Jove, don't you look grand. Feeling as good I hope."

"Right as rain. How's Jake holding up?"

"Like an expectant father." He tossed her a handful of energy gels. "Rein in your engines this morning. Hold something back for Saturday."

"You got it."

He took a step back toward his van, pivoted, then circled around to Simon's van. "Crikey! Me mind's a jumble. Your start time's been bumped up a minute. Julie's out of course, and Tim scratched Sydney. Her prognosis is bloody awful."

"How awful?"

"She's got sepsis. Her doctor suspects blood-doping—but on the cheery side, she's in with a small chance."

"Do you have any idea who helped her?"

"Who said she had help?"

"It's virtually impossible to bleed yourself into a quart-sized baggie without help. How well do you know Tim?"

"Well enough to say your implication is absurd."

———————

LOGAN CHECKED THE brake pads on her bike for clearance and tires for air. Satisfied with the space between the pad and metal and hardness of the rubber, she cradled her helmet, shouldered her bike, and set off toward the starting box. She'd taken only a handful of steps when Simon blasted out of his van, leapt off the landing, and crab-walked her way.

"Hang on, girlie. Catch me up."

She laid her bike on the gravel. "What's up?"

"Saw you and Reilly cozying up to pretty boy this morning. Got somethin' for him."

He pressed a fistful of crumpled papers into her hand.

"Why me? You cozied up to him too—over your porridge."

"Got better things to fill me time with than playing postie."

She looked at the mess in her hand. "Are they important?"

A vein in his forehead bulged. "Can't say. I ain't a snoop like some. Found 'em crammed underneath me microwave. Pretty boy don't know Drake and I swapped vans."

"You and Drake were mates?"

"Drinking buddies is more apt."

"Do you know why he quit?"

"A man's got a right to his privacy. 'Sides we all got dreams."

She jammed the papers back into his calloused hand. "Well, pretty boy will have to wait until after Jake's race. Be a peach and stuff those papers into my carryall, pretty please?"

He wrestled one of Jake's carryalls off the bottom step.

"Not that one." She pointed to an identical bag on the top step. "That one is mine."

He crammed the papers into the side pocket and grumbled off.

"Hey, you hanging around for the race?" she called after him.

"Heck no," he growled. "Got better things to do with me time than stand around and watch you manhandle a bike."

SHE WAS WITHIN twenty feet of the starting box when she leaned her bike against a convenient oak tree and lifted her helmet onto her head, getting an unwelcome shock. The clip on the strap was gone. She cursed. The bloody thing had worked fine on her morning ride. She ran through her options—beg, borrow, steal—or forfeit her time and go back to bed.

She peered down the roadway. Fay White stood behind the check-in table, straightening a row of boxes. Grabbing up her bike, she tapped her way down the tarmac.

"Hi, Fay."

"Hi—checking in?"

"That depends." She held up her busted helmet.

"Helmets are mandatory."

"Got any extras back there?"

"No, but you can use mine."

"You're not racing this morning?"

"Nope, Tim grounded me." Fay ducked underneath the table.

The official's tent stood a few feet from the finish line. Jake stood alongside the timing strip as the melodious voice of a second cowboy erupted over the sound system with the next rider's name, finishing time, and current standing. Jake caught her eye and gave her a thumbs up. Logan acknowledged him with a smile. A couple more cowboys stood just inside the vestibule clutching pale-blue carryalls. She glanced at her watch—T-minus four minutes. Her nerves spiraled up.

Out on the course, Reilly's turquoise jersey bobbed in the distance. In the starting box, Allison's friend Davis Morgan held the seat post of Rachel's bike, while Allison stood at the foot of the ramp awaiting her turn behind Logan, leaving Taylor as the last racer. On the ground, Fay's hiney inched backward as she hauled back a Diamond Dust carryall in each hand.

T-minus two minutes.

Fay straddled the first bag between her legs, pulled back the zipper, and peered inside. Her eyes grew impossibly wide, and her jaw froze. She zipped it halfway, tossed it aside, grabbed up the second bag, and pulled out one of Team Continental's blue, silver, and black helmets. "Here you go, but I'd better warn you—Jake can disqualify you for using another team's gear."

She clipped it in place. "I'll chance it. It's only practice—and thanks. You're a lifesaver."

SHE STREAKED PAST Allison, positioned her front tire behind the start line, and clipped into her pedals as Davis's hands closed around her seat post.

"Five... four... three... two... one... you're off."

The ramp was a blur. The moment her front tire hit the blacktop, she positioned herself along the length of the top tube, tucked in her elbows and knees, and rested her hands on the handlebar drops. Her eyes homed in on the horizon, while her fingers worked the rear-cog shifter on the right drop, clicking the lever in and out of easier or harder gears to keep her heart rate from soaring into its red zone as she maintained a steady cadence. When the gnarly turn before the turnaround came into view, her timer flashed 24:47—twenty-three seconds ahead of her goal. The fifty-four front gear was bang on. Just short of the turnaround, she tapped her brakes, folded her inside leg into a *V*, and coasted around the orange cone. Clear, she straightened her leg, clicked into a more difficult gear, sprinted up her cadence, geared up, settled back down into the drops, and climbed. She'd no sooner crested the top, when she dropped the chain into a more difficult gear and reclaimed her comfortable rhythm. She cruised into a third-place finish, less than four seconds behind Reilly's second-place time. Taylor placed fourth, and Allison finished with the best time—fractions of a second ahead of Reilly.

While Grant handed out packets of recovery gel, Jake—binoculars hanging from a strap around his neck—hovered, checking the sound system, timing strip, and overhead banners. Logan avoided him, washing down one of Grant's coffee-flavored gels with water from the cache he kept on ice in a cooler across from the finish line. Fay was nowhere in sight, and the check-in table was packed away in the bed of Jake's Ridgeline. She left Fay's helmet with Grant to return, shouldered her bike, and moved beneath the oak tree to do her post-race stretches.

She was into her final cobra, when Jake hunted her down, gripping a Diamond Dust carryall in one hand and a clipboard in the other.

"Great ride, beautiful. Given any more thought to a meal together?"

"I have, and I'm sorry if I misled you, but there never will be an *us*—for any meal or anything else."

Leaving Jake with his mouth agape, Logan bounced up from her stretch, hoisted her bike, and searched out Reilly, standing beside the Jeep loading the trainers into the cargo bay. She'd just slammed the door shut when Logan strolled up and racked their bikes in the cage—Reilly's on the inside peg, her own on the outside.

"Fabulous ride," she said. "Whatever you're doing, keep doing it."

Reilly's laugh was lighthearted. "Thanks. You, too. Like I said—*way-more-trained-up* is a good thing."

"Yes, it is. We can both go into Saturday's race with a lot of confidence."

"Include Allison in that 'we.' This is the first time trial she's won in years. She's usually bottom twenty."

"She's probably way-more-trained-up, too. Want to hit the hot tubs?"

"No can do. *Siesta* then lunch with the sheriff." Reilly's eyebrows lifted in a Groucho Marx leer.

Logan burst out laughing. "Where does this leave the gambler?"

"With a two-nine off-suit."

SHE COOLED DOWN underneath a tepid shower, combed tangles from her hair, and tugged on her bathing suit. When she opened the screen door, he backed her up onto the bed, and she melted into his heat.

CHAPTER 9

A SHORT STROLL past Reilly's cabin brought Logan to the hot tubs. With the male cyclists still on the course, dozens of females splashed about in various stages of undress. Every so often shrill laughter cut through the high-pitched buzz. She draped her towel alongside a vacant tub, climbed inside, and dipped underneath the water, groaning with pleasure as the strong sprays kneaded her spent muscles. As she broke the surface, Allison's tear-stained face stared back at her. Julie's teammate had traded in her team kit for a cranberry swimsuit that created a long, smooth line between her broad shoulders and slim hips. The blond ringlets curling around her face made her look more like a graceful ballerina than a formidable cyclist.

Logan scooched closer. "Hey, why the tears? If Jake's race is any indication, you're peaking at the perfect time."

Allison burrowed her head into the folds of a thick towel. "We cheated."

"We? You and who else? You're the only one sitting on the saddle. Besides, that's impossible. The sensor that records the moment your front tire breaks the electrical current is invincible."

"We didn't... me... mess... with my... fin... finishing... time."

"You didn't. Well, that's good to know. The only other way you can cheat is to bribe an official, but there wasn't one to bribe this morning.

Oh, I see. Jake made a mistake. He penciled another rider's time into your slot, and you didn't say anything."

Allison brought her face out of the towel. "It wasn't any of those things. Davis sent me down the ramp early."

"How early?"

"About forty seconds."

"And nobody noticed?"

She gave her head a hard shake, sending her curls airborne. "Not even Tim. Every racer but Taylor was already out on the course, and as usual, he was all over her. Maybe y'all figured I wasn't a threat, that I wasn't going to do well. Whatever the reason, I wasn't on anyone's radar. Getting away with it—well, that was the easy part. Everyone—riders, coaches, officials, and spectators—assume a racer goes off at her designated time. Davis knew Jake hadn't designated anyone to check the exact second I went down the ramp."

"Jake followed protocol, and in informal races like this one, the counter and holder are usually the same guy."

Allison's blond head bobbed. "Exactly why we knew we could pull it off—if Davis could wheedle his way in as the holder. The only time anyone notices a racer go down the ramp is if she's late. Most everyone listens to the counter. They don't watch the clock. I told Davis he'd have a minute to play with between your start time and mine. So, he let you go on the button at eighty thirty-five then went right into my ten-second countdown."

"Giving you more like fifty seconds than forty. That's like loping a quarter-mile off the course. Cheating to win a race is so unlike you. Whatever made you to do it?"

"Julie."

"Julie is dead."

"She wasn't when we planned it."

"Was this your revenge because she told Tim you doped?"

"You know about that?"

"Taylor told me. She also said Julie had no proof, but despite that, Continental didn't offer you a contract for next year."

"Davis overheard Julie and Tim arguing about it Tuesday night after supper. Tim believed her."

"So what? He has nothing to take to the Federation but Julie's trumped up words. You'll never get falsely suspended on that alone. The way things stand now, you're finally free to sign with another team—get yourself into a better situation. Riders come and go—change teams—on a yearly basis."

Allison sucked up the last of her sniffles. "Does Reilly know?"

"She knows Julie accused you, but we both know you'd never do anything as stupid as recycle your own blood. The risk of infection is enormous. Was that all Davis overheard Tuesday night?"

"He said there was more, but it had nothing to do with me. I'd taken a lot of guff from Julie over the years, but her doping accusation was the last straw. Davis and I decided to get back at her where it would hurt the most—her ego. She might've been the reigning national champion, but even she couldn't overcome a big time deficit. Can you imagine how livid she'd have been if I'd beat her Saturday? Jake's mock time trial was the perfect opportunity to try it out before the championship. If Jake had busted us, Davis could simply say he'd made a novice mistake."

"Yeah, but again, Julie isn't racing Saturday."

"I know, but Davis said we should try it anyway—see if we could pull it off." Allison fisted away leftover tears. "What I didn't figure on was feeling this badly afterward. I want to tell Jake, but Davis says if I do, he could lose his job."

"If this morning's race was the real deal, I'd haul you in front of Jake myself—but it wasn't. It was practice and mostly for Jake and his crew. My advice is to tell Davis to ask Jake for a different assignment on Saturday and then ride your best and see if you can win legitimately."

"I hoped you'd say that because Davis is really going to need his job after we're married next weekend."

Married. She hadn't seen *that* coming. Yet she could hardly condemn Allison for throwing over her career for a man she'd known less than a week since she was about to do the same thing for a man she'd known only one night.

She gathered Allison in for a hug. "I'm thrilled for you, but what's the rush? Think about it. If this man you're about to marry cheated so you could win a mock race, could he have killed the woman trying to destroy your real career?"

"Gosh, I'm pretty sure Davis wouldn't do something like that."

"Pretty sure? If I were in your shoes, I'd want to make damn sure."

"Are you going to tell Reilly about the cheating?"

"No, because you're going to tell her."

"I will. I promise, first chance I get. Thanks for believing in me. It means a lot." Allison scooped up her towel. "I better go eat. If you've got some free time after lunch, can we meet again? There's something else I need to tell you. Something that happened years ago."

"Does it involve Julie?"

"How'd you know?"

"Because none of us will get back to anything that feels normal until her death is resolved. How about we meet up on the courtyard around one o'clock?"

"Works for me."

BACK IN HER cabin, Logan turned in her swimsuit for a pair of tangerine shorts and a comfy sweatshirt, shoved her feet into flip-flops, and headed out to snag some downtime from murder, mayhem, and men.

It wasn't to be. Cortland Krause sat on a picnic table in the courtyard. When he saw her, he waved her over.

She pointed at the covered dishes on the table. "What's this?"

"I had Griffin prepare a special lunch to make amends to your Reilly, but it is a wasted gesture. She is with the big sheriff, yes?"

"Yes, but gluttony aside, you won't get anywhere with her if you pull another stunt like the one you pulled on her this morning."

"But I speak the truth. Did I say wrong?"

"You didn't say enough. Nobody throws his friend underneath the bus without an ulterior motive, and you can bet Reilly won't rest until she uncovers yours. If you're serious about making amends, start with me. If I believe you, I'll put in a good word with Reilly on your behalf."

"What is it you wish to know?"

"Start with where you were yesterday morning."

"In my van, tuning bikes."

"Maybe that's where Reilly deposited you after Julie gave you that very public slap, but that's not where Julie found you a half-hour later. In her version, she went to your van because the shifters on her new bike wouldn't shift. You weren't there, so she took it to Simon."

"Julie is still alive when you find her, and she tells you this?"

"She told Simon when she dropped off her bike. He told us when Reilly and I went to pick up our bikes."

"I caution you not to believe the words of Julie Easton. It is true, I did leave, but only for a few minutes and only to visit with Theo. He is worried I am overextended. A day turnaround between Jake's event and the championship leaves no room for error."

"What kind of error?"

"If I need a part, there is no time to get it. Now it comes true. We are down one bike."

"Somebody crashed?"

"Guy Young steered his bike into a rock. His crumpled front fork suggests he didn't swing sharply enough at the descent before the turnaround. He must've sailed straight into a boulder." He shrugged. "Perhaps his brakes locked up. It happens. He is most fortunate not to be crumpled himself. If he is concussed, his chance of a medical clearance before Saturday is iffy."

"That's too bad, but let's say I believe you...."

"Let's say... you accuse me of lying too?"

"I'm not there yet. So okay, you *saw* Tim early Wednesday morning—that still leaves a big window unaccounted for." She snatched up her plate. "But right now, I don't have time to play cat and mouse with you. Not only am I not good at it, I'm starving. I've got thirty minutes left on my ninety-minute post-race clock to refuel—so, let's eat."

With the pent-up excitement of grade-schoolers on a field trip, they peeked under the lids at Griffin's offerings before choosing one of his half-pound hamburgers. The tantalizing aroma of roasted onions, mushrooms, red peppers, and melted cheese made her mouth water. Cutting her sandwich in half, she munched happily as he loaded his plate with potato chips and house salad—a concoction of mixed lettuce greens, raw onion rings, and sweet gherkins topped with bits of diced ham, Swiss cheese, and hard-cooked eggs.

Crunching her way through her own mound of chips, she studied the landscaped beds bordering the flagstone courtyard. Thorny raspberry canes hid patches of mint and strawberries, and red-breasted robins jumped in and out of the bushes chirping for gratuitous crumbs.

"Before I forget, Simon gave me some papers for you—papers he found in his van. He said they belonged to Drake, so you should have them. They're in my cabin. Come get them after my nap. As for Reilly, your only hope now is to play it straight with her, and then maybe she'll let you beg her for a first date."

Logan banged through the screen door into the kitchen. Griffin sat at the counter, prodding the keyboard on a laptop with a chocolate-smeared finger.

"Mind if I mix up some chocolate milk?"

"I will fetch the syrup for you." Disappearing into the pantry, he returned in short order with a gallon of chocolate syrup. "Are you and the handsome mechanic enjoying my food?"

"Your special hamburger is incredible."

He beamed. "Perhaps you'd like another piece of my special chocolate cake for dessert?"

"I won't say *no*." She moved to the refrigerator and poured milk into a large glass.

"You are always welcome here, my dear—particularly now that you are part of our household again."

"About that. I don't see us doing anything differently, do you? Unless you want to, of course."

"Should I think of something, I will run it by you first."

"I'm sure that's not necessary, but it's sweet. Thank you for making me feel useful."

While she mixed swirls of chocolate into the milk, he cut her a generous slice of cake and set it beside her glass. "Are you pleased with your race this morning?"

"Very."

He clapped his hands. "Then all goes as planned."

"I'm glad you feel that way." She kissed him lightly on his cheek and left with her cake and milk.

A SHORT TIME later, she returned to the kitchen with her empty plate and glass. Griffin was no longer there. She stepped back out on the courtyard, gathered up the rest of their dirty dishes, stepped back inside, and dropped them into the grimy sink. Then, she went back to the courtyard to wait for Allison. She whiled away the time eating cherries from a bowl filled with finger fruits. When the cherries were gone, she started on the grapes.

"I won't betray Davis."

She turned around. Allison stood behind her, half hidden by a planter box. She'd exchanged her red bathing suit for a pink eyelet blouse and skinny jeans.

Allison moved to the bench and helped herself to a strawberry. "How much do you know about Julie's past?"

"Not a thing."

"Well, you know how dangerous our sport is."

"I do."

"And you know how stubborn Julie was."

"Actually, I don't. The only time we saw each other was at a race, where I only saw the determined side of Julie—followed by her backside when she beat me."

"Well, you have my word that Julie was very stubborn. Look no further than the way she manhandled her bikes—big chain rings, low cadences. After twelve years in the sport, it's a medical miracle she has… had any knee joints left. As far back as I can remember, Julie never listened to any coach, even as a junior cyclist, and that included any sports doctor who dared tell her how to ride her bike. She either muscled her way to a win or fell off the peloton—the big loser. On our long races, she demanded we do most of the work to make her look good—even then she rarely won. She was great at time trials but awful on climbs and breakaways." Allison chewed nervously on her polished lips. "Remember the Tour of Idaho?"

"Sure I do. It was touted as America's grand tour for women."

"Well, one of our veterans got herself pregnant and quit midseason. The team signed this terrific climber as her replacement. She was young and without much experience riding in a peloton. To make it worse, the course featured some steep drop-offs without a sniff of a guardrail or embankment. That day we were in the mountains, and as I'd already pulled Julie halfway up one long climb, I'd dropped off the back. Boy, was I whipped. The newbie was up next, but Julie couldn't keep up with the girl's relentless pace, not with those big gears she favored. Her legs must've been screaming because I remember watching her rock from side to side as she fought to hold her line. Wheels crossed, a bike skidded off the road, and the young girl flew over the handlebars." Allison's voice grew sad with remembrance. "God it was awful. Coach said she broke her neck and died instantly."

"Are you saying Julie bumped the girl's bike intentionally?"

Allison shrugged. "It's also possible the newbie panicked and locked up her wheel."

"But if she'd braked too violently, she would've fallen over on the road with the bike on top of her and her feet still clipped into the pedals—not off a cliff."

"I agree that's what usually happens, especially on a steep hill when there's little time to clip out, but the only thing I saw for sure was Julie's front wheel ramming into the girl's rear one. At the very least, why did Julie let the newbie take the line next to the drop-off? If she'd fallen back onto the road, she'd have broken a rib or a collarbone, maybe sustained minor road rash. Normal injuries."

"Julie may have showed poor judgment, but that's not the same as deliberately running another cyclist off the road. Did the local sheriff investigate?"

"Highway patrol did. The officers found nothing conclusive, certainly not enough to ruin Julie's life, too. They ruled it an accident."

"Do you remember the girl's name?"

"No. It's been more than ten years. Like you said, cyclists rotate in and out of teams all the time."

"Did you tell this to Chief Byrd?"

"No, he never asked me for ancient history."

In the silence that followed, the screams of the wind mingled with the thunder of pounding hooves against the hard-packed earth.

"Davis and Jake's brother are working the horses. Want to meet Slade? He's nothing like Jake. Slade is quiet and patient. I'm headed that way right now to lend a hand."

"I'll pass." She snared a few more grapes. "Do you want me to pass your story onto Reilly?"

"Do what you think is best—but if you do, please tell her that's all I remember."

She placed a hand on her friend's shoulder. "Be happy, Allison. Really, it's *not* about the bike."

Yesterday, she would have cut out her tongue rather than utter such blasphemy.

SHE SPENT SOME time in her cabin, exchanging her lightweight clothes for stouter jeans, a sweater, and boots, then swept her hair into its customary ponytail. On her way outside, she kicked her dirty clothes underneath the nightstand.

She returned to the kitchen. Griffin was still MIA.

She banged out the screen door, made her way across the courtyard, and then strolled down the road leading to the stable, but when she arrived at the fork leading into the forest, she took Jake's suggestion and turned onto the footpath. The first half-mile took her through tall larch trees shedding their golden needles. So wrapped up by the vibrant fall colors, she soon forgot to look where she was stepping and nearly pitched over when a splintered stump snared her shoelace. She brushed herself off and double-tied both shoelaces, then moved ahead with more caution. At one point, she scared up a mule deer. It leapt over the brush with the grace of a ballerina. Overhead, an eagle with the wingspan of a condor streaked across the sun, and a red-tailed hawk screeched to its mate. She zigzagged around elk scat and huckleberry bushes laden with tufts of bear fur. Squishy mud beneath her boots harbored the sunken prints of a wolf pack. A few yards farther, the prints vanished slyly among the rocks.

The greenhouse Jake had mentioned was an A-frame situated less than a half mile from the turnoff. Stacks of firewood stood by the open door. Inside, the floor-to-ceiling canopy of clear plastic gave her the feeling she'd stepped into a soap bubble. Planters filled with bright foliage stretched throughout the structure, and a makeshift kitchenette sat to the right of the entryway. Whoever was in charge of it hadn't planted a single rose or tulip—not even one twisting tomato vine. Other than the pink azaleas and golden buttercups growing in beds nearest the door, she didn't recognize any of the other flowers blooming in the additional eight beds. Perhaps Griffin was its caretaker, and these plants were the cultivars for his *special* teas.

The presence of a beekeeper's bonnet and gloves hanging from pegs near the door suggested the apiary was nearby. On her way outside, she accidentally knocked over a pole with a hook at one end that had the bad manners to block her path. Setting it right, she went in search of the apiary.

The natural bee habitat—fifty yards down the road—came as a surprise. The grove of long-needle pines stretched over a plot of land roughly the size of a baseball diamond. Hollowed-out tree cavities formed the framework for the bees' densely packed honeycombs, and thousands of hexagonal cells made up each teardrop hive. The bees had smoothed the bark around each hive and attached the honeycombs with brown resin to plug unwanted spaces and defend against intruders. Scores of hives dotted each tree, starting a few feet from the ground and rising up as high as she could reach.

As ominous clouds began to chase away the blue sky, she headed back toward her cabin for her mandatory nap. She was threading her way around a clump of thorny bushes when she noticed a caravan of spiny cockleburs hitchhiking on her shoelaces. After plucking them off, she continued walking until she stubbed her toe on a rock and planted her face into a pile of decaying leaves. At some point, the snow-dog shot out of the woods and lashed out his paw, trying to tempt her into a game of hide and seek.

She brushed her way clear of the leaves. "Not today, Fido."

His liver-colored nose nudged her thigh. She ran her fingers through his tangled coat and uncovered a clip-on collar. A silver tag shaped as a bone held the word *Cerberus*—the same Cerberus that guarded the Gates to Hades. Somebody on the ranch had a wicked sense of humor.

"Cerberus, where is your sweet sister?"

He sprinted down the road, prancing back a few minutes later with Fay at his side.

The dog made a show of sniffing Fay's pale tracksuit before shooting off into the trees. Fay joined her alongside the leaves.

"I see Cerberus found you too," Logan said. "Thanks again for the helmet. Did Grant get it back to you?"

"He did, and you're welcome. Glad it worked out."

"Listen, you knew Julie better than I did. Is there any chance she hid her bike before she went into the tunnel where Reilly and I found her?"

"Hid it? No way. The Julie I knew would've flaunted it. Despite appearances, Julie didn't care *about* things—she cared about *possessing* things and making her teammates feel insignificant." She plucked a golden maple leaf from the pile and held it up to the sunlight. "I guess this means the sheriff hasn't recovered her bike yet."

"If he has, he isn't sharing. Jake retrieved the wheels though." Reilly's warning about not appearing eager bubbled up, and she feigned a yawn. "I'm heading back for a nap. If you're going that way, we can walk together."

"No, thanks. I'm just starting out."

Her next yawn was the real deal. "Gosh, I'm beat. If we don't get a chance to talk again before Saturday, good luck on your race."

"Oh, I'm not racing then either. Tim took away my bikes."

"You told me he grounded you. I thought that was just until Saturday."

"It's worse than that. He said I can't have my bikes until I put on at least five pounds of muscle and stop my two-a-days. If you ask me, that's pretty shortsighted of him. With Julie dead, Sydney in the hospital, and me grounded, we haven't a chance in hell of earning enough points as a team to participate in any of next year's premier races."

"But next year is still months away. By then, you and Sydney will both be back on your bikes."

"We've no guarantee of that." Fay dashed the leaf to the ground. "Damn it! If Julie had died a year—even a few months—ago, I'd be racing this week, not wasting my time in hospitals getting pumped full of junk."

"That junk is nutrients. Without it you'd be dead. How dare you blame Julie for your eating disorder."

"She is to blame. She said I was fat and that if I lost a few pounds, I'd be a better lead-out for her. She wouldn't let it go. She also said if I didn't start doing what Continental was paying me to do, she'd have Tim replace me."

"You're a grown woman. Why didn't you stand up to her?"

"Nobody stood up to Julie without repercussions."

"Still, that doesn't explain today... this minute... Saturday's race. Julie is dead, and you're still not eating. If you really want to ride your bike again, stop blaming a dead woman for your own failing and throw a McBurger into your mouth."

"Don't you think I've tried?"

Logan reined in her irritation. "I'm sorry. I've no idea what you're going through. Maybe you have tried. I only know you're seriously sick, and Tim had no recourse...."

The retort of a gunshot sang out.

The weight of Fay falling against her tipped Logan off balance. She sprawled into the leaves, fingers splayed. Her arm felt as if it were on fire. She sprang to her feet. Blood stained her sweater and dripped from her fingertips. She clawed at the sleeve to expose her arm. The bullet had gouged out a flap in the crook of her elbow, miraculously missing her artery by narrow millimeters.

Fay!

Logan fell to her knees beside the pile of leaves as Cerberus bolted out from behind a boulder. Together they dug furiously—leaves flying everywhere—until Fay's bright-blue sneakers came into view.

"Cerberus, STOP!"

The dog drew back his paw and lowered himself onto his belly, tail twitching back and forth on the damp ground.

She reached into her pocket and threw him a stale peanut. "Good boy."

Brushing away the last bits of debris, she gently rotated Fay so her face turned upward. Blood spurted from a charred hole beneath her collarbone, spilling over the pale fabric of her tracksuit. Logan checked for a pulse. Which of them had deflected the bullet was anyone's guess, but that fortuitous twist had spared both their lives.

She hauled off her own bloody sweater and bound it tightly across Fay's shoulder. Then, she lugged over a fallen bough, lifted Fay's legs onto it, and folded the woman's arms across her chest.

"Cerberus, sit."

The snow-dog inched forward and spread himself alongside Fay.

"Even better, pooch. Now, guard!"

The snow-dog laid his head down on his paws. With a final glance at the injured woman and obedient guardian, she sprinted toward the stable for all she was worth.

CHAPTER 10

THE SATINY FOLDS of her bathing suit conjured up the image of her supple curves and velvety skin. Jake sifted through the rest of her cast-off clothes, his frustration mounting.

He wanted her bad.

Her icy aloofness had only served to fuel the fire burning inside him. Usually women came on to him—but not her, the one he wanted. Something about her was different. She was reserved but unpretentious, familiar yet alien, alluring but forbidden—a woman to be finessed, not trapped. She'd made that abundantly clear.

The cyclist's death was an unforeseen snag, yet the Cycling Federation had given him the nod to go ahead with the race—welcome news, since he needed the revenue it had brought in if he hoped to expand his hospitality business. With his brother's swift veto of a casino in Two Medicine, he'd no other choice but to open the ranch to newcomers—not a bad decision, since it had brought her to him. The contract he'd negotiated with the aluminum plant was an unforeseen bonanza.

He dropped her swimsuit on the bed and made his way over to the kitchen, where he ate a club sandwich while Griffin drove a knife into his heart with the news she'd lunched with the good-looking mechanic. When he'd finished, he placed his dish in the sink, strode past the gun cabinet—reconsidered—turned around, and left through the screen door.

SLADE PACED SNOW Runner sideways along the footpath, using the stallion to block his brother's retreat. "Why?"

Jake scowled up at him. "She enjoys the hunt, too."

"Keep your distance from her."

"How do you know anything of her?"

"I will take to my grave that which you will spend a lifetime longing for." He ran his hand across the sole of his boot. A film of silvery dust clung to his fingers. He held his hand in front of his brother's scowl. "Keeping our ancient lands and waters pure is not a sidebar of our existence but the reason the Great Creator entrusted the Blue Planet to the Old Man."

Jake pushed it away. "Prehistoric twaddle. Do not waste your second say on this triviality, brother." With an agility borne out of a lifetime of outdoor toil, he bolted around Snow Runner.

Slade slid off the stallion and tracked Jake through the trees. He'd raised an arm to strike a blow when the sight of her thrashing toward them threw him into a panic. He threw his brother to the ground, hurdled over him, and ran.

Dark splotches stained the lace on her bra, and crimson slashes marred her silky skin. Her hair was sticky with blood, dirt, and leaves. The sharp metallic scent of death eclipsed her.

"*Nuttah!*"

HIS RAW TERROR slammed into her with the force of a sledgehammer. He lifted her into him and pressed his lips against hers, letting his strong life force surge through her.

When his grip loosened, she slipped to the ground. "It's not me. It's Fay. She needs our help."

He pulled her back. "Give me your arm."

She held out her injured arm. He ripped off his shirt and bound the soft fabric around her wound—each turn brought her world back into focus.

A few feet away, Jake glowered at them from behind his mask of hatred. "You are naive if you think my arcane brother can please a woman like you."

The sharp crack of his brother's hand as it collided with Jake's cheek delivered an apoplectic warning. "If you ever force your touch on her, you will die by her hand or mine. Go call our cousin."

Red-faced, Jake launched himself toward the dining hall.

Her husband's burning eyes simmered. "Show me."

They backtracked though the trees until the injured woman came into view. Cerberus still held fast to his post. Logan praised the dog, then knelt beside Fay and checked again to make sure the woman's heart still beat.

He dropped to a knee beside her. "Keep her warm. I will get medicine."

She gathered Fay into a close embrace.

A gentle breeze had kicked up by the time he returned, holding a weed in each hand. Silky threads ran up and down the stems. A white blossom topped each stalk.

"The ancients used yarrow to staunch bleeding in the battlefield." He removed a leather pouch from his belt and set it between them. "Get Merenale, please."

She laid Fay gently in his arms and took up the pouch. With the snow-dog's help, she found a running stream on the other side of the clearing, close to the gorge. She soaked the pouch full and ran back to the trees. In her absence, he'd spread Fay across the soft leaves, hollowed out a bowl in a stump, and filled it with shredded yarrow. She relinquished the pouch.

He dribbled water over the yarrow, then gently folded the mixture together to form a soft paste. "Please remove my shirt."

When her arm was once again bare, he pressed half the paste to her wound then redressed her arm. Turning his attention to Fay, he removed

Logan's sweater, then the girl's jacket, and cleansed away the blood until he'd exposed the bullet hole beneath her collarbone. Any evidence of a bullet was invisible to the naked eye. He packed the other half of the yarrow into the wound.

"This one's spirit holds tight to her life force." He wrapped Fay back into her jacket, laid Logan's bloody sweater on top of her, then gathered Logan into his lap. "Tell me what happened."

She told him.

His eyes cast over Fay. "What do you know of this woman?"

"She was kind to me."

"From which direction did the bullet come?"

She pointed in the direction of the greenhouse.

"A muffled or sharp retort?"

"Sharp, loud—but not deafening."

"Please remain." He moved toward the clearing south of the greenhouse.

She hugged her knees to her chest and closed her eyes. When she opened them again, he knelt behind her, shifting through leaves. After a minute, he stood, taking her with him. "You stood here?"

"Yes. I walked in a diagonal line from the apiary and ran into Fay, who joined me from the road."

He pointed toward the stream. "Trampled ground near the clearing suggests the shooter stood close—close enough to put a bullet in your back."

She swallowed, hard. "So it was Fay he wanted to harm."

"I believe so."

"But why? What could she have…?"

Chief Byrd's sudden appearance cut short their exchange. If he was surprised to see Julie's teammate lying prostate and bloody on the ground, he gave nothing away. A burly young man with hair the color of rusty barbed wire followed in his slipstream. Both wore backpacks over tan uniforms and carried a stretcher between them. His cousin introduced the man as Deputy Joe Amundsen, then went down on a knee and ran his hands over Fay.

"Not a relaxing way to spend an afternoon, is it, ma'am," Joe said.

"Logan, and no it isn't. Neither of us had the slightest warning."

"A hunter most likely, though local folks know better than to shoot this close to the buildings." He shrugged off his backpack. "Ambulance is on its way. Won't be but a few minutes."

"Thank you, Deputy.

"Joe."

The sheriff straightened, giving his cousin a guarded look as he set his sunglasses in place. An almost imperceptible nod of her husband's head acknowledged the look.

"The old ways have spared her life for now," the sheriff said as he passed to help Joe bundle the injured woman in blankets.

They lifted her gently onto the stretcher. While Joe buckled the straps tethering Fay to the stretcher, Slade rejoined his cousin in the clearing.

She moved beside Joe. "I'm sorry to disrupt your day like this."

"Tough way to start a friendship." He brought a notebook from a pocket tucked inside his leather jacket. "Can you tell me about it?

"Not much to tell. I went for a walk. Jake had mentioned a greenhouse I was eager to see. I bumped into Fay, and we got to talking."

"About what?"

"Her illness. Her coach had taken away her bikes and forbade her from training or racing. She wasn't happy about it. We'd pretty much come to the end of what there was to say about her situation when the gunshot ran out. She fell against me, and we both landed in those leaves." She pointed to the blanket of bloodstained leaves at their feet.

"You mentioned her illness. What's the thumbnail on that?"

"Anorexia—she's starving herself."

"Why?"

"Logically, anorexia is an illness that only affects people who can afford to eat. Fay blamed her downward spiral on Julie Easton. She claimed Julie bullied her into losing weight. Fay went overboard. Their coach might be able to fill in any missing details."

He looked down at Fay's withered face. From the depths of her soft cocoon, she looked like a mummy unearthed after five millenniums in an airless tomb. "What's your history with Miss White?"

"Until today, overlapping racing schedules. The most words we'd ever exchanged came this morning when my helmet broke, and I borrowed hers."

"Where's that helmet now?"

"Back with Fay. I left it with my coach to return."

Joe had tucked his notebook away, when his phone rang. He picked up with a "Yep… ETA eight minutes," then buttoned it away as he moved to the bottom half of the stretcher. "Ambulance is waiting. Best get a move on."

The ambulance was parked at the fork in the road. While one EMT fussed over Fay, the other fussed over Logan—cleaning the wound, applying a disinfectant dressing, then bandaging her arm. "Flesh wounds like this one bleed like crazy but rarely do any damage other than to leave a jagged scar."

Free to go, she dumped her bloodied sweater into the plastic bag Joe held out and returned to her cabin with Slade at her side.

UNDER THE CASCADE of hot water, he sponged gently around the kiss of the bullet. When he lay beside her, she curled into him. Even after a shower, the scents of rawhide and pine lingered.

"I'm sorry I came between you and your brother."

"My brother has chosen to embrace the worst of his bloodlines. If he doesn't find his humanity soon, he will walk alone in this lifetime." He kissed her gently. "I did not expect such violence to accompany your homecoming. Please remain vigilant. I will come for you tonight."

HE WAS GONE when she awoke. She padded to the window. The sun still ruled from her throne in the heavens. She jumped back into the warm bed, rolled over, and drifted back to sleep.

The next time she awoke, shadows climbed into the room. She stretched lazily, rolled out of bed, and plodded into the bathroom with her bloody jeans. She held them underneath a stream of cold water as blood swirled indolently down the drain. When the water ran clear, she rolled them in a towel and carried them outside to the stoop.

Inside, she tugged on her last pair of clean shorts, then hunted for a serviceable laundry container. A wedge of black plastic crammed underneath an old book on the shelf turned into a trash bag big enough to hold everything. With the evening meal still hours away, she flopped onto the bed and tackled the old book—*Poisonous Plants of the Northwest*.

Somewhere between azaleas and foxglove, the screen door opened, ushering in a rush of cool air and Reilly's Romeo. She jammed the book underneath the pillow.

He pointed to her bandaged arm. "What's this? Did you crash?" His frown leaked out. "Why is your skin so pale? Today, when we are together, you are the picture of health. Now... well, now... you are death. Did you catch a bug?"

"Sit down, and I'll give you the horse's mouth version."

He crossed to the refrigerator, pulled out a bottle of water, and lobbed it onto the pillow. "Drink that. You must hydrate. I bet a bundle on you."

She twisted off the cap and drank thirstily as he sprawled over the hamper.

"Somebody took a shot at me and Fay in the forest." She placed the empty bottle on the nightstand. "Fay got the worst of it."

"She dies too?"

"No, but she absorbed the brunt of the bullet. She's on her way to the hospital in Plains."

"How bad are you?"

"A flesh wound."

He scowled. "All this violence is unsettling… an accident surely."

"Chief Byrd is looking into it."

"Does he expect to find a connection to Julie's death?"

"Ask him."

"Why did Jake not cancel the race?"

"Because it's not just a race—it's nationals. He's already invested significant time and money to make sure our races comes off. Somehow he convinced the Federation Julie's death had nothing to do with their championships or his ranch." She retrieved her carryall from the closet. "I'm sure Tim read you the riot act about Fay and her bikes."

"He tells me to lock them away. Yet today she is no better off on her own two feet than on my two wheels."

"It's certainly a case of 'out of the frying pan into the fire.' Before today's incident, the sheriff might've worked up a good case against Fay. She blamed Julie for her eating disorder."

"It is not an easy thing—this playing detective." He helped himself to a can of Mountain Dew from the refrigerator. "Now, where are these papers you hold for me?"

She dug out the papers Simon's greasy hands had soiled and his annoyance had crumpled. "They're a mess." She smoothed out each sheet and aligned them on the bedcover. "There—hey, do you see what I see?"

He joined her beside the bed. "You have the discerning eye. Please help me piece them right."

Working together, they rearranged each sheet into the image of Julie's one-of-a-kind bike.

"Holy Toledo!" she said. "I never saw this coming. Why would Drake hide a blueprint of a bike Julie designed?"

"Our error may be in believing what Julie wanted us to believe."

"But the bike exists, and she planned to submit a patent. Are you saying Julie stole the design from Drake, or that Drake didn't hide it?"

"We have only Simon's word they switched vehicles"—he tidied the papers into a manageable pile—"and a more likely supposition is someone else designed Julie's bike."

"And let Julie take the credit?"

"*Let* is the nicest possibility."

"What's another—blackmail?"

"Julie was a bully, yes—but was she more? Monday night I see her flaunt this very machine in Theo's face. They argue. Theo comes away crazed with worry. Was it a stolen design that derailed him. Bah! How could it be? He has known of such a design for months. No, to rattle my stoic friend, Julie's mischief must go deeper than purloined geometry."

"You do know you just said a bunch of nothing, don't you?"

"Then I will say it like your friend Simon so that you might better understand—'how the hells do I know what's running around in that she-woman's head?'"

His guttural massacre of the King's English made her laugh.

He swept up the papers and strode toward the door. "It is good to hear you laugh once more. It shows me you're not badly hurt. I will hope Fay recovers swiftly as well. Now I must leave you. Please thank Simon for me."

She stood with her arms akimbo, frowning at him. "Come back here with those papers."

His hesitant stride brought him as far as the nightstand. "They are safer with me than you."

"I've no intention of keeping them. Regardless of who originally owned those papers, they are now part of an ongoing murder investigation. Anything that has to do with Julie or her missing bike belongs with Chief Byrd."

"Yet I must insist on keeping them."

"Why? Did you come down with a sudden attack of employer loyalty? Continental pays you to fix its bikes, not chase down missing property of questionable pedigree."

He cast his eyes at the floor. "Ah, you call my bluff."

"Bluff—what bluff? If I did, it was purely unintentional—and another thing… drop this cloak-and-dagger act you put on whenever you're with me or Reilly. That alone will go a long way in getting you that first date with her. She doesn't suffer fools gladly."

The smile he sent her way would have melted the heart of a Siberian snow queen. "It will be as you wish between us, but you must promise me you will not tell Reilly, as she is bound by legalities you are not."

"Pinky swear."

"What is this pinky swear?"

"It's the highest regard of all promises. The Anglo version of the Japanese "cut off your finger" promise."

"Ah, then I accept your pinky swear. My true profession is as an investigator for the Cycling Federation. As such, everything that transpires at these championships is my business—including a hidden blueprint, a missing machine, and especially the death of a licensed cyclist."

She blinked, giving his admission a moment to sink in. "Will you entertain a compromise? I'll get Reilly to scratch you off her naughty list, and in return, you'll give her the papers for safekeeping. Underneath her gun-toting righteousness, she's fair-minded to a fault."

"It will be as you say but with one caveat. I will keep these papers until seven o'clock, at which time, you will drive us into Two Medicine, and I will present them to Reilly so she no longer questions my integrity."

"Make it six, and you're on. Meet me at my Jeep—the white one. It's unlocked."

———

SHE WALKED THE short distance to Reilly's cabin on the off chance her friend had returned, but when she stepped inside and found it empty, she sought out Griffin instead.

He sat behind the counter in the kitchen elbow-deep in grated cheese. She cleared her throat.

"My dear!" He unfolded himself from a stool and hurried over, embracing her with a warm hug.

When he released her and returned to his task, she took in the bowls of salsa, guacamole, refried beans, and tortilla chips on the countertop. "Bad timing?"

"I'm a man. I would never say *no* to a visit from a beautiful woman." He pointed to the neatly organized countertop. "See, I have banished my messes."

The canvas bags of flour, sugar, and cornmeal now lived in the pantry, and the appliances lazed in order of height on the shelves. Not a jam jar, honey pot, or poison tin in sight.

She smiled at him. "How do you like it?"

"It grows on me."

"I'm here to help, but before you say yes, you should know I can't cook. I've never even tried, so give me something simple. It'll be less stressful on both of us."

"I have a foolproof job for you." He pointed to a stack of flour tortillas resting on the countertop. "Heat those."

"In the microwave?"

"If you please. Thirty seconds per stack. Use these." He handed her a pair of tongs. "Clean plates are in the dishwasher."

She busied herself piling up tortillas, pausing as he removed a baking dish from underneath the counter and dumped in shredded chicken, diced peppers, colorful cheeses, and secret spices. "What are we making?"

"Pollo Fingers. Jake wishes a Mexican buffet to go with his games."

"What games?"

"His gambling night."

"That's tonight? Gee, with all that's been going on I forgot."

"Understandable." His dark eyes crept over the rims of his turquoise cheaters. "Jake ate his sandwich in my kitchen after you left. He wanted to know if I'd fed you."

"Something tells me those weren't his exact words."

"What does it matter? Jake is a hoverer. Too blinded by his own ambitions to see what has been going on underneath his own nose. You have chosen wisely."

"I think so, too, but it's always nice to hear a second opinion, especially when it agrees with mine."

He pulled a pygmy-sized bottle of Diet Coke from the refrigerator. "Here. I thought it best to stock up."

"Thanks." She kissed his cheek. "You, in particular, make me feel like I'm home."

"We all wish that for you, even Jake—although he envisioned a different outcome."

"He's made that perfectly clear. Do you mind if I skip your Mexican dinner tonight? I've some errands to run in Two Medicine."

He pointed to the bandage on her arm. "Jake told me of another incident, one in which you were hurt. Will you visit a healer?"

"The EMT who treated me said it was only a flesh wound. Fay didn't fare as well."

"Who is this Fay?"

"Julie's teammate. She doesn't eat, so I'm not surprised you haven't met her."

"Julie Easton was a most disagreeable woman. She argues with her teammates. She throws herself at Jake. She cares only for her needs. A woman like that gives many people reason to find her disagreeable, to want to cause her harm—but this other woman, this Fay—I may not know her, but I know of her. She is the one I call the 'shadow woman.' She lurks behind the others whenever they are about."

"She is unhappy."

"She is not right in her head, but she is not unaware. She watches the movements of the others like the cougar sizes up the ailing deer."

As the microwave timer rang out its last ding, she removed the first plate and slipped in a second, reset the timer, then hopped onto a stool, awaiting the next batch. With the tortillas warmed to Griffin's satisfaction, she helped him fill, roll, and cut his Pollo Fingers.

After the last one had been sliced, she sat on a stool and danced a carving knife between her fingers. "How would you like a permanent helper?"

When the tip of the knife landed dangerously close to her pinkie, he slipped the blade from her hand. "I think it best if we discuss your proposal after the race Saturday."

"I suppose a few more days on your own won't hurt." She laughed. "How is it some culinary-challenged woman like me hasn't snatched you up already?"

"How do you know one has not?" He poured out a coffee from a percolator heating on the stove."It's good you and Miss Allison will stay on with us. We could use a lightening of spirit."

She crossed to the back wall and lifted the broom from its peg. "About my friend Allison and her friend Davis Morgan. Is he a good man?"

"He survived his share of troubles until he came to us. His work with the horses suits his wild nature, but like myself and the other men on the ranch, he has no wish to sleep alone."

She swiped the broom over a patch of floor, coming away with a few strands of cheese."You're very good at evading the point."

"Diplomacy comes in handy with incomers who bring with them narrow-view preconceptions about us and our way of life. Now, I must shoo you away so I can focus on my sourdough pancakes for your breakfast."

SHE RETURNED THE broom to its peg on her way out the screen door. Taylor sat on a bench, sipping sweet tea from a tumbler. A few yards away, Tim's platinum hair flashed as he moved off the courtyard.

Her approach brought Taylor to her feet. "Y'all hear the news about Sydney?"

"She didn't… isn't…?"

"No, thank the Lord. The hospital will release her tomorrow."

"Any word on Fay? I assume Tim told you about the incident in the woods this afternoon, before he snuck off."

"Can't keep something like that under wraps. Lordy, first Julie, now Fay. Getting so it ain't safe to take a breath of fresh air no more."

"The sheriff is considering it an unfortunate accident, a stray bullet from a hunting rifle, until something contradicts that."

"Incidental or intentional, dead is dead. Thank the Lord you were Johnny-on-the-spot."

"When did Tim take away her bikes?"

"Some time ago. Fay raced some of the flatter spring classics on the Continent with us, but by May, her performances had dropped off along with her appetite. Tim sent her to the team doctor. His diagnosis was she'd caught some foreign bug she couldn't shake. By June, *not eating much* swiftly morphed into *at all*—poor woman. Tim wised up. Fay hasn't ridden with us since."

"If she's unable to race, why is she still traveling with the team?"

"Because Tim can't stop her. She's paying her own way—or stalking us, depending on how you want to look at it."

SHORTLY BEFORE SIX o'clock, Logan returned to her cabin, retrieved her dirty laundry, and set out for the Jeep, but as she came abreast of the Craftsman, Jake sat on the porch swing, slumped against the pillows. Deep grooves cut into the flesh around his mouth, and worry lines pleated his forehead. Her presence brought the dogs flying out of the bushes and up the staircase, where they sniffed his jeans as if he'd hemmed them with tenderloins. She trailed after them, stopping on the last step to let the dogs dance about at her ankles. She gave the snow-dog a welcoming pat, then went down on a knee and whispered a name into the hound's floppy ear. Again, the dog's tail whipped back and forth. The memory had come to her in a dream. *Geneva* was the name of the ginger dog, and she was the *other's* guardian.

"What can my brother give you that I can't?" Jake asked as he traded in the porch swing for his worn boots.

God, the man was insufferable.

She turned to leave, but as a wave of unease washed over her, she reined in her angst and studied him with an impassive expression. Destiny had bonded her to these lands and this man's brother for eternity. She needed to make Jake understand he wasn't part of the deal.

"Your brother, the animals, and these lands are my world now. Please look elsewhere for your happiness."

CHAPTER 11

L OGAN BACKED THE Jeep into a slot near the laundromat. While her laundry sudsed and churned, she and Cort ducked into the ice-cream shop, bought a huckleberry milkshake for her and a banana split for him, and then sat on a bench near the dam to enjoy them.

The village offered few amenities—a collection of art galleries and pubs, flanked by a jewelry store, a gun shop that claimed 'ammo was them,' a café dishing up home-style cooking, and a movie theater with a marquee advertising Midnight Madness—*Creature from the Black Lagoon* and *The Thing*.

He nudged her arm. "With its quaintness and Edwardian streetlamps, Two Medicine is not unlike my hometown."

"Do you miss it?"

His jaw slid forward. "America is the land of the free where I can steer my own ship and change course at will. It is also a country of many quaint towns. Someday I shall find one that suits me."

"Quaint, yes—but not cycling friendly—narrow streets, dirt footpaths, wooden walkways, and the nearest hospital comes with a three-hour drive through rugged terrain. That's a long time to hurt. Any news on Guy Young?"

"He is okay. His head is right, his shoulder not so much, but his bike— it is unsalvageable. He goes home." He pointed to a Swiss Chalet in the distance. "What's that?"

"Not sure. Railroad tracks run behind the ice-cream shop, so maybe it's a train station."

He tossed his plastic dish into a handy trashcan and stretched slowly off the bench. "I shall explore this quaint village… who knows, perhaps we will reunite someday… while you do what you came to do. Do not hurry. When I grow bored, I retire to your Jeep."

"What about the blueprint?"

"In the glove box. Perhaps it is best if you keep me out of it. Simon gave them to you, not me. I can add nothing to his story."

"What about Reilly's absolution for your sins?"

He grinned his Prince Charming grin. "I leave my fate with the fair constable in your capable hands." He dropped a kiss in her palm, crossed the street, and passed through the doors of the art gallery.

Logan backtracked inside the ice-cream shop, bought a chocolate milkshake, and returned to the Jeep. He'd slipped the papers inside a zip-lock bag. She seized the bag and then followed the wooden planks to the sheriff's headquarters behind an arched doorway at the north end of Main Street, hesitating in front of the picture window cut into the brick facade.

The room was a blur of red oak. Only the walls, painted a mouthwatering shade of caramel, had escaped the carpenter's hammer. Discarded coffee mugs, Styrofoam food containers, pens and pencils, and cardboard boxes cluttered the desktops and spilled onto the windowsills. Reilly sat alone at one of a pair of desks flanking the fireplace, aglow with sputtering embers. Logan passed inside.

"Well, look what the wind blew in." Reilly set aside the turkey wrap in her hand to point at the milkshake Logan had set beside the keyboard. "For me?"

"I owe you for all the Diet Cokes I've pinched this week."

Reilly took a happy suck on her milkshake. "Hmm, I love it when they hold the trigger down on the chocolate syrup." She waved a hand at the bandage on Logan's arm. "Hurt much?"

Logan shot her a questioning glance.

"Hey, it's a two-man outfit. No secrets bounce off these walls."

"It's nothing more than an ugly scratch. If you read Joe's report, you know the bullet was meant for Fay."

"The bigger question is what was she doing wandering around the Enchanted Forest? Doesn't she have a bike race to nap for?"

"Tim forbade her from riding until she fattens up."

"Then why is she here?"

"She's traveling with the team on her own nickel."

"Separation anxiety?"

"File it under 'how the hells do I know what's running around in that she-woman's head?'"

Reilly burst out laughing. "Is it too much to suggest to the sheriff we wrap all this up"—she made a smearing motion over Logan's bandaged arm—"as straying into the path of an innocent bullet?"

"Define *innocent bullet*."

"One that's fired from a rifle engaged in innocent target practice. Around these parts, when it isn't deer season, it's elk season. If not elk, then bear—not bear, then duck, and so on. In between, it's practice."

"Too much blood has been shed to use a modifier like *innocent*." As a sudden twinge of pain shot through her arm, Logan grimaced. "Griffin said something interesting to me a short while ago. He said Fay was sick but not unaware. What if she saw or heard something she wasn't supposed to see or hear?"

"Like Julie's killer making off with her bike? How could she? The logistics are all wrong. Assuming Fay was stranded on main site, how did see anything that was going on twenty miles away? She had no car or bike."

"She could've borrowed either."

"Let's say she did. How would Julie's killer know Fay saw something? She's thin to the point of invisible."

Logan grinned. "That's where you come in. I offer up wild, unsubstantiated speculations, and you and the sheriff run your tail off trying to prove me right or wrong."

"We will if you give us something to work with—like what Fay saw, heard, or knows that the killer doesn't want us to know."

"If I knew that, we'd be having a different conversation." She gave her fingers a loud snap. "Maybe it's not any of those things. Maybe it's what she did."

"Which is?"

"She came to the race. It's the only thing that fits since she's done nothing else."

"Are you sure she didn't intimate the identity of Julie's killer before she stopped talking?"

"Only if she was incriminating herself. She blames… blamed Julie for her anorexia, but it came across as a *woe is me*, not a confession."

"People who do stupid things usually see themselves as victims, not idiots." Reilly pushed the turkey wrap toward Logan. "Here, eat this. You need it more than I do."

"Thanks." She took a generous bite. "Hmm, turkey, spinach, bacon, and cranberries glued together with gobs of fat. Yum! You sure know how to pick 'em." She wiped mayonnaise from her chin. "How'd you wrangle up such a great sandwich in this burg?"

"The café. Its ambiance is right out of the wild west, but the food is terrific. Between Griffin and that café, you won't starve up here."

"Starving is the least of my worries. Any update on Fay?"

"Stable, but guarded—medico for *iffy*—but hey, she's still breathing, so that's something."

"She's not talking yet?"

"Oh, sure. On the rare occasion she's not demanding to be released, she claims she saw nothing that can help us because the sun blinded her."

"But that's impossible. She was facing the mountains. The sun doesn't move that way until later in the evening."

Reilly backhanded chocolate ice cream from her lips. "The risk of infection with a bullet wound is high, which means Fay isn't going anywhere for a good long while—plenty of time for her to come to her senses, although how much sense can a woman who refuses to eat have?"

"Which brings us full circle—trying to make sense of Julie's death." Logan set Simon's papers on the desktop. "Simon found these in his van, which in a past life belonged to Tom Drake, which—in Simon's world—entitles Romeo to anything Drake left behind, even if it factors into a murder investigation."

Reilly poked her pencil at them. "It'll save time if you tell me what they are."

"How do you know I know?"

"Because you're almost as nosy as I am."

"Put them together, and it's the design blueprint for Julie's bike."

"Drake stole them?"

"That's a fresh take. We thought Julie might've done the stealing."

"We?"

"Romeo and me. I left him wandering the village. He invited himself along hoping you'd exonerate him from any wrongdoing if he turned them over."

"Why isn't he here?"

"Because somewhere between the maraschino cherries and strawberry sauce on his banana split, he got cold feet. He said he had nothing to add. I can vouch for that. I've barely let them out of my sight since Simon shoved them into my carryall."

"Define *barely*."

"I left my carryall on Simon's porch during the race, then tucked it into my cabin after the race. Romeo strolled in around four o'clock, and I turned them over to him. They were in his possession until he put them in the glove box of my Jeep at six o'clock."

Reilly tapped the plastic bag. "Why didn't Simon give them to Romeo as soon as he found them?"

"That's a question for Simon. For what it's worth, we both know how he works—the path of least resistance."

"Why didn't you give them to Romeo straightaway?"

"Because I had a more urgent problem. The clip from my helmet fell off right before my start time. Lucky for me, Fay was working registration and loaned me her helmet."

"Talk about waking up on the wrong side of the bed." Reilly reached for the papers.

"Hey, aren't you going to dust them for prints?"

"What good will that do? More skin has touched these papers than Santa's lap. Help me put them together."

They quickly recreated the blueprint. When the last piece was in place, Reilly pulled out her phone and snapped off some shots. "Yep, that's Julie's bike all right. So, who took what—Julie or Drake?"

"Since Julie was a habitual liar—bulldozing and bullying her way through every obstacle that fell in her path—it's impossible for me to think she designed anything, and since the only words I've ever exchanged with Drake are 'good morning,' I've no idea what he's capable of, but if Simon can put a bike together blindfolded, Drake probably can, too. If I had to choose, I'd go with Julie as your thief."

"What about the bike?"

"Julie *had* the bike. She wanted its pedigree."

"What about a third option? Somebody other than Drake designed the bike, Julie stole the blueprint and hid it in Simon's van, then that somebody—not knowing she'd hid them—killed her when she refused to return them."

"Six of one, half a dozen of the other. Now you're left with only one conundrum—how did this somebody smuggle out Julie's bike frame, and where is it now?"

RETURNING TO THE laundromat, Logan dumped her damp clothes into a dryer. Her first step back outside brought Rachel out of the ammo shop and across Main Street, squawking like an angry goose.

"You can tell Reilly I'm taking care of Tim's situation with immigration, so there's no need to make more trouble for him."

"Can't Tim fight his own battles?"

"Why should he when he has me?" She held out her left hand. A diamond ring sparkled gaudily on her third finger. "We're engaged."

"Well, I hate to throw a wet blanket on your impending nuptials, but with Julie's death, Tim's problems have escalated way beyond immigration issues."

Rachel reared backward. "Tim was Julie's coach—period."

"Several witnesses have come forth to swear they saw *your* teammate and *your* fiancé arguing on numerous occasions. As team captain and coach, Julie and Tim spent a lot of time together—alone... in his van." Logan crossed her fingers behind her back. "The line of investigation Chief Byrd favors is that Julie uncovered something about Tim—something *not* for public consumption—and tried a spot of blackmail on him, but he wasn't having it and killed her."

"That's absurd!"

"Hey, I'm only the messenger. If you've got something that will exonerate Tim, tell Reilly. She's in the sheriff's office, but if I were in your sneakers, I'd give it awhile. She's kind of busy right now reserving a cell at Deer Lodge Federal Penitentiary for your fiancé."

LOGAN WEAVED IN and out of shops, walking past everything from huckleberry tea bags to ceramic ducks toting bottles of wine. Her favorite store was Sir Chop-A-Lot, which sold an array of kitchen gadgetry and cookware she couldn't name and certainly didn't know how to use but nonetheless conjured up an atmosphere of homespun coziness that appealed to her. She ambled up and down the aisles, sniffing up overtones of cinnamon and cloves mixed with the pungent scents of orange, lemon, cherry, and pumpkin.

A bottle of marinade with garlic cloves trapped inside caught her eye. She removed it from its dusty ring and turned it upside-down then right-side-up, launching the garlic into the oil like alien pods floating about in zero gravity.

A hand fell on her shoulder. "You look lost."

She set the bottle carefully back in place and smiled up at the crinkled face of a valkyrie. The woman's coppery eyes held the burnished glint of newly minted pennies caught in the rain.

"Clueless actually."

A smile tugged at the valkyrie's lips. "We offer cooking lessons on Wednesday night."

"Sounds lovely, but I've got Griffin."

"Griffin Jaeger at the Diamond Dust?"

"Yes, Griffin is my cook. It's good to know he gets out once in a while. I was beginning to think he chained himself to his pots and pans."

"Griffin keeps my shop in the black. What happened to the brothers?"

"Happened?"

"You said *my* cook. You the new owner?"

"Not exactly." She seized up the bottle of garlic aliens, plucked a package of greenies off the shelf, and dug out her wallet. "I'll take this stuff."

She hit the fudge shop next and bought a pound of coffee-filled truffles from a petite blond woman who peppered every sentence with "you betcha." On Main Street, she crossed inside the Blue Moon jewelry store. Skirting the displays of religious crosses, wedding rings, and diving watches, she hesitated at a cabinet filled with gold pendants. Rows of beautifully crafted butterflies, penguins, and tulips nestled in petite foam trays and miniature cars, boats, and trains zoom-zoomed from delicate gold chains. She stepped over to a display case containing signature rings made of tungsten carbide as a man's voice drifted over.

"Tungsten carbide is scratch resistant."

She turned to find Tim Richard standing behind her. "I prefer shinier bits."

He laughed. "I'm glad I ran into you. Would you please give Reilly a message for me? Tell her I'm done hiding. Lies have destroyed my team, maybe my future with Rachel."

Julie was dead, Fay was fighting to breathe, Sydney faced a lengthy rehab, and this bozo was worried about his own prospects? *Bloody self-serving sod.* She reined in her irritation. Reilly had told her to look and listen, not piss-off perfectly good suspects.

"I'll see what I can do," she lied. "Good news about Sydney, right?"

"Much of the credit goes to you—the same can be said of Fay." His frosty eyes swept over the not-so-hidden security cameras hooked to the vaulted ceiling. "I'm afraid you're in for a disappointment if you champion Sydney. This doping episode isn't her first."

He fished a fistful of business cards from the rack, pushed one into her hand, jammed the rest into his pocket, and then tugged her backward, away from the prying ears of the sales clerk behind the register. She chalked up his weird behavior to nerves.

"When Sydney was a junior cyclist on the national team, her coach found dirty needles in her room. She served her mandatory eighteen-month suspension. After that, she was damaged goods. Continental gave her a second chance as a favor to her uncle, Tom Drake."

"Her third-place finish last month proves she has potential."

"If Sydney doped for this championship, she probably doped for Moriarty too. This offense is officially her second. I doubt the Federation will restrain her punishment to a slap on the wrist and another suspension."

"Have you tried to find out who helped her recycle her blood?"

"None of her teammates would do such a thing."

"Well, somebody did. Blood-doping takes four hands. Past experience has shown it's not uncommon for an entire team to use performance-enhancing techniques—the one-for-all and all-for-one mentality. Is that what you and Julie argued about? Was it Julie who instigated a doping plan for herself and her teammates—and not Allison? You told her to stop, and Julie being Julie, refused. It would explain why you're not putting up a bigger stink about your immigration status, or lack thereof. If you keep Reilly busy looking into your past, your present will remain in the shadows."

His stoic mask fell away. "Even if all these things you say prove true, they still do not add up to a motive to murder my best cyclist."

"It does if Julie followed her refusal to stop doping with her threat to blame you. If it came down to your word against hers, and the blood tests bore out the fact that five of your female cyclists had doped, you'd come across as the liar. You *are* responsible for your team's actions."

"My only crime was to give Julie what she asked for. If it will put me in good standing with the authorities, I will tell you of Julie's fraudulence, but not here and not now. Tomorrow morning on the course, near the turnaround—eleven o'clock."

"Reilly will want to tag along."

"No cops."

"Before I agree to something that moronic, tell me where you were at the time someone was bludgeoning Julie."

"With Grant, riding my bike."

"Early on, but what about later?"

"I rode back in. The demands on my time are never-ending."

He skated through the door.

She hung back, jammed the business card into her wallet, then crossed the street to the laundromat. Her bloodstained bag was worthless for carting clean clothes. Not as organized as Reilly, who would have air-expressed a sexy negligee and hamper to the ranch anticipating both a reunion with a lost husband and trip to the laundromat, she looked above, behind, and between each row of machines for a sack not sticky with body fluids or—at the very least—a serviceable box. She'd resigned herself to making several trips between the laundromat and her Jeep when a brunette in a plaid-flannel shirt hurried over holding a basket made of tree bark.

"This *mocuck* sure could use a good home." The woman set it on the window ledge. "It's been living in my lost 'n found for ages."

Logan made quick work of packing up her clothes as she thanked the woman for her kindness.

After dumping the *mocuck* in her Jeep, she jogged over to the library. Peter Pan had vacated his post to a formidable-looking woman with a cap of black, gray, and wild curls. Logan scooted up to the desk and explained what she wanted.

"This way, hon." The woman led her over to a bank of gray-metal filing cabinets, pulled out a drawer, and pointed out a row of microfiche. "Readers are in the back."

Logan found her comfy chair by the fire and pawed her way through the local newspaper archives for the state of Idaho, counting back ten years plus two more for good measure. Twenty-five minutes later, she'd found three Idaho periodicals that held promise—*The Priest Lake Call, Idaho Grange News,* and *Boise Daily Reminder.* Carrying herself to a reader, she inserted the microfiche under, over, and around the spool, flipped a couple of switches, and scanned the print.

The *Reminder* was a religious newsletter. *The Call* devoted its printed word to duck hunting. She struck gold with the *Idaho Grange News.* The fatality had been significant enough to make the front page, and thanks to the valkyrie in the kitchen shop, Logan had no difficulty finding the name of the young girl who'd broken her neck at the Tour of Idaho ten years past. The verbiage regurgitated Allison's version of the accident. She pressed the *print* icon, pocketed her copy, and returned the box of microfiche to the cabinet.

On her return trip, Romeo was asleep in the Jeep's passenger seat. Careful not to wake him, she pulled her stadium blanket from underneath the driver's seat and draped it over him. Then, she hopped into the driver's seat, turned the key in the ignition, and let the Jeep have its freedom back to the ranch.

CHAPTER 12

THE UNEXPECTED APPEARANCE of Jake jogging along the footpath as Logan approached her cabin gave her a jolt. He wore navy shorts and an abbreviated tank top that showed off his six-pack abs. Though not as slim as his brother, or as bulky as Romeo, Jake's muscular legs ate up the terrain at a frightening pace. She hung back. Fortunately he hadn't seen her, or if he had, he'd willfully ignored her.

Back inside her cabin, she threw herself on the bed and pulled the quilt to her chin.

She had barely drifted off when Reilly banged inside, lowered herself beside Logan, and stuffed a pillow behind her head. "Did you hear about Guy's crash?"

Logan shook herself fully awake. "I did. How is he?"

"Okay. Road rash, a bum shoulder—minor stuff."

"With the tens of thousands of miles we cycle every year, the odds of crashing from fatigue alone are high. Add winding descents, gale-force winds, rough roads, blind curves, giant boulders, and heavy traffic into the mix, and those odds escalate."

"Don't forget riding while injured. We're lucky Grant is such a great coach." Reilly laughed. "I remember when you first signed on, and he practiced bumping his front wheel into your rear wheel, crossing his front wheel into your front wheel, and making you lay down your bike—

over and over. You were so pissed, I thought you were going to tear up your contract right in his face."

"And I remember showing up at our races black and blue. Maybe that's what happened to Anna. She came to the Tour of Idaho injured and lost her line."

Reilly gawked in surprise. "Griffin's sister was a cyclist, and she died at a race?"

She repeated Allison's story. "Julie was certainly there. Whether she was responsible…."

"Whatever happened, it's beyond sad." Reilly pointed at the discarded book. "Witchcraft, really?"

Logan vaulted off the bed and stuffed her feet into sneakers. "Come on. I want to show you something."

"But I just got here."

She was already halfway out the door when she stopped to make sure Reilly was following.

"Where are we going?"

"To the greenhouse, so you can tell me I'm crazy."

Reilly leaned against the doorjamb. "We don't need to waste calories hoofing around in the dark for that. You're crazy. It's part of your charm."

"I'm not kidding. The welfare of a man I'm fond of is at stake."

"Your slinky stranger?"

"My brilliant cook."

"Crikey—serous stuff then. Lead the way."

Neither of them spoke again until they came upon the greenhouse. Someone had turned on the rosy grow lights since her last visit, bathing the building in a gauzy pink glow. Her hand was on the doorknob when Reilly shoved her aside, both hands gripped around the Smith & Wesson as she melted among the flowerbeds.

Reilly reappeared as swiftly as she'd vanished, holstered the gun, and motioned her inside. "We're alone. Whatever you got to say, say it fast. This place is spooky—capital S spooky."

They crossed inside, where Logan pointed at the explosion of pink blooms. "What are these?"

"Really? That's why you brought us here? To spring a botanical quiz on me? I'm a bicycling cop, not a horticulturalist. You've got exactly ten seconds to tell me what we're doing here before me and this ghostly garden part ways."

"Those pink things are azaleas, and these yellow things"—she brushed her fingers over a golden blossom in the neighboring flowerbed—"are buttercups, and they're both poisonous. So is this timber milk vetch"—she pointed to a bed of wispy fern-like greenery budding with bell-shaped flowers—"and that yellow ragwort with the orange centers next to you. North America offers up more than seven hundred species of poisonous plants, and at least twenty of them are growing in this greenhouse. Griffin is harvesting poisonous honey."

"How can you possibly know that?"

"Because the apiary is next door. The bees use the nectar from these poisonous blossoms to make their honey. Griffin had planned to poison Julie, but something stopped him."

GIVING INTO REILLY's uneasiness, they slipped out of the greenhouse and tromped back through the forest to Logan's cabin, where Reilly lowered herself onto the hamper with the soft quilt draped across her lap. "Griffin planned to kill Julie because he held her responsible for Anna's death—is that where this is going?"

"Revenge is a powerful motive."

"Are you sure this poisonous-honey rubbish isn't the result of too much reading... well, reading period? Would it kill you to turn on the boob tube once in a blue moon and get stupid with the rest of us?"

"Be serious. Is it a crime to destroy evidence?"

"Of course it's a crime, but what evidence, and who destroyed it?"

"Griffin. He slapped that honeypot from my hand at our tea party, remember? Now, every scrap of honey that was on those shelves in his kitchen is gone."

"You want me to arrest a man because he destroyed evidence of a murder he planned but didn't commit?"

"I never said he didn't kill Julie. I said he planned to poison her but changed his mind, or something changed it for him."

"Before or after he lured her into that tunnel with his naughty cake in his imaginary car?"

"He could've borrowed something from somebody—bike, car, scooter."

"Let's back up a linear mile, please. Do you have anything to shore up Allison's faded memories and your overactive imagination that Julie was in *any fashion* responsible for Anna's death?"

She brought out the newspaper article and dropped it into Reilly's lap. "Only this."

While Reilly read, Logan paced, her eyes straying through the screen door where the fireflies sparkled up the jet-black night.

"This newspaper article claims the Highway Patrol found no evidence to fault Julie," Reilly said as Logan stopped pacing.

"Griffin wouldn't care. He was desperate to blame somebody for Anna's death. Julie was in his line of fire. So you see, he's known *of* Julie for more than a decade. What's more, he had access to the Federation's website. The address is right there on Anna's racing license, and the Federation posts the location and date for each championship race the November before the upcoming racing year. It also explains Griffin's presence on the ranch *uninvited* in January of this year."

"All right already. Let's say you're right, and Julie was in some way responsible for Anna's death. How would Griffin know she'd show up here?"

"Pre-registration."

"You're not going to give this up until either Griffin confesses or we prove otherwise, are you?"

"I need to know without a doubt."

Reilly fluttered the printout. "May I keep this?"

"Please do."

"The best I can do is to get us a copy of the official report. New eyes might turn up something, but don't expect a miracle. Anna's death isn't a cold case—it's an icicle."

"Does Griffin have a satisfactory alibi for the time Julie died?"

Reilly withdrew her notebook and tossed it to Logan. "Last page. Read it while I phone Reko."

"Reko?"

"Chief Byrd. His father was a Norseman who never went home."

"His mother?"

"We aren't cozy enough yet to swap family histories." The bang of the screen door heralded Reilly's exit.

Griffin was not a nine-to-five guy. He was a five-to-nine guy. From five to ten Wednesday morning, he'd labored away in his kitchen dipping, grilling, flipping, and flopping slabs of French toast. He'd taken himself out for brunch between 10:30 and 11:30, then spent the rest of the day prepping for lunch and dinner. Jake had detailed some of his men to help set up the buffet, then wash up. Otherwise, Griffin had spent his day alone.

As second bang heralded Reilly's return. "What do you think?"

"I think Griffin lives in culinary purgatory." She flipped the notebook back to Reilly.

"The sheriff estimates Julie's killer needed at least forty minutes to drive to the turnaround, go into that tunnel, kill her, and hustle away with her bike. Given access to a motorized vehicle, Griffin could've found the time." She sucked in a breath. "Before you gave me that article, I couldn't imagine the Magic Chef killing anyone. Now, not so much, especially when I tell you Julie's neck was broken before someone impaled her."

"Broken!" Logan exclaimed. "My God, what a monster."

Reilly helped herself to a coffee truffle. "Sure you don't want one of these? Caffeine and chocolate together are natural mood—"

She held up her hand. "I'm more interested in why Chief Byrd withheld that fact at our first meet and dump."

Reilly shrugged. "Not my place to question his methods."

"Where does this leave Griffin?"

"Death-dealing honey aside, your Magic Chef is safe for now."

Reilly had returned to her own cabin by the time Logan changed from shorts to jeans, pulled on thick socks and hiking boots, and yanked open the screen door. This time when she stumbled into him, he kissed her until she was lightheaded.

She glanced at the bed. "Perhaps we should stay here."

"It is safer if we do not. Although the moon no longer claims you nor the sun me, I do not wish to broadcast our past union or the events leading up to our reunion."

"Okay, stranger—take me to your man cave."

Their first steps outside brought Cerberus and Geneva rushing into the room and onto the bed. While Cerberus squirmed his way down into the pillows, Geneva made nesting circles before she settled in.

Logan brought out the bag of greenies from the nightstand. "Come on, guys. First one to the glass house gets a treat."

The animals bounded off the bed and dashed out into the night with the humans following at a much slower pace. They'd made it as far as the dirt road when the Doberman pup shot out of the aspen grove, her ears pinned back and her muzzle twisted into a lopsided grin. She wiggled between the older dogs, and together, they weaved their way toward the mountains.

"Does the pup belong to Jeremy?" she asked.

"She hasn't chosen yet."

"Is that how it works here—everybody chooses?"

"How could it be otherwise?"

"What about the colt with the blue eyes?"

"He has already chosen."

The news left her deflated.

His amber eyes sparkled. "He has chosen you."

"Me?" She threw her arms around his neck, wondering what her *other* had done or said a thousand years ago that had made him choose her too. "How do you know?"

"Jeremy told me of your return and also of your bond with the tobiano colt. Of course, you may refuse my gift. A woman always has second say."

"No way. If I wasn't totally onboard with this belonging thing before, I sure am now."

Another quarter-mile brought them to the glass house, where the dogs lounged on the doormat, curled one into the other like nesting Matryoshaka dolls. When she pulled open the door, they scampered inside and jostled for a place on the hearth rug.

She spread herself lengthwise across the leather sofa. "Was Allison's choice as wise as mine?"

He laid beside her and gathered her close. "Davis was orphaned at a young age to search out his own path. It ended with me at the Diamond Dust. He has a natural affinity with animals and has proven his fierce loyalty to me. I believe he will display the same love and loyalty to your friend."

"If someone wronged someone he cared for, would he seek revenge?"

"Revenge, never. It is not our way. Nor do I believe he would kill a woman under most circumstances."

"What about a man?"

"The Old Man and the Old Woman left us with many reasons to kill a man."

CHAPTER 13

FRIDAY MORNING BROUGHT Reilly to the door of Logan's cabin carrying a bakery-sized box filled with breakfast burritos to kick off calories-be-damned day—the eating holiday they'd invented that fell on the day before a big race... well, any race.

Settling in on the hamper, Reilly helped herself to a burrito and took an ample bite, slopping eggs and cheese onto her chin. "If only I had a mocha latte to wash it down with."

Logan pulled a bag out from underneath the nightstand.

Reilly's hazel eyes lit up. "No way!"

"Simon dropped them off only minutes ago. It's his way of telling us he bet a bundle on us too, so one of us better win tomorrow. How'd you score the burritos?"

"Your Magic Chef."

"You didn't threaten him, did you?"

"Of course not. A man's entitled to spend his last days of freedom chained to his stove."

She smothered her giggle in caffeine.

"Short ride today. Any ideas?"

"Let's ride out to the workshop. It's an easy pedal from the entrance—fifteen miles tops."

"In a hurry to get back?"

"I'm meeting Tim."

"A date?"

"Another meet and dump. I ran into him in the jewelry store last night. He was edgy. We arranged to meet this morning so he could tell me of 'Julie's fraudulence' without the intrusion of prying ears."

"Whose ears?"

"The sales clerk."

"That guy is weird. Okay, we're in. When and where?"

"'Fraid not."

"You don't want me?"

"Not me—Tim. He unfriended you… well, cops in general."

"Can't say I like the idea, but as Simon says 'nuthin' I can does about it, cause yous is all growed-up.' Promise me you'll be extra careful around him, okay?"

She crossed her heart. "Were you able to fill in the gap between the time Tim defected and when he took up with Continental?"

Reilly grabbed her notebook and flipped to a dog-eared page. "His IRS returns state he worked for the Whitfield Metal Laboratory in Idaho from 2010 to 2012. His supervisor Frank Demars confirmed it."

"A man on the lam files income tax returns?"

"It's illegal not to. Those filings and his ability to lie fluently in German, English, French, and Spanish probably kept him off everyone's radar. Demars said Tim walked into the lab one day and asked for a job. Whitfield's had a vacancy, and he took a chance. Tim volunteered for a lot of overtime. Demars said it was the best hire he ever made… until Tim walked out a few years later."

"Nothing after that?"

"Not until he showed up on Continental's payroll."

The day dawned bright and crisp. A pair of ambulances stood inside the front gate, a churlish reminder of the dangers that lie around every corner.

Reilly checked her watch. "A bit early for the Grim Reaper's chariot."

"One cyclist is dead, two more are in the hospital, and another is going home from injuries sustained in a crash. My math says it's too late."

Turning east at the entrance, they enjoyed a short stretch of flat road that swiftly gave way to rolling hills. Another few miles took them over mild climbs and sweeping downhills. A few storm clouds passed overhead, dusting them with corn snow. The unseasonal cold snap did nothing to diminish the grandeur of the rugged mountains or their symbiotic neighbors, the dark forestlands and verdant meadows living off the affluence. The last descent took them into a basin where the tentacles of the storm hadn't reached.

Logan twisted around in the saddle at the same time the sun burst out amid the snowflakes, creating a crystalline fog over the craggy formations. "The fog is rolling in. You'd better lead if you don't want us to get lost."

"You don't know where the workshop is?"

"I know it's east of the dining hall as the crow flies."

Reilly stuck her hand up. "Stop. We're going to fix this right now."

They unclipped, dismounted, and dragged their bikes to the side of the road.

"How is it you get lost so easily?" Reilly asked.

"Easily, my arse—it's hard work. I start out knowing where I am...."

"That's a relief."

"And I usually know where I'm going, but unless it's a straight line, I can't reconcile the here to the there."

Reilly laughed. "Do you know how wacky that sounds?"

"Only to you—the human compass."

"Use landmarks." Reilly turned and faced the mountains. "Look. The Canadian Rockies are north, so left is west—where the sun sets—and right is east, where the sun rises."

"Where are the cabins?"

"Right now, west—behind us."

"So if we keep riding into the sun, we'll hit the workshop."

"Eventually, although you do get that the sun moves south then west, right?"

"See, it's words like *eventually* that do me in. Eventually, I second-guess myself, and the next thing I know I'm lost on a shortcut that at best was a figment of my overactive imagination."

"Four words for you, girlie—*don't go outside alone.*"

They set off again, drafting off each other's slipstreams. On her third pull, Logan dropped back as Reilly pulled forward.

"Pull out my gloves—will you, pretty please?" Reilly said.

Logan unzipped the pocket that ran across the back of Reilly's jacket and dug around. "Here." She passed off the fingerless gloves, then squinted into the bright sunlight as an errant piece of muffler appeared on the road in front of them. "Look out!"

Logan swerved left to miss it as Reilly sped off right. Catching up, Logan moved abreast of Reilly and slowed her pedal cadence. Up ahead, a lone cyclist closed in on a copper roof set off to the north side of the road. The rider had disappeared from their view by the time they came abreast of the workshop. They stopped, unclipped, dismounted, and leaned their bikes against some pines. When Reilly plunged down a narrow elk trail littered with droppings, Logan tramped behind her until they came to a river. A few stout tree limbs—victims of a past storm—blocked their egress. Logan dipped her hand in the water and stirred up the silvery glitter that twinkled up from the bottom.

Meanwhile, Reilly had moved west to jump across a narrowing that landed her on the opposite bank. She gestured to Logan. "Over here."

Logan crossed at the same spot, but instead of following Reilly west along the river, she walked northeast until she arrived at the workshop, a vaulted rectangle covered in green metal with a north-facing door. Elephant ears, yarrow, and knapweed grew profusely in the dirt pushed up against its walls. A field of plastic drums took up a patch of land east of the structure, several upended by recent winds. She walked to the closest drum and gave it a thump. It returned a hollow cough. She tried lifting it. It yielded to her touch. She set it back down and tried a few more. Most proved empty or partially filled. She wove around them to the door and punched the wall switch.

Reilly joined her as the door chugged open. "So, okay, we've officially crossed the line between snooping and B and E."

"Relax, we've got an in with the caretakers."

The shop was so vast Jeremy could have driven an RV into it and still squeezed in the state of Rhode Island. The walls were painted soft green, but everything else was gray—the concrete floor, conveyer belts, stainless countertops, and stacks of aluminum cylinders pushed against the walls. The air held the acrid bit of ammonia with overtones of turpentine. A water cistern rose up in a back corner. A monstrous piece of machinery equipped with a water tank took up a good chunk of real estate near the front. More silver specks carpeted the bottom of the tank.

Reilly pointed them out. "I never got a chance to tell you what the lab uncovered on that partial brake pad you found in the river. With Julie's bike still missing, we can't verify its origin, but since it's made of a unique alloy, the sheriff is acting like it did. Joe traced the silvery glitz back to the blades on Jeremy's saws, which are made of a fiber-mesh composite with industrial-grade diamonds glued onto the grid. The trace amounts of arsenic and antimony in the analysis are contaminants of the aluminum Jeremy cuts up for fencing. The sheriff figures the wheel of Julie's bike picked it up and transferred it to the pad. The pad broke off, and half of it ended up in the river—the part you found."

"What about the composition of the brake pad? Does it contain carbon?"

"Yes, but not any run-of-the-mill carbon compound—carbon mixed with vanadium. The inside of the pad was made of Babbitt's metal to reduce friction."

When Reilly wandered off, Logan snaked around cabinets and poked inside drawers that held an assortment of man essentials—hammers, blades, wrenches, chisels, screwdrivers, knives, nails, and duct tape in assorted neon colors of raspberry, lime, lemon, and tangerine.

Eventually, she joined Reilly by the cistern. "Any chance Julie did what we're doing?"

"Snoop where she had no business snooping? Every chance. Not only is it vintage Julie, it goes a long way in explaining that glitter the lab found on her brake pad."

Back outside, Taylor carefully picked her way around the maze of plastic drums. She was dressed in her team kit with a hands-off headset clipped to her ear.

Reilly joined her, while Logan secured the door. "Top of the morning to you. What brings you out this way?"

"Same as you I suspect—boredom. Lordy, I wish this championship were over and done with. Who would've thunk a dead Julie would be more troublesome than a live one?"

The willowy redhead moved on, picking her way across the river and back toward the road.

"Lordy," Reilly said, "whatever did Miss Georgia Peach mean by that?"

They'd reunited with their bikes as Jeremy stepped onto the path from behind a tree. The Doberman pup lagged behind him, leaping playfully over fallen boughs until it spotted Reilly. The dog gave out a frisky bark and fell on her shoes, nibbling on the Velcro straps.

The ear-to-ear grin Jeremy gave Reilly pleated his face like a broken-down accordion. "Josie seeks purpose."

"Well, she isn't going to find it licking my shoes." She scooped up the puppy and cooed baby gibberish into its face.

He gathered Reilly—still clutching the Doberman—into a tight hug. "You will be leaving us soon, *Ksikkihkini*—but will take many hearts with you."

———————

"WHAT DO YOU suppose *Kemosahbee* meant by that?" Reilly asked after man and dog had moved on.

Logan laughed. "If I knew stuff like that, I'd bottle it and sell it on Etsy."

Reilly tapped her phone. "Nine thirty... only ninety minutes left before your date with Tim."

"Will you stop it with this date thing? If my meet and dump was with Allison, you wouldn't call it a date."

"If Allison was involved, there'd be no cloak and dagger. So where is this clandestine tryst?"

"On the course."

"Geez Louise! That's a good fifteen miles northwest of where we are now. So much for an easy pedal."

"Then we better haul some you-know-what to get me there on time."

They mounted up and sped back down the road that had brought them to the workshop. A few miles farther on, the ringtone of Reilly's phone made them brake and clip out.

"This"—Logan pointed at the singing phone—"is exactly why I don't carry one of those things. We can't even do a blooming bike ride in peace."

Reilly waved off her protest with a "yes" to the caller. "Today? When? Eleven. Jeremy's veranda. Got it." She dropped the phone into her pocket. "You're not the only one with a date."

The miles flew by as they sped west, then north down a road Reilly assured her was a shortcut. Logan was skeptical until the patch of rocks where the paper wasps had stung her loomed on the horizon. Once again, they braked and unclipped from the pedals.

"Turn left at those rocks, and you'll eventually come to the turnaround. You can find your way back from there, can't you?"

"Ride straight south until I run out of pavement at the hot tubs."

"Yep, with no shortcuts to tempt you... not even a service road." Reilly brought out a pair of gels and offered one to Logan, who shook her head. "You know, all your talk of dates has got me thinking."

"Not my talk, your talk."

"Somebody's talk. Julie called her luncheon tête-à-tête a date, right?"

"Bragged is more apt."

"Then odds are she was with a man—because that is *so* Julie, right?"

"Right, but which man?"

"I'm good with eliminating Grant. He has trained us too hard and respects us too much to do away with the only woman who might've beaten us. Besides, what's in it for him if we win—thirty seconds in front of a mike and a sound bit on ESPN if it's a slow week. Nobody commits murder for that."

"A win for one of us also means he gets to keep his job. Motive aside, Grant has an unimpeachable alibi—Katy and Sabrina. Tim too."

"Katy and Sabrina insist they were with Grant the whole morning, but at some point Tim dropped off."

"That's what he told me too—'too many demands on his time,' is how he put it. What about the others? Did their alibis check out?"

"Romeo was in his van *alone*, Sydney was asleep in her cabin *alone*, Fay was out wandering *alone*, and Taylor and Allison were out riding—but not with each other."

"Rachel?"

"In her cabin studying—*alone*. She's graduating from medical school this December. Simon told us he fixed Julie's shifters, got a coffee in the dining hall, chatted up Griffin, strolled around the ranch, and then returned to his van—*alone*."

"You're not seriously considering Simon, are you?"

"We're seriously considering everyone. That's how it's done. Like the others, Simon also saw Julie that morning when she dropped off her bike for him to fix and again when she picked it up after he'd fixed it."

"Maybe her killer didn't take the bike. The way Jake runs his mouth, he probably gave that railroad speech, or its facsimile, to every Tom, Dick, and Harriet who got off the bus. How do we know someone else didn't wander into that tunnel, find Julie dead or dying, and simply ride off on the bike for a joy ride?"

"Nobody rode off on Julie's bike because her *killer* left the wheels behind, remember?"

"Touché. What about Davis Morgan?"

"Allison's friend?"

"Fiancé. She told you what they did yesterday, right?"

"She did." Reilly rolled her eyes. "What were they thinking?"

"Isn't that the bazillion-dollar question. Allison has always won her races through hard work and brilliant racing tactics. It's more likely Davis Morgan came up with the idea to cheat, and she covered for him. He might be worth a second look."

Not ten minutes later, Reilly's phone sang out again. This time they kept riding as she pulled it from her pocket. "Thanks. Right. Bye." Reilly pressed the end-call button. "That was Joe. The fax on Anna's death came in. Highway Patrol confirmed Allison's story. Julie was the cyclist who bumped Anna off the cliff."

She turned a draconian eye on her friend.

Reilly crossed her heart. "I swear on my badge I won't do anything about Griffin until I talk to you first."

"Does that mean we're still on for lunch?"

"Only a fool would forfeit the Magic Chef's eats on calories-be-damned day."

CHAPTER 14

L OGAN TURNED LEFT at the fork in the road. Overhead, the sky simmered like blue glass, and the sun was swollen with heat. She was hot, edgy, and hungry—familiar territory as race day drew near. Whatever Tim had to tell her had better be worth the extra calories she'd burned to get here. She used the wait visualizing the course—a long stretch of road with a slight gradient, several miles of rolling hills, a shallow climb, and a plunging downhill to the turnaround, then back in reverse order.

Eleven ten, and still Tim hadn't turned up. She practiced the harder climb—the downhill that turned into an uphill on the return leg—several times, varying gears and cadences until she found several she could push at eighty-five rpm. After the fifth attempt, she continued riding south, tackling the rolling hills in reverse order. When they were done, she made a sweeping turn and rode back toward the turnaround. As the steep descent came into view, she relaxed into her saddle.

An engine rumbled behind her.

She geared up on the rear cog, spun up her speed, and surrendered every inch of the road she could spare to the approaching vehicle while holding her line on the road.

Again, the engine revved—a deafening rumble hinting of a van or truck. A whispered hum followed as a dark shadow crept threateningly over her rear wheel, then her saddle, and finally her handlebars.

She sat heavy and slowed to a crawl, keeping a tight grip on the handlebars in anticipation of the truck's backdraft, which would fishtail her rear wheel when it passed. Then, she soft-pedaled to maintain her balance.

The shadow retreated. The engine stilled.

Fed up with the truck's cat-and-mouse tactics, she rose on the pedals and twisted around. The truck had dropped back several lengths and now idled on the road. As the engine gave out a violent rev, the truck charged forward—bearing down on her at full throttle.

THE BUMPER OF the truck was only yards away when Logan launched herself toward a bank of sand, fell short, hit the gravel first, and then tumbled into a growth of prickly lettuce. As the truck sped past, she rolled out of the thorny bed and melted into the sunbaked earth. For a while, the hard gravel gave way in her mind to his soft waterbed, and she fell blissfully asleep. When she awoke, her head throbbed like a jackhammer. She lifted her shoulders. The rocks in the distance tilted, then straightened. She fell back down to the tortured cry of an angry fox. More time passed before she took stock of her pain—a gash in her mouth, an ache in her thigh. She stood in stages—pressing forward onto her knees, inching up into a crouch, and finally rising onto her shoes— shivering, lightheaded, and bleeding.

Her bike lay across the road, where the truck had tossed it like a leaf in a windstorm. The collision with the truck's bumper had pleated its rear wheel and mangled the spokes. She lurched toward it, collapsed onto the gravel, plucked out the water bottles, and drank thirstily.

When she pulled up her knees, a pain shot from her thigh down to her ankle. She struggled on, inching backward across the gravel to the sandy embankment, where she fished out her last candy bar, tore off the wrapping, and let the sweet-salty blend of buttery caramel and roasted peanuts work its magic underneath the noonday sun.

THE LACK OF physical evidence at the crime scene had prompted the sheriff to send his deputy back out to the ranges. Joe Amundsen steered his truck toward the tall woman zigzagging across the tarmac. She was the same woman who'd deflected a bullet less than twenty-four hours earlier—Logan, Slade's friend. Her shirt and shorts were ripped clean through, and blood dribbled down her arm from yesterday's wound.

He braked the truck to a stop, yanked open the door, and sprinted a short distance down the road. Her hair was a tangled nest of thorns, gravel, and dirt underneath a helmet cracked like an eggshell. An acrid scent of fear laced with peanuts enveloped her. No bones sticking out, only a skinless patch on her leg where the shorts had ripped away and yesterday's bandage hanging from her arm.

"Are you okay?"

She stared up at him as if he was a Jovian God. "You've no idea how glad I am to see you."

"Fall off your bike?"

"I lost my line and had to bail out," she lied. "My legs are a bit wobbly. Could you lend me yours?"

He tucked her against his side, holding tight to her hand. "Come on. We're off to the hospital."

She wrenched herself free. "No! I can't leave him."

"Leave who? Is there someone out here with you?"

"Tim… we were supposed to meet, but he blew… er, he didn't come."

His grip on her tightened. "I'll run you back in, then drive back out and take a second look for Tim—I promise."

They'd reached his truck when he lifted her gently onto the passenger seat and buckled her in. "Still okay?"

She nodded.

He returned to the road, lifted her bike into the bed of the truck, ran around to the driver's side, and buckled himself in. "Looks bad."

"Simon can fix anything."

"In time for your race?"

"I'll race a different bike tomorrow, one configured specifically for a time trial. Simon keeps those bikes under lock and key."

"No harm then."

She flexed her well-muscled legs. "No harm."

He turned the key in the ignition. Her eyelids felt like sandbags weighing her down. She let them drop, vaguely aware he'd reined in the car's Motor City impulses and crept them back to the main entrance in silence.

JOE EASED THE truck alongside the ambulance. "Sit tight. Jake's up in his office. I'll only be a minute."

She clutched his arm. "Jake's got his hands full with the race. Try Griffin. He's sure to be in his kitchen." She released his arm. "Thanks again. If you hadn't shown up when you did... well, thanks. What brought you out to course?"

"The chief wanted another sweep of the crime scene. Listen, I don't know how long I'll be, so if you start to feel poorly, Jake is only a stone's throw away."

After he'd gone, she used the passenger seat as a springboard to push herself out onto solid ground. She reached the truck bed as a silver truck drove through the entrance. Taylor sat behind the wheel. She parked it in front of the Craftsman, then set off on foot across the meadow. Logan wrenched open the back gate and yanked her bike to the ground. She slammed the tailgate shut as Griffin grew up beside her.

He held up an icy bottle of Diet Coke. "Drink this, my dear."

She seized it from him and drank greedily. "You're a lifesaver... a thousand thanks. Where's Joe?"

"Guarding my chocolate soufflé." He lifted her broken bike. "Where may I trash this?"

"Shh! Simon might hear you. He's got the ears of a bat and the disposition of a saltwater crocodile." She glared down at the mangled rear wheel. "Put it on Jeremy's veranda, please. I'll deal with Simon later."

The river was within view when Logan lagged behind.

"What is it?" Griffin asked.

She pointed to Taylor and Tim sitting side by side on a rock. "Let's not disturb them." She pressed the empty Diet Coke bottle on him. "I'll be fine the rest of the way alone. Go back to your soufflé."

She'd limped to within twenty yards of the glass house when the dogs trotted up to her with their tails wagging. "Hi, guys—hungry?"

The wagging hit fever pitch.

"Me too."

They dashed inside the house and took their places near the fire while she ripped off her shoes, jacket, and helmet and padded into the kitchen. She fixed herself a jumbo glass of ice-cold Diet Coke, filled the dogs' bowls with dry kibble and baked chicken, and refreshed their water. The glass was almost empty when she walked into the bathroom and stripped off her torn clothes, dumping them and the bloody bandage into the trash. Underneath the harsh spray of the shower, she spent most of her time untangling her hair while she rehearsed some lies that would satisfy Simon.

Today would be the first time in eight years she'd returned a bike in pieces. With more than thirty-years-experience as a mechanic, he'd seen all kinds of bikes sustain all kinds of damage in all kinds of ways. If he found out somebody had deliberately tried to injure her, Simon would tattle to Grant, who in turn would scratch her from tomorrow's race. If she told him she'd lost her line on the road and fallen victim to a ditch, he'd bemoan her klutziness but keep his mouth shut. The race of truth was her event, and she wouldn't let anyone steal it from her.

She dabbed antibiotic cream onto the fresh crop of superficial scrapes and scratches that covered her arms and legs, bandaged yesterday's flesh wound, then tackled the road rash on her thigh, painstakingly tweezing out each piece of gravel before splashing hydrogen peroxide over the worst of it. The bruise blossoming underneath the road rash was her only cause for concern. She padded back into the kitchen and removed an ice pack from the freezer. Back in the bedroom, she crawled underneath the bedcovers, placed the ice pack atop her thigh, and fell instantly asleep.

HIS HEAT AROUSED her to wakefulness. After uncoiling the soft cocoon of blankets that enveloped her, he danced his fingertips over her ankles and knees. When he caressed her thigh, she clamped her lips together so she wouldn't cry out. By the time he'd splayed his palm on her breastbone she wanted him so badly she pulled him down on her, but as their legs collided, she yelped. He leaned away, his topaz eyes blazing. As she arched toward him, he met her halfway, and this time she made no sound when he held her against him and freed her hair from its bondage.

Sometime later, he kissed her awake. "You friend has sent word. You must go to her, but first I must treat your injuries so you can ride tomorrow."

"Treat them with what?"

"Our medicine."

He crawled back into his discarded jeans and disappeared through the French doors. She returned to the closet to find more of her clothes hanging from rods and stuffed away in cubbyholes. She plucked out a fresh pair of jeans and a long-sleeved shirt and returned to the bed. He waited, armed with a tray that held a cup filled with a pale-green liquid, a pile of shiny green leaves, and bag of cotton pads.

"Please lie back," he said.

She relished the sensation of his warm touch on her naked skin, until he came to her thigh. She bolted upright. "What are those?" She pointed to the leaves, now arranged as a *T* with the crossbar running horizontally along her hipbone.

"Cleavers. Like yarrow, the leaves reduce bleeding and swelling." He pressed a glossy leaf similar to the pod of a snow pea into her hand. "Let them work their magic while I cleanse your other wounds."

She closed her eyes as he dribbled the liquid over her cuts and scrapes, but when his fingertips caressed the cut on her forehead, she opened her eyes to find his lips hovering above hers.

"Belonging to each other does not mean you must sacrifice your dreams, *Nuttah*."

She pulled him down beside her. "For now, you're all the dream I can handle."

CHAPTER 15

IN LATE AFTERNOON, the dining room was pleasantly stale. A handful of cowboys kibitzed near the fireplace. Diamond Dust carryalls and wide-brimmed Stetsons sprawled on the window seat and spilled onto the floor like spent dominoes. Suede gloves, empty soup bowls, half-eaten bread crusts, and cracker crumbs littered the tabletops. A quartet of male cyclists wearing the gold-and-green jerseys of Team CR7 laughed boisterously at a table flooded with lazy sunlight. Outside in the courtyard, a stout man wearing a Las Vegas Raiders jersey sat on a bench holding hands with a petite brunette wearing a Los Angeles Chargers jersey.

Reilly was nowhere in sight.

As cowboys and cyclists bustled away, Logan sank into a chair near the buffet and listened to the furnace ping out its pulsating beat like a drum soloist tuning up to an empty café.

Fifteen minutes ticked off the arts-and-craft clock hanging above the fireplace—still no Reilly.

The wave of adrenaline and sugar that had sustained her for hours had long since ebbed. Even worse, her thirty-six-hour window for pre-race eating was closing fast. She helped herself to a bowl of tomato soup and a tuna on rye from the buffet and carried the tray to a table closer to the warmth of the fire. Griffin had loaded his soup with chunks of tomatoes and seasoned it with a hint of cloves. She'd scraped the bowl clean when Rachel rushed inside and headed straight for her table. She hadn't come alone. The aromas of sunscreen, bananas, and fingernail polish traveled with her, along with a stony glare that would've made the Gorgon sisters proud.

They settled down on the neighboring chair. "Where's Reilly? I need to tell her something."

"She's running late."

Rachel inched a hand beside the tuna sandwich. "You gonna eat that?"

Logan kept back half and pushed the plate toward Rachel. "Where's Tim?"

"On his way to Plains. Somebody had to pick up Sydney and check on Fay."

"You're sure?"

"About Tim? He's not tagged with a computer chip if that's what you're asking."

"In light of his propensity for vanishing, maybe you should consider it."

Rachel burst out laughing. "God, I needed that! It's been far too gloomy around this place lately."

"There's three good reasons for that—Julie, Sydney, and Fay. Did Tim use public transit?"

"No, he took Jake's truck."

"Jake was okay with that?"

"If he wasn't, why give us a set of spare keys?" Rachel took a bite from the sandwich. "Gosh, this is good. I haven't tasted a decent rye bread since I left Chicago."

"You're from the Midwest?"

"Born and raised."

"Is that where you met Tim?"

"No, we hooked up in South Carolina. I was on a family vacation, and Tim was working for Continental Tire in Fort Mill. One day we met up on the road. I was riding for a developmental team back then. He told me Continental was sponsoring a team and asked if I was interested. When my time as a junior was up, we reconnected."

"When was this?"

"Seven years ago."

"Any regrets?"

"Plenty. He never bothered to tell me I'd be cycling my butt off for Julie. Without that grief, I'd have done more on my bike and argued less off it. It worked out though. I put myself through medical school, and of course, I grew closer to Tim."

"Does that mean you'll be trading in your bike for a stethoscope soon?"

"Not right away. Julie's death has opened up some opportunities for us veterans, and I'm still relatively young. Even if she hadn't died, Julie's expiration date as a cyclist had passed. She showed up here fat and slow. If she'd lost this championship, Continental was ready to cut her loose. Now, with Allison packing it in, I'm the only veteran left. I'll give it two more years on the condition I'm promoted to captain and Tim builds the team around me."

"What about your medical career?"

"I've got a two-year grace period on my residencies."

"Where does that leave Taylor, Fay, and Sydney?"

"Continental already cut Sydney loose. If she gets herself together, another team will sign her. Fay's gone. No team will touch her in her present condition. Anorexia is a tough illness to beat. The success-to-failure rate is fifty-fifty." Rachel stole a furtive glance at the entryway. "Taylor—no idea. She's reticent about her future plans. Hell, she's reticent about everything, except that damn modeling gig she's after." She poked the last rye crust between her lips. "It looks like Reilly isn't coming. Would you mind passing something along?"

"About Julie?"

"About the manner in which Julie was killed. Whoever killed my former teammate had a working knowledge of physiology. If he'd driven the spikes in straight instead of on a slant, her arteries would've sealed off. She wouldn't have bleed out so quickly. Julie might've survived six, even up to twelve hours—plenty of time for someone to find her and get help."

Not with a broken neck. Logan played along. "Maybe her killer had poor upper-body strength. Lots of cyclists do. Hitting something at an angle takes less oomph than hitting it head on."

"Whatever… it was just an idea. Still, we can both agree that even Julie—nasty as she was—didn't deserve that kind of sendoff."

RACHEL HAD BARELY stepped into the courtyard before Reilly stormed inside and threw herself into Rachel's still warm chair. An impassioned exhibition of slapping her hand down on the tabletop followed her angry entrance. Logan knew better than to horn in on Reilly's theatrics when she was in one of her moods. Her friend might be a miser with words, but when it came to drama, Reilly was law-enforcement's counterpart to Harold Lloyd.

After a witless battle with her jacket, Reilly hurled it to the floor. "Don't say another word… not one stinking word… to anyone who has ever said as much as 'howdy' to Julie Easton."

Then, she burst into tears.

For once, Logan kept her mouth shut and waited for the storm to pass.

The rumbling of Reilly's stomach put an end to it. She straightened, plucked the napkin from Logan's tray, and blew her nose furiously. "Have you eaten?"

"Not nearly enough. Let's go." She closed the snap on her jeans and dumped her dirty dishes on the cart before her return to the buffet.

"Is that limp you're rocking the worst of it?"

"Pretty much."

"What about yesterday's carnage?"

"A distant memory."

"Then you're still racing tomorrow?"

"Unless Grant scratches me. You'll keep your mouth shut, won't you?"

"Of course, but will Simon?"

"I'll deal with Simon."

"What are you going to tell him?"

"I'm a klutz."

"I'd buy it, even if Joe didn't."

"He didn't?"

"If you'd bailed like you told him you did, or done a face-plant into a ditch, the front of your bike would've sustained the damage, not the rear-end. That means something hit you from behind. What was it?"

"A truck."

Logan set a bowl of beef barley soup onto her tray as Reilly seized her arm. "Oh, my God! Look what your Magic Chef put out." Reilly pointed to an ice bucket filled with bottles of chocolate milk. "I love that man!" She seized up an armful and set them on her tray alongside a grilled cheese sandwich.

Logan did likewise. Thanks to Griffin's generosity, calories-be-damned day was in full swing.

This time she made quick work of her sandwich while it was still hot and then dabbed a napkin to her lips. "Rachel stopped by to give you a message. She says we're barking up the wrong tree."

"The Tim tree?"

"The illiterate tree." She repeated Rachel's remark.

"Anyone who can point and click a mouse can ferret out that kind of stuff on the Internet. Half my life as a cop is spent looking up obscure facts about obscure things."

"What's the other half?"

"Driving around." Reilly twisted the cap from her first bottle of milk and took a noisy sip. "Hmm, so good. Joe's report included a line about Tim that said nothing. Did he, or did he not, show up?"

"Not in any way I know of. Rachel said he took Jake's truck over to Plains to pick up Sydney."

"What about the truck that hit you? Did you see anything that will help us differentiate it from the five million other trucks sold in the state of Montana each year?"

"Like what?"

"Was it light or dark?"

"Pass… too many shadows, but the bumper was rounded."

"Shiny or dull?"

"It makes a difference?"

"Legal requirements outlawed chrome fenders in the 90s."

"Pass."

"Did you see the driver?"

"Nope."

"Not even a shadow?"

"Nope. I was too busy staying alive."

"Then it wasn't Tim. His bright hair shines like a glow stick."

"He could've worn a hoodie." Logan took a last lick on her spoon. "Why are you so late?"

"Taylor stormed into my cabin at the nth minute complaining you sabotaged her."

"Sabotaged her—how?"

"That cryptic remark she made to us about Julie being a bigger pain in her *tochus* now that she's dead made me take a closer look at that Sapphire Rose gig. Originally, SR thought about using Julie as their next pinup girl. Its rep—the guy in the three-piece suit at Moriarty—stuck around long enough to see her clip you at the finish line. He was impressed. It wasn't a slam-dunk, but Julie was in his top three candidates to go forward, depending on the outcome of tomorrow's race. Julie's death caused a reshuffling of the candidates. You head up his current list."

She laughed. "To quote Katy, you 'pull my boot.'"

"Taylor claims she stood a better chance against fat Julie than she does against you. She's fuming and blames you for every star out of alignment in her universe."

"But I never talked to anyone from Sapphire Rose, nor would I accept anything it offered."

"But you did open your mouth and let condemning words fly out, didn't you? The fact you didn't simply shoo when she stomped her foot ignited her ire. She said you hung around, eavesdropped on her call, and suggested SR choose a winner as their pinup girl... not a loser like her." Reilly picked up her jacket and loaded in the remaining bottles of chocolate milk.

"Where are you off to now?"

"A meet and dump with Grant. You?"

"Simon."

"Good luck... and oh, by the way, the background report on your Magic Chef is on your connubial bed."

LOGAN CLEANED UP their messes and left through the front door, taking the footpath past Reilly's cabin, then continuing on to the Craftsman, where Allison paced back and forth on the veranda. The square-cut bodice of her pale-lavender dress showed off her small waist, while its flowing skirt fluttered with the graceful undulations of a jellyfish with each of her jerky movements. Sometime between yesterday and today, Allison had cut off her long, thick braid. What was left of her hair fell to her chin, the edges feathered unevenly along her jaw line. Clear gloss downplayed her full lips, and blended layers of blue and taupe shadows changed her soft gray eyes into smoky circles.

Logan made her way slowly up the stairs and collapsed onto the porch swing. "Wow, you clean up good. New life, new look?"

"It'll be easier with the horses and my new job."

"You got a job already... doing what?"

"It's not for sure yet, but Davis said a new fitness center is going up in Two Medicine. He knows one of its owners and can get me an interview to teach some cycling classes if I'm interested."

"That sounds great."

Allison lowered herself on the opposite end of the swing and gave her a myopic squint. "You're looking kind of beat up. I heard how you and Fay got in the way of somebody's target practice, but this looks more serious. Did you crash?"

"I did—lost my line, hit a ditch, and the rest was a painful blur."

"Still racing tomorrow?"

"I'll see how sore I am in the morning."

Allison squirmed uncomfortably. "I took your advice and told Reilly about what Davis and I did yesterday. Then I told Tim, and he told Jake. I offered to disqualify myself from the championship, but Jake said I could race—his wedding present to me. He's kind of a romantic, you know?"

"How did Davis make out?"

"He works for Slade. Jake may be the older brother, but when it comes to the horses, he has no say. Still, Davis made it clear to Jake he doesn't want to be involved with tomorrow's race."

"I'm happy it turned out okay for you. If our paths don't cross again, good luck on your ride."

"You too… if you can pedal."

"Fingers crossed. So why are you all gussied up?"

"Davis and I are shopping for rings today. Two Medicine has a nice…." The sudden appearance of a burgundy Colorado truck pulling into the loading zone shot Allison off the swing. "That's Davis. Got to go."

She flew down the stairs and onto the footpath as Davis hopped down from the driver's seat, opened the passenger door, and then helped Allison inside. Back behind the wheel, he gunned the engine and peeled the truck out the front entrance.

CHAPTER 16

FAILING TO FIND her bike on Jeremy's veranda, she tapped on the door of Simon's van while she rehearsed her lie, but by the time the door cracked open to reveal his beady eyes, she was so mixed up she wasn't sure what would fly out of her mouth.

A minute passed in which he slipped onto the landing and crushed her against him. "Dang! Never been so happy to see a girlie in all me life." Beefy tears spilled down his cheeks, twisting his face into the muse of tragedy. "Tell me you ain't gonna forfeit the race tomorrow."

She untangled herself from his embrace. "Relax, your bet is still good."

His relief was palpable, and he sagged visibly.

"About my bike…."

"What about it? Griffin towed her in." He stepped back inside, returning with her mangled tire."

"You're not upset?"

"Heck no, weren't your fault." He flung the damaged wheel into the steel drum below the landing. "Some fool rear-ended you."

"How bad is it?"

"Frame's still sound."

"So we're only out the cost of a wheel? That's not too bad… certainly not bad enough to tell Grant…."

"Not tells the boss?" He dug around in his scalp. "Dunno."

"How much will it cost me?"

He recoiled. "Cost you… why it won't cost you a queen's fart. Got plenty of me own dosh stashed away. Now them brothers… seeings as winter's coming… well, maybe they could…."

"What makes you think I have any sway here?"

"I got eyes."

"Griffin told you, didn't he?"

"Might've."

She screwed up her eyes. "Let's get this over with."

"Oh, all right! With the end of racing season creeping up, I'll be needing somewhere to hole up. Think you could sweet talk them brothers into letting me stay on here for a few months? I ain't asking for a handout, mind you. I'm right handy with me toolkit."

"I'll see what I can do."

She'd negotiated the first step when his hand landed on her shoulder, and he spun her around. She caught her sneaker on a loose board and tipped forward, lashing out for the railing to keep upright.

"Better odds against a truck," she muttered.

He cupped his ear. "What's that?"

"My God… anything else, duck?"

"Me common sense told me to put another century on Officer Reilly in case you were out of action." He shot her a crafty wink. "You might dazzle them city slickers with your pedal work, but that don't mean you're any kind of Babe Didrikson."

"You do know Mildred played golf, right?"

"Mildred? Who the hells is that she-woman?"

———————————

LOGAN HAD SET off on the footpath that ended at the stable when Cerberus dove off the veranda and pranced to her side. They took a circuitous route to the cabin Davis Morgan had slipped out of Tuesday night. Along the way, the sun's brilliant glow played across the bands of creamy quartz slicing through the darker granite to render the gorge less sinister in daylight. Small, gray doves cooed in the treetops, while a blue grouse strutted angrily around her sneakers. She kicked the air beside it, but the feisty bird held its ground.

Who owned the carryall he'd taken away, and why he'd taken it was something she'd let slip through the cracks. Allison might not care if the man she was about to marry was a murderer, but Logan did, and if her hunch panned out, she'd eliminate Griffin from Reilly's naughty list, despite the trouble she'd stirred up to put him there.

The dog led her through the aspen grove to the screen door of the cabin, then abandoned her and backtracked through the trees. The sickly fragrance of Julie's jasmine-scented perfume still haunted the room. Logan nudged the door farther open. Two days without Julie had left behind an aura of neglect and stillness that made the hair on the back of her neck stand up. She stood in the doorway, clenching and unclenching her fingers until the comforting sounds of Cerberus pawing busily in the underbrush made her feel less vulnerable.

Julie's suitcase, helmet, and shoes lay on the bed. The Silver Bullet basked in the sunlight alongside the window. She crossed over to it, went down on a knee, and counted the teeth on the front chain ring—fifty-six, not sixty as Julie had bragged on—yet still impressive. She slid over to the bed and swept her hand underneath the box springs, bringing back a handful of dust bunnies. The space behind the linen cabinet contained more grime. The small bathroom revealed nothing other than fluffy pink towels and horseshoe-shaped soaps. The cabinet underneath the basin held toilet tissue, Kleenex, and air freshener.

Logan jumped up on the bed, pulled a book from the shelf, and flipped through its pages. When nothing fell out, she dropped it on the bedcover and pulled out another, methodically working her way through all eight books before she tackled the nightstand. An open bag of jellybeans and a framed photograph of Team Continental snuggled the back panel. She dropped the candy in the waste bin and spent some time with the photograph.

Taylor, then Tim, and finally Julie knelt in the front row. Julie's arm rested lightly on Tim's shoulder, but his arm was wrapped around Taylor's waist. A healthier-looking Sydney stood behind Julie. Next came Allison and then Rachel, standing apart from the others like an orphaned waif. Fay and Tom Drake were not in the frame. Logan unfastened the latch holding the picture in place and slipped it out. The date on the back read July 27—the day of the Moriarty race.

She tidied up her mess, set the empty frame on top of Julie's suitcase, and pulled the door shut behind her as she welcomed the sunlight outside.

THE EMPTY CORRAL lead her into the stable. With nothing on her schedule for the rest of the day other than her team dinner and a good night's sleep, she looked around for something on which to rest her aching leg. She'd just laid down on the prickly hay when a lazy drawl disrupted her daydreaming.

"Never figured you for a horsewoman, *sha.*"

Taylor sat on a bench inside a stall, oiling a well-worn saddle.

Logan joined her, propping her injured leg against the half door. "You either. Been at it long?"

"Most of my life. You?"

"Half that. Listen… about that Sapphire Rose gig. I'm not interested. Neither is Reilly."

Taylor set the oily cloth on the doorsill. "Oh, Lordy! I only used you as an excuse so I didn't have to admit to the sheriff I had a good reason to want Julie gone."

"Not a good reason, a million good reasons—if you land that cover-girl job. Still, it wasn't my intention to steal anything from you." She removed the photograph from her pocket, smoothed out the creases, and then plucked out another lie. "Jake came across this picture in Julie's cabin. Would you like it?" She set it carefully beside the cloth.

"Why would I…? Oh." Her gaze fell to the photo. "I see. You want to know if Tim and I were…."

"Not were, *are*."

"We *were*—past tense. We… er, it lasted a few days after Moriarty."

"Before or after his engagement to Rachel?"

Taylor twisted the cap on the bottle of Neatsfoot oil. "Rachel may be his main meal, but Tim likes his side dishes. As far as I'm concerned, he can dine elsewhere."

"Rachel isn't riding much this week. Is she injured?"

"If she is, it's a well-kept secret. Tim says she prioritizes studying over everything these days."

"What about you… if you model for Sapphire Rose, will you give up cycling?"

"Heck no. One of the conditions of my contract will be to stay relevant. If anything, I'll need to work harder on my bike."

"You're okay with that?"

"Oh, I'm more than okay with it. Part of my pillow talk with Tim included a new peaking schedule."

Logan smiled. "If your fourth-place finish yesterday is a reflection of the hard work you've already put in, you'll do Sapphire Rose proud tomorrow."

THEIR TALK TURNED to details of the race course and the impact the weather might have on their racing strategies until Taylor returned the saddle to its cubbyhole and headed back to main site. When all that remained of her presence was a cloud of Oriental scent, Logan made a bed for herself on the hay, while Cerberus nosed around in the stalls. When she grew tired of doing nothing, she left the dog sleeping fitfully in the corner and hauled herself up the ladder to the upstairs landing. The doorknob turned easily in her hand. She passed inside the apartment, leaving the door ajar.

The main room was white with black accents—recliner, big TV, area rug, coffee table—a man cave... more specifically Davis Morgan's cave. A microwave and a shelf filled with cereal boxes took up a side wall. The footprint of a Murphy bed cut into the wall behind the recliner. Another door led into a tiny bathroom. Bright yellow towels softened the cold harshness of the white tiles. A cosmetic bag lay on the vanity. She unhooked the clasp. Allison's smoky-eyeshadow palette and tubes of glossy lip oil lay on the bottom.

If Davis hadn't destroyed the carryall he'd taken from Julie's cabin, it would be here or in Allison's cabin. She stepped around the shower and slid open the door to a small linen closet.

A pale-blue carryall hid in plain sight.

Her fingers curled around the strap as the door behind her creaked.

"I APOLOGIZE FOR the cheating, ma'am."

She pressed the closet door shut. He stood just inside the doorway. His dark jeans and black shirt were a striking foil to his pale eyes. His going-to-town boots were also black with silver studs emblazoned on the outer seams. Like Jake, Davis wore a Stetson, only his was gray and tilted backward, exposing a spacious forehead.

"Please, call me Logan."

"Davis... er, ma'am."

Two bodies in the tiny bathroom were one too many. As he stepped toward her, she sailed around him to claim a patch of wood in front of the recliner. He slipped in beside her with the Diamond Dust carryall in hand. She fell into the recliner and pressed her back against its soft leather.

"I figured someone would come lookin' for it. I just never figured on you."

"I had a head start. I saw you steal out of Julie's cabin with it Tuesday night."

His tongue darted out to wet his cracked lips. "Would you like something to drink?"

"Water, if it's not too much trouble."

He set the carryall on the throw rug and made for a mini fridge in the corner. She scooted it closer and pulled back the zipper as he returned with a bottled water in one hand and a can of beer in the other. She felt herself blush.

"Don't be embarrassed. I meant for you to have it."

"Me… why?"

"Allison said we can trust you, and Julie is dead. She can't hurt my gal no more."

She took a hesitant glimpse inside the bag. "I didn't know what to expect, but this stuff wasn't on the list. Mind if I dump it out? Nothing looks used."

"Go right ahead."

She slipped off the chair and held the bag upside down. A cache of sterile needles and plastic bags—each empty, except for a squirt of colorless anti-blood-clotting liquid—spilled out.

"Pockets are full of stuff, too."

An economy box of Band-Aid strips, a blue latex tourniquet, a bulk package of cotton pads, an amber bottle filled with rubbing alcohol, and a torn business card joined the jumble on the rug. She plucked up the card and jammed it into her pocket.

"Can I confess something to you, Logan?"

"I'd prefer you confess to Chief Byrd."

"Can't. Got Allison to think of. You're my best bet of keeping her out of the mess I've made of things. She don't deserve no more trouble. That"—he kicked the carryall—"is my fault. So was the cheating. It was a stupid thing to do."

"Yes, it was, but Allison said you were able to work it out with Jake."

"Only because I tend the horses, something Jake leaves to his brother." He crushed the empty can. "Me and Allison… we got serious real fast. She likes what I like, and she wants the kind of life I got here on the ranch. Can you understand that?"

She smiled up at him. "Oh, I'm a big believer in love at first sight."

"Then you'll get why I did what I did. Tuesday night after supper, Allison stayed behind with her teammates, leaving me to settle down on Jeremy's porch swing. Ain't been at it but two shakes when Julie came down the footpath with Tim on her heels. Words flew between them something fierce. They didn't know I heard them, or maybe they did but didn't care. The upshot was Julie accused Allison of doping—siphoning off her own blood and putting it back in before she raced. Can you imagine?"

"I can. The proof is on your floor."

"Only it wasn't Allison who'd done the doping."

"No, she's too smart to do something that dumb."

"Yeah, that's what I thought, too, but that wasn't the end of it. Julie said Allison had recruited some of her teammates to do it too. By then I was real sore. Whatever it took, I was going to have it out with her. I was up on my boots when Tim said something that made me think maybe things weren't so bad for Allison. He said he wasn't going to take Julie's word for nothing. That she'd lied before. He wanted proof. Well, ol' Julie let out that witchy cackle of hers and told him to look in Allison's cabin the next morning, and he'd find his proof."

"So, this mess is what Julie threw together to incriminate Allison?"

"That's how I figured it. After Allison and I parted ways for the night, I headed to Julie's cabin, but she wasn't there. Locking doors isn't something we do this far north, so it was easy for me get inside. Heck, I didn't even have to sneak in. I never meant to do anything other than wait, and at first, that's all I did. Then I got tired of sitting, so I poked around… like what you just done when I caught you." His gray eyes shifted to the bag. "*That* was right behind the door. Julie was fixin' to plant that junk in Allison's cabin. So I took it. That wicked woman couldn't plant what she didn't have, could she? After the news of her death broke, and after Allison told me she told you about the cheating, I had to come clean too." His toothy smile splashed disorderly dimples across his cheeks. "Allison told me I had more audacity than sense. We had a good laugh over that."

"If Tim didn't believe Julie and never told their sponsor, and Julie never had a chance to plant this junk in Allison's cabin, why did Continental pull Allison's contract?"

"The company didn't just single out Allison, and it ain't a done deal. All of Continental's contracts are in jeopardy, even Tim's. Allison told me the money it pulls in from tire sales is peanuts compared to what it had hoped to pull in from its new line of high-end bike frames, but something put a hiccup in its plan, so it's considering pulling its sponsorship... another reason Allison said it was a good time to step away."

The rumbling of the walls warned of the horses' return.

Davis tossed their empty containers into a bin set next to a pile of newspapers. "Are we good here? Cuz if we're not, we'll have to talk later. Slade needs my help with the horses right now."

"We're good."

"What should we do with that stuff?"

"I wouldn't muddy up the waters at this point. Why not wait until nightfall, steal back into Julie's cabin, and put it back where you found it? If anybody catches you at it, tell them I asked you to pack up Julie's things."

He grinned back at her. "Allison was right. You do see things for what they are."

"I don't know about that. I only know Allison wouldn't marry a murderer."

He blushed.

She rose up on her boots. "Just out of curiosity, what happened to the ring-buying expedition?"

"Allison said we could make better use of our money than wasting it on some glittery rocks. We treated ourselves to some huckleberry milkshakes and came home."

CHAPTER 17

S LADE GREETED HER at the bottom of the ladder with a slow kiss. Afterward, he led her to the hay bales. "We must talk."

"Too bad. Kissing is more fun."

He kissed her again—quicker, harder. "Please... it is a matter of urgency."

She brushed a stray piece of straw from the back of his hand, allowing her fingers to linger. "I'm listening."

"With our joining, our lands are now once again underneath your custodianship."

"Does our trouble involve your brother?"

"You know?"

"You argued with him, and my husband is not a man easily angered." She told him about the empty drums and twinkling waters. "We haven't spent much time together, but within this small window, I have realized you and I and our lands are intertwined."

"My brother is many things—good and bad—but his pollution of our Merenale is a blatant disregard for our heritage. I have negotiated a contract to reclaim the diamond fraction of our waste and dispose of the contaminates, but my brother believes we waste our resources on something that returns no value."

"What can I do?"

"As my honored consort, you have *second say* in all that belongs to our people. Will you speak to him?"

"You ask so little of me. Of course I will."

THEY JOINED DAVIS in the corral. While the men tended to the horses, she spent time with her tobiano colt, throwing out a few names. He responded with a rude toss of his head, his mane whipping insolently across her face.

She laughed. "Aren't you the finicky one."

He snorted and raced around the corral, finally collapsing onto the ground in a gangly heap.

A sudden wind gust blew past, bringing in a tumble of debris. Slade moved in beside her. "Much pain?"

"The worst has passed."

"You are strong of mind. Tomorrow, your body will do as you wish." He rose and offered his hand. "Now, we will ride together, so when your colt is ready, you will be, too."

Slipping the reins onto an Appaloosa stallion, he led the animal out of the corral and onto the dirt pad. Like her colt, the horse's coloring was rich sable with the leopard-spotted pattern characteristic of his breed spreading out over his muzzle, the length of his postern, and his hindquarters. Sable and tan stripes ran vertically down each hoof. Slade mounted the stallion then lifted her in front of him. Her legs rested lightly against his as they straddled the horse.

He dropped the reins into her hands. "Do not force Sahaptin. Keep your wrist soft, pulling and slacking the reins with little force. With your colt, you will change directions only slightly. When he is older, you will ask that he turn more sharply gathering his hind legs. Today, my legs will serve as yours. If you wish to go right, I will squeeze my left leg against him, as you rein right. Right leg, left rein will signal Sahaptin to move in the opposite direction."

They worked the horse tentatively at first, but as she relaxed into the animal's rhythm, she increased the frequency and sharpness of the turns. If Slade realized the woman reining the horse was as experienced as the animal he'd chosen, he didn't let on. Near the end of the session, she guided Sahaptin through a series of sharp ninety-degree turns.

He dismounted first and then helped her off the stallion. "You have played me."

"I learned a trick or two during my exile."

"Your *other* rode bareback."

"The passage of the centuries has made me rusty."

THE BACKGROUND REPORT Reilly had put together on Griffin lay atop their bed in the glass house. When Slade left to clean up, she sprawled across the bed and gave it her undivided attention.

Griffin had been born and raised on Kauai in the Hawaiian Islands. His father was a retired naval officer and his mother a native Samoan. Together, they had operated the only tourist resort on the island—the *Coconut Plantation.* Anna had been nine years Griffin's junior, and at age fifteen, the family had moved to Denver—a hop, skip, and jump away from Boulder, the cycling Mecca of America. During those years, Griffin had worked in a potpourri of restaurants, diners, and bistros.

Many years after Anna's death, Griffin had packed a suitcase with his bib overalls, an autographed copy of Fannie Farmer's cookbook, and his set of Wustof knives, bought a one-way ticket on Alaskan Airlines to Glacier International Airport, and taxied out to the ranch, where Jake had found him asleep on Jeremy's veranda, his head resting on his suitcase and arms hugging his beloved Fannie—*according to Black Bart*—Reilly had penciled in. *No mention of a culinary arts school or any school for that matter.*

When Slade passed through the bedroom, she laid the paper on the nightstand and took her turn in the shower. Afterward, she scooped up their discarded clothes and the torn business card from Julie's carryall that had fallen beside the wastebasket. Gold letters on the navy face spelled out *Jasper Leister*. The numbers +353 277 0313 lay below the letters. A Gmail address came next. The reverse side held *ffee* printed in white typewriter font. Below that came *oom*. Someone had penned in a series of columns and rows filled with letters and numbers around and over them.

She dressed in jeans and a copper-and-green-swirl wrap blouse, jammed the card down into her pocket, and gave Slade the keys to the Jeep for an errand he claimed he couldn't put off. In return, he gave her a goodbye kiss that ate up considerable time. Sometime during the exchange, the dogs sprinted over from the orchard.

As LOGAN WALKED along the river, the dogs trotted obediently at her side, ignoring the call of the wild to listen to an untiring woodpecker drill out quarter notes on the trunk of a golden pine. They arrived at the dining hall to find Griffin pacing back and forth across its porch. He waved to her, moved down the staircase, took her arm, and marched her through the tall grasses around back to the meadow, as the dogs zigzagged in front of them.

"I must confess to you," he said. "I do not want to start our time together dancing a tango of deceit."

"I want that, too, but if your confession has anything to do with Julie's death, tell Chief Byrd—not me."

"Only after you and I have talked. If you still think I must go to my… the sheriff, I will do as you wish."

"Why me?" She turned on her heels and stepped toward the courtyard, the dogs dancing a few yards in front of her.

Again, Griffin caught up, then stepped in front of her, blocking her way. When she stopped, the dogs stopped, too, flanking her dutifully on each side, ears lifted, noses twitching.

"It is your purpose to listen. You are our unifying light. Your word governs all."

"Are you saying I have *second say* in everything that concerns the ranch?"

"On *all* tribal matters. You are the only woman among the brothers. The Old Man and the Old Woman decreed it shall be so to ensure balance and harmony. We have no other council, other than the elders, who engage themselves in another purpose."

"What happened before I came home?"

"Much disagreement, much fighting, much wandering." He looked to the courtyard, where a glut of cyclists flooded the flagstones. "You are still between worlds, and I have overwhelmed you—for that, I apologize, but my transgression comes with a sense of urgency. Might I suggest the greenhouse—nine o'clock."

"Can we make it eight thirty? I have to get some sleep tonight."

"Of course." He dropped a chaise kiss on her cheek. "Your homecoming gives me great comfort. Now, I must see to my food. Cooking in the mountains is challenging. If you leave something too long—puff—it turns into mush."

She waited until he'd returned to his kitchen before she freed the dogs into the night. They dashed off toward the river and splashed about like joyous preschoolers. Not yet nightfall, she spent a few minutes enjoying the serenade of a great-horned owl hoot, hoot, hooting from a hidden bough, then returned to her cabin, flopped on her bed, and pulled out her wallet, bringing the torn card with it. She set her wallet on the nightstand.

The cramped script in the first column on the reverse side read $Ti5Al25Sn$, $Ti6Al25$, $Ti84Mo3Al6.8C2(9)V6.2$, $Ti2C4$, $94Ti6Al$, $93TiAlV4.2C2.8V$, $94.5Ti3AlC2.5$, $TiO2$. The other markings were incomprehensible numbers, except for one—the scientific symbol for degree. Her time in college had required her to memorize bits and pieces of the Periodic Table of Elements. The letters Al, Cr, and Ti were scientific abbreviations for aluminum, chromium, and titanium, and C,

Mo, and *V* for carbon, molybdenum, and vanadium. She was struggling with the symbol *Sn* when the screen door banged open. She shoved the card underneath the pillow, then jumped from the bed. Tim stood by the hamper, a sheepish grin running across his boyish face.

She jumped from the bed to lean against the nightstand, arms crossed. "Where were you this morning?"

"Rachel got one of her migraines. I drove to the pharmacy in Two Medicine for her medicine." His face screwed up. "You are agitated. Did something happen?"

"Nothing that matters, but since you're here, what did you want to tell me?"

"Only that you should not believe anything Julie may have told you. She was an accomplished liar. Her latest lie accused Allison of doping. She was about to make a false claim for something she didn't own. Julie couldn't even pedal her bike properly, how did she expect anyone to believe she knew anything about wind foils and metal alloys."

"Perhaps she knew enough to sound convincing."

"A good liar always mixes a spoonful of truth in with her falsehoods."

She slid the torn card out from underneath the pillow. "Since you're here, maybe you can help me with this, seeing as you worked in a metals laboratory."

"Who told you that?"

"You're in this country illegally, and you take umbrage in the fact someone's pried into your employment record? Earth to Tim. A woman is dead. None of us have escaped the sheriff's scrutiny. For a man whose team is in dire straits, your self-centeredness staggers me."

"I apologize for allowing my own troubles to blind me to my true responsibilities. Forgive me. Now, what do you need from me?"

She held out the card. "Tell me the significance of these symbols."

He held it at arm's length, then brought it closer, his face bunching together. "May I first inquire as to where you found this?"

"In a pile of junk. I'm familiar with some of the chemical symbols, but the alpha-numeric groupings baffle me."

"Each string of shorthand is a chemical code... a recipe for a compound. I assume you are only interested in those compounds that relate to a bike."

"That's a good starting point."

His finger landed on the grouping $96Ti4Al$. "I believe you and I talked of this earlier. Only this one can be used in a bike frame."

"Titanium and aluminum. What do the numbers mean?"

"Percentages.   Ninety-six   percent   titanium   and   four percent aluminum."

She pointed to the "9" surrounded by parentheses in the grouping $Ti84Mo3Al6.8C2(9)V6.2$. "This?"

"A type of carbon—Type 9, similar to substituting whole-wheat flour for all-purpose flour in a bread recipe."

"Is it possible to embed a metal like titanium into carbon fiber to improve strength and durability?"

"In theory, all is possible. The question then becomes one of necessity. TiAl bikes have proven themselves durable over many years. What is the benefit of adding extraneous elements like carbon and molybdenum? Would this benefit nullify the additional weight and cost? Still, it could be done this way... and yet, once it was done, many years of testing would be required to ensure the materials, and the products of their use, are robust and structurally safe. If you believe I am the liar, and Julie told the truth when she bragged of a unique alloy and *her* design, then tell Reilly to talk with Continental's legal team. One of our lawyers will confirm Continental would never allow Julie to ride a bike made of an untested alloy—consider the liability."

"A disconnect exists somewhere. A bike that costs upward of twenty-five thousand dollars is pricey for a reason, yet the people who should know something about that reason insist otherwise."

"Pre-manufacturing development in the lab and wind-tunnel testing on a prototype can greatly push up the price of a bike."

"If Continental didn't formulate the alloy, could she have procured it somewhere else?"

"Our job requires extensive travel. Julie may have uncovered this unique alloy overseas. How she brought a sample back with her, even if she did, is a matter of speculation." He glanced at his watch and then at the door. "Now, if you'll excuse me, I must hurry to collect Rachel for the evening meal. If I do not run into you again, good luck tomorrow. Even injured, you slot in as the race favorite now."

The door had banged shut when she plucked up a directory from the stack underneath the nightstand and flopped crosswise across the bed. She flipped to the section labeled *Pharmacies*. Two listings jumped out at her—neither one carried an address in Two Medicine. She reached into the drawer of the nightstand and lifted out her laptop. A few minutes on Google convinced her the business card originated in Europe—Ireland specifically.

She threw what remained of the card into the trashcan as she left her cabin. The Women's Cycling Federation didn't race in Ireland.

CHAPTER 18

LOGAN DROPPED INTO the chair beside Reilly in time to catch the tail end of a heated exchange between Grant and Simon that centered around the escalating cost of bikes relative to the diminishing return on investment. Grant argued the human motor won the race, not the bike that weighed a few grams less. Simon championed the machine.

"Did you have time to read my report?" Reilly whispered.

She nodded.

"There's nothing in it to suggest Griffin is a crazed killer. On paper, he comes across as a very stable guy dedicated to his craft."

"I'm happy you feel that way because I've got a favor to ask of you. Griffin wants to confess something to me, and I want you with me when he does."

"You're finally thinking straight. Walking unwittingly into a dangerous situation is excusable... going in with both eyes open is moronic. Where and when?"

"The greenhouse at eight thirty."

"We'll leave your cabin at a ten past." Reilly jabbed her head toward the courtyard. "Let's take a walk. I've got something to tell you, and I don't want witnesses around when I do."

"Does this something concern Slade and Jeremy?"

"How'd you know?"

"'We're seriously considering everyone,' remember? You've demonstrated remarkable restraint until now, which means it's serious."

"Straight up?"

"Unvarnished."

"Black Bart and Jeremy alibi each other. They were both at the corral putting together fencing until eleven thirty, which leaves only your man without anyone to vouch for him."

Logan reminded herself Reilly was doing a thankless job and not getting paid one red cent for her efforts.

They settled on opposite ends of a bench.

"Slade has no alibi... not for the time of Julie's death or your accident. He and Davis work solo, and Allison was with *her* man—not *your* man."

"Slade is not a murderer. Besides, he does have an alibi for the time Fay was shot—his brother."

Reilly shook her head. "Black Bart says they were together for only a few minutes before you blasted onto the scene, leaving plenty of time for him to shoot Fay and ride his faithful steed back to the road to argue with his brother."

"What did he do with the rifle?"

"Ditched it. He must know the Enchanted Forest like the back of his hand."

"Did you find a connection between Slade and Julie? Or Slade and Fay? He had no reason to harm either woman. They were two of a hundred-plus incomers—soon to be gone."

"You can't deny he wears his animosity toward outsiders like a crucifix. Other than you, and maybe Allison, he's never said *boo* to the rest of us. He and his brother were already at odds over this championship. Failing to talk Jake out of hosting it, he sacrificed Julie to stop the race. It's logical to assume the death of a cyclist would make the Federation pull out, but in our crazy world, the race must go on."

"Then what... he shot Fay for sport?" Logan fought hard to rein in her anger. "If you really believe Slade is a killer, talking to me isn't going to change your mind. Haul him in." She jumped from the bench and pounded toward the sliding door.

"Hey, I'm sorry," Reilly said, catching her as she crossed inside. "I gave you the bad news first."

"What's the good news?"

"Logistics rule him out. He has a driver's license but prefers to travel horseback. So yes, it's possible he shot Fay, hopped onto his trusty steed, and made it back to the road in time to fight with his brother, but when it comes to Julie, he didn't park Snow Runner outside the tunnel, do the deed, load up her bike, and ride off across the outback. Joe didn't uncover any hoof prints at the crime scene."

"He didn't need a trusty steed. He donned a cape and flew off to his Fortress of Solitude with Julie's frame tucked securely underneath his arm."

Reilly laughed. "Your man may be a lot of things, but Superman isn't one of them."

"If that's your idea of an apology, keep it—and if you still want my help—you ought to try leading with 'I know you have better judgement than to fall in love with a cold-blooded killer.'"

Reilly auditioned a sheepish grin. "If it's any consolation to you, Romeo has no alibi either. Nobody remembers seeing him coming or going or staying put."

"He was with me."

Reilly goggled at her. "Why didn't you say so?"

"You didn't ask."

"What were you doing together, if you don't mind my noisiness, and even if you do…?"

"The day Fay was shot, Romeo asked Griffin to prepare a special lunch for you—his way of apologizing for being a jerk at breakfast—but you stood him up. You've been too preoccupied with the sheriff's everything to notice Romeo is crazy about you."

"He never mentioned either of those things."

"He wouldn't because he's another nice guy, which is why I don't understand why you are so eager to send him to the electric chair too."

"There you go again—defending a man you've known less than a week."

"Geez Louise! There's no pleasing you tonight, is there?"

"You know it's not about that."

"Then why aren't you crucifying the obvious suspect—Tim Richard?"

"Obvious—why? Because he stood you up?"

"Among other things. He came to my cabin less than an hour ago to make his excuses. Rachel came down with a sudden migraine. He drove Jake's truck to the pharmacy in Two Medicine to get her medicine... but guess what? There is no pharmacy in the village." As Jake's cowboys bustled out of the kitchen, Logan gripped Reilly's arm. "Come on. Chow's on, and if the smell of garlic means anything, it's your favorite—Italian."

They scrambled into their seats as bowls of spaghetti, baskets of garlic breadsticks, and tureens of spicy tomato sauce as thick as glue appeared onto the table. Sweet basil, diced onions, green peppers, crushed tomatoes, Italian sausage, and tender meatballs swam in the savory sauce.

Grinning, they unsnapped the top buttons on their jeans and dug in.

Reilly piled a meatball the size of a tennis ball onto her plate and nudged Logan. "Are you sure—"

She pushed her finger against Reilly's lips. "One hour. No murder, shootings, or mishaps. No alibis either."

———

ACROSS THE TABLE, Katy and Sabrina filled up on salad and bread, while Simon toyed with a breadstick. The cadre of junior cyclists had grouped at the far end of the table, socially trapped by an army of i-toys bombarding them with tedious digital gossip.

Logan forked her way through a plate of pasta covered in greasy red sauce. At the neighboring table, Allison scoured a newspaper, and Taylor flipped through the glossy pages of a fashion magazine. Tim had his nose buried inside a notebook, while Rachel picked at a plate of oily salad. Romeo's stunning physique was conspicuously absent.

When Grant stacked his dishes, Logan pushed aside her plate.

"National weather service forewarns a corker of a storm will lay siege to us tomorrow. Shouldn't affect the juniors, and the ladies may be spared. Sadly gents, but it looks like you'll get the worst of it." He segued seamlessly from the weather to registration, then handed out warm-up scripts and training plans for the remainder of the season.

Simon stood up next. "Listen up. Your racing bikes are ready to go and racked according to racing numbers. You can start picking them up at dawn outside my van."

At seven o'clock on the dot, Logan's moratorium on murder ended, and she let Reilly hustle her toward the exit. "Come on. Let's do some chocolate."

They shuffled out at the tail end of the mass exodus and settled on the porch to close out calories-be-damned day with a mug of Griffin's strong brew and Logan's last dark chocolate bar.

Reilly skinned back the foil wrapper. "We've got an hour. What do you want to do with it?"

"Examine every bumper of every truck in the parking lot."

"Seriously?"

"No stone unturned."

They returned inside, deposited their empty mugs on the cart, then moved back outside onto the footpath, making their way to the Craftsman in silence.

Reilly stopped short of the parking area, packed end to end with late-model vehicles. "*Oy vie.*"

Logan counted sixty-seven in all, including the ambulances—which had blossomed by two. Twenty-four of the vehicles were trucks, Jake's Ridgeline among them. Davis Morgan's burgundy Colorado was backed up in front of the Craftsman. "We'll divvy it up. It'll go faster."

Logan worked her way from right to left along each row, running her fingers over fenders marred with water drops and bird droppings, yet only the occasional dent or scratch. She'd reached the end of the third row when Jake stepped from the Craftsman. His hand remained on the door as he held it open and allowed a petite woman with a blond bob to pass. Something about the woman's teary light eyes, mustard-colored jumpsuit, and silvery sandals reminded Logan of Julie. A man with a budding paunch and a receding hairline wearing a Sun Devils t-shirt with its fiery golden pitchfork stepped out next. They lingered on the porch until Jake reached into his pocket and pressed something into the woman's hand. With a wave toward the dining hall, he escorted them off the veranda and then over to Julie's SUV, where he helped the woman into the passenger seat, then gave the man a firm handshake and the door a hard slam before he waved them off. A moment later, he melted into the shadows on the veranda, then moved around to the back and vanished among the trees.

Logan continued her tour of the parking lot. A number of bumpers sported rental stickers. She hit pay dirt with a silver Ford F-250. The fender sported a few dollar-sized dents, tarry freckles, and deep scratches cut into a darker undercarriage.

She flagged Reilly over. "Over here."

Reilly pulled out her phone, clicked off a few photos, and tapped on the keyboard.

"What'd you just do?"

"Texted the chief." Reilly had barely tucked away her phone when it sang out again. She plucked it out, read the display, and frowned. "Uh-oh. The chief recognized the plate number. It's registered to *Kemosahbee*."

"Crapola."

"It's not all bad. Those scratches and dents could be normal wear and tear. Even if they aren't, only one in a bazillion chances *Kemosahbee* was behind the wheel if and when it took out your bike. When the men of the Diamond Dust aren't behind the wheel, it's parked out here, keys in the ignition."

"So anybody could've hopped inside and tried to run me over?"

"I don't make this stuff up."

"Where was *Kemosahbee* after we left him this morning?"

"Somewhere on the ranch, but I didn't see this truck parked out at the workshop when we ran into him, did you?"

"No."

"So unless someone brought him back here, it's unlikely he was the driver."

"You packed a lot of unknown into that *unlikely*."

They saved Davis Morgan's truck for last.

Logan rang her fingers over the split bumper. It was pristine. "Nope."

"You're sure?"

"It's two-tone—red on the top and black on the bottom. I would've remembered something like that, and I don't."

IT WAS JUST after eight o'clock when they started out for the greenhouse. Logan forged ahead, lighting up the footpath with a flashlight she'd fished out of her Jeep.

Reilly's hurried footfalls came up behind her. "Slow down! What's your rush?"

"I don't want Griffin to see you."

"Then why am I here?"

"I need a witness... a mute witness. Once we get there, find a hidey-hole we can both live with."

They'd reached the gorge when a shadow emerged from Julie's cabin. Reilly seized Logan's arm. "Isn't that Romeo skulking out of Julie's place?"

"It's his shadow, but that's as far as I'll go." She dragged Reilly toward the fork in the road. "Forget about him."

"First your Magic Chief, now Romeo."

"First what?"

"First you get me all worked up that one or the other killed Julie, then you throw a bucket of ice water over all of us."

"That's a tad dramatic."

"Whatever. You do realize that alibi you gave Romeo is full of holes. He had plenty—"

"You can forget that alibi too. He doesn't need it."

"Why not?"

"Because he's off limits… untouchable."

Reilly flopped down on a log and folded her arms. "Says who?"

"Says me… and don't make me tell you… I pinkie swore."

Reilly grinned. "There is no pinkie-swearing in a murder investigation."

Overhead, the slate sky darkened to pale smoke as storm clouds pressed in.

"Now you tell me." Logan perched on a stump within arm's length of Reilly. "Remember when I questioned his career choice?"

"I recall your incongruity with the fact he had downgraded from racing bikes to fixing them and my response, along with the fact his background check didn't turn up anything fishy."

"You didn't dig deep enough. Romeo is an investigator for the Cycling Federation posing as a mechanic."

"He's a gumshoe? Wow, I didn't see *that* coming! Hot dog! This changes everything."

"How so?"

"In my cockamamie theory, he designed Julie's bike, Julie stole the blueprint to patent under her own name, and it all came to a head with that very public slap the morning she died." Reilly pushed herself off the log with a grunt. "Boy, was I wrong. So, what brought him to nationals?"

Logan forfeited her stump. "I didn't ask, and he didn't tell. What I can tell you is he couldn't wait to get out of my cabin with that blueprint."

Reilly brought out a packet of gum and shook out a few pieces. When Logan refused the offer, Reilly skinned off the wrappers and folded both pieces into her mouth. "We better get going."

The greenhouse loomed in the distance. Five minutes later, they walked inside. She slapped the flashlight into Reilly's hand. "Hide where you can hear us but we can't see you. If Griffin suspects you tagged along, he might not talk freely."

Reilly concealed herself near the north end of the greenhouse between a bed of sneezeweed and another of cock's comb. In the dark of night, Griffin's fuzzy pink bubble jived with cacophony. The refrigerator hummed, the fire crackled, and water gurgled into the beds. Logan stood her ground until a shadow loomed in the doorway, sending her staggering backward against the sink.

"No good comes of bumbling around in the dark, my dear." Griffin pushed through the screen door and groped for the light switch, releasing a flood of fluorescent lighting to chase away the rosy glow.

"When did you find out the Diamond Dust was hosting the championship?" she asked.

"December."

"December," she said.

He gave her a quizzical look. "I'm not so many years your senior that my ears have failed me."

His big-hearted humor made her relax, until he reached for the pole with the menacing hook and brandished it over her head. Much to her relief, he angled it into the louvered slats above the door, shutting out the chilly air leaking in.

"Before you confess anything, give me a *yes* or *no*. Did you turn up on Jeremy's doorstep to kill Julie Easton because you blamed her for sending Anna down that cliff?"

He slumped against a flowerbed, sending the pole crashing onto the dirt. "You must understand it was Anna's first race."

"I do understand. I haven't forgotten what it's like to be a novice besieged with nervous excitement. I still get nervous." She set her hand on his arm. "Tell me what you saw that suggested Julie ran Anna off the road?"

"I saw nothing!"

The emptiness of his words was damning enough.

"Anna was—as you say—jittery that morning. Her hands shook when she ate my French toast, yet when she was on her bike, her unease fell away. She flew up the mountain like a cheetah on wheels then"—he choked back a sob—"she tumbled off the cliff."

A wave of heartache for needless loss washed over her. "I'm so, so sorry."

Sloppy tears dribbled down his cheeks. "What I know is that Julie Easton did nothing to protect my sister. If Anna could ride faster than everyone, she rode faster. She knew nothing of the politics of that world. She didn't know her *job* was to make Julie Easton look good on a bike—and what of Julie Easton's job? Why did she not keep my Anna safe?"

"I don't know. Did she use poor judgment when she didn't look out for Anna—yes, but all that is behind you now. Your sister is gone, and Julie's faults died with her. I am sick with worry that you may end this life in a prison cell. Please tell me you did not murder her."

"I wanted to kill her, but I was forced to let her live."

"You left Julie alive? You're sure?"

"Of course I'm sure." He waggled his fingers. "I am not so celibate that I have forgotten the difference between a woman who breathes and one that doesn't."

"Then what did you mean 'you were forced to let Julie live?'"

"Bah! To look at that vile woman with all her bulges, you would never imagine how fussy she could be about my food. She turned her nose up at my *special* Greek salad, plucking out only the olives—*those* she ate."

"Let's skip to the poison dessert. Did you make your special baklava?"

"But how?" His eyebrow cocked. "Ah, the honey."

"Were you her lunch date?"

"Yes, we fixed it up Tuesday night after you left me. She, too, wandered into my kitchen."

"What did she want?"

He shrugged. "What do you think? She was not a woman who embraced tact."

"Really."

"In the past, my dark looks and statuesque physique have not gone unappreciated. 'Hooking up,' she called it. You said yourself my appeal is to the culinary-challenged. Julie was one of that legion."

"Was it you who suggested the tunnel?"

"The tunnel was her choice. The picnic was my idea." He relaxed against the curtain of the sink. "After breakfast, I packed up our lunch and helped myself to Jeremy's truck. It's a very comfortable method of conveyance—roomy with good mpg's and all the trimmings. We met near the river north of the basin and journeyed to the tunnel on foot."

"Did you see Julie's bike?"

"I don't remember a bike."

"Her yellow jacket?"

His feral curls bobbed *no*.

"A backpack?"

"Nothing other than the soiled jumper."

"What broke up your picnic?"

"Nothing."

"But you said…."

"*She* stymied me. How was I to know the woman did not eat pastry? I poisoned the wrong food."

"Then what?"

He shrugged. "I tidied up."

"Julie?"

"She talked."

"About what?"

"I have no idea. I wasn't there to be entertained."

"Then what?"

"I drove back to my kitchen."

"To do what—whip up a ptomaine steak?"

"Of course not. *That* would have been a waste of good beef."

Geneva lay by the woodpile outside the front door.

Griffin gave the hound's muzzle a gentle pat. "We're good?"

"We're good, and for what it's worth, I'm thrilled Julie stymied you." She hugged him tightly. "Promise me you won't do anything like that *ever* again."

Griffin was gone by the time Reilly slipped from her hidey-hole and brushed petals from her jeans. "I knew there was a reason I detested that woman. Who doesn't like a gooey pastry?"

Women and dog raced back to Reilly's cabin where Reilly crawled out of her jacket and jeans, then tucked her gun underneath the pillow and herself under the bedcovers. When she jerked her phone from the tangle in her purse, Geneva wrestled it from her hand and dropped it into Logan's lap. Reilly flung a stink eye at the hound. Geneva retaliated by hunkering down across her legs.

Logan palmed the phone. "Griffin is not your guy."

"You believe him?"

"His story is too messy not to be true. Besides, he was dead set on killing Julie. He had no reason to take her bike."

"He might've taken it to throw us off track." Reilly opened the drawer of the nightstand, brought out a bottle of antihistamines, and popped a pink tablet between her lips, chasing it with a swig of water.

"What else did the sheriff find out about Julie's bike?"

"Nothing else because he doesn't have it, remember?"

"Right. So, other than the analysis on that brake pad, you know nothing about the mysterious metal alloy Julie bragged on about when we changed her flat?"

"Actually, we do. The rep from Continental finally upchucked the nuts he'd been hoarding. Julie showed up at the factory in Dayton with the raw materials for her bike stashed in the cab of her SUV." Reilly tapped her watch. "Two minutes, and I'm off with the sandman, so if you're going somewhere with this, get there." She pushed Geneva's head away, inciting the dog to scoot up and give Reilly's face a good slobbering.

"I found a torn card with some chemical notations on it."

"Julie stole something else?" She held out her hand. "Gimme."

"No can do."

"Why not?"

"I junked it."

CHAPTER 19

GENEVA SET A furious pace through the forest to the glass house. Slade sat on the terrace, watching the stars burn out. When Logan flew into his arms, he kissed her as if she'd been gone another millennium. Later, when he opened the doors, Geneva darted inside to join Cerberus on the hearth rug.

Slade stretched out on the sofa, pulling her on top of him. "Are you ready?"

"For the race?"

"For us."

"We're past due, don't you think?"

He laughed. "This version of you is much lighter. You are welcome to join us in our work with the horses while you seek your purpose here."

"I can't just wander around as my *other* did?"

"You can if you wish. The land will welcome you." He smoothed back her hair, letting his hand linger on her cheek. "My brother does not understand why you have chosen me and our old world when you could have chosen him and remained in your new world."

"The answer to that is simple, my dear husband—because you are the brother who waited for me."

THEY WERE GETTING ready for bed when a discarded blue-and-gold Montana State T-shirt in the laundry basket caught her eye.

She touched his hand. "You're a college man? I didn't see *that* coming. What was your major?"

"Ancient Studies."

"Cheater. What about your cousin?"

"We are of the same twelvemonth. He studied law."

"Your brother?"

"A younger Jake sought purpose as a healer."

"A doctor?"

"No, an animal healer."

"What happened?"

"He, too, got lost, but he was not taken."

THE JOINING HAD put a stop to the horsemen, except for one. He was not of the others and only appeared when the sun reigned high—a half-man, half-specter as pale as his gray Carthusian mount.

Logan awoke troubled. Beside her, Slade stirred.

He gathered her close. "You saw him?"

"Since our joining. Do you know him?"

"His soul touches mine. You do not feel it?"

"I'm not on the same page with you yet."

"Your reshaping is a slow process."

"Is there anything else you know that I should?"

"I observed the woman."

"Julie?"

He nodded. "She made no attempt to mask her true self, and her disagreeable temperament made her an easy human to discard, yet death waited for her here—on our tribal lands."

SATURDAY MORNING, HE arose before dawn, dressed, and stepped outside into the grayness.

HE RETURNED AN hour later, slipped underneath the bedcovers, and kissed her awake.

"Hmm." She snuggled against him. "I could get used to your wake-up call."

Still groggy from her night of broken sleep, she dragged herself into the shower. Even underneath the pounding spray, her leg no longer ached. Balancing on her good leg, she moved her injured leg up then down. It moved freely without pain.

In the bedroom, she donned racing shorts and jersey, moved to the French doors, and threw them open. A misty veil of fog rushed at her like a lost child. She slammed them shut, then inched herself into a pair of jeans.

Her carryall—filled with her heart-rate monitor, spare shoes, an Allen-wrench set, and a new helmet—lay on the sofa across from the fireplace. Slade had driven to Kalispell and back to get her the helmet while she'd been at supper. She added another pair of cycling shorts and warm-up pants, dropped in her spare helmet, and checked the side pocket for Grant's scripted warm-up. Unable to find her cycling license in her wallet, she tried her jacket but found only her emergency stash of candy bars, a spare tube, a set of lever wrenches, a three-pronged Allen wrench, and two CO_2 cartridges. She conjured up her pre-race routine at Moriarty.

A spoke on her rear wheel had broken during her warm-up. Fortunately, Simon had driven up in a support car, popped off her damaged wheel, and slid in a spare, freeing her to vault to the sign-in table with minutes to spare. Afterward, she'd shoved the license into the glove box of her Jeep. She hunted down her key ring in the pocket of Slade's jeans, along with a new set of spare keys and a receipt for her new helmet.

In the kitchen, she loaded up her pockets with energy gels and shoved some bottled water into the pockets of her carryall. She splashed a dollop of cream into her coffee to save a few heartbeats for the race and relaxed on the sofa to study the western sky. Fluffy clouds streaked with bands of gray and smears of blue had replaced the morning's mist, and the bickering squawks of camp-robbing blue jays dive-bombing through the orchard framed her pensive mood in chaos. Slade strolled in, looking sultry in dark jeans and a wine-colored shirt. The dogs traipsed in behind him.

"Morning guys," she said. "Want some eats?"

Tails wagged.

She settled greenies, mugs, coffee, and cream onto a tray. While Slade jostled with the dogs, she toasted up English muffins and then piled on huckleberry jam. They spent a pleasant half-hour sharing coffee and muffins, while Cerberus wrestled with his bone, as if he'd unearthed a twenty-foot python, and Geneva licked the flavors off hers layer by layer like an archeologist peeling back time.

BILLOWING CLOUDS ESCORTED Logan to her cabin, where she liberated the torn card from the trashcan and continued on to Reilly's cabin as a few random raindrops fell from the sky. Reilly stood alongside the hamper sorting clothes with one hand and holding a tall latte in the other. Logan folded a pile of rumpled shirts into uneven lumps and handed them to Reilly while her friend rehashed the sheriff's news.

"Chief Byrd believes Tom Drake helped Sydney blood-dope."

"Not Julie?"

"No evidence to suggest it, although Julie's itinerary argues she doped too. Neither Drake or Sydney will admit it, but Joe stayed up most of the night checking air flights. No trips for Tom Drake, but plenty for Sydney. She visited him regularly this past month in Portland and whenever she had a big race on her calendar. Julie punched a round-trip ticket between Phoenix and Portland, too, arriving last Friday."

"Did Joe get a hold of Tom Drake?"

"Last night. Drake is staying at The Lodge on Whitefish Lake. He checked in Monday evening figuring on doing some angling. He'd planned on driving up here to watch Sydney race. He'd no idea she'd taken ill. He admitted Julie visited him in Portland after our race in Moriarty."

"Since her car is here, she probably left it in Portland and drove here from there. It explains how the Silver Bullet came to be in her cabin too. What about the blueprint of Julie's bike?"

"Drake maintains he knows nothing about any of that—who designed Julie's bike, who hid the blueprint. He claimed he boxed up his things before he gave the van to Simon." Reilly slammed the lid on the hamper. "Any uncle who puts the life of his own niece in jeopardy redefines the term despicable."

"You'll get no argument from me on that score, although in Tom Drake's version, one item jumps out—he had no reason to kill Julie."

"Or at least no reason you made up for him."

THEY WERE AMONG the first in line at the sign-in table, which Jake had set up on the veranda of the Craftsman. He sat alone behind a wooden trestle table. A cardboard box rested in front of him beside a clipboard. A male cyclist dressed in a red-and-gold kit stood on the opposite side with goose pimples puckering his bare skin.

Reilly shivered in the light drizzle. "Let's hope the snow holds off until after we race."

"Since we're wishing, why not ask for sunshine?"

"Because I used up all my Pollyanna asking the beaver to heal you."

"The Blackfoot healer?"

"I guess so. Chief Byrd told me the beaver is the spiritual medium for the powers of the other medicine animals. Since you were pressed for time, I went right to the top."

She laughed. "Whatever you did worked, and I'm grateful." She kicked out her leg. "See?"

"How's your arm?"

"An occasional twinge. Your mojo is firing on all cylinders."

Reilly dug some folded papers from her jeans and pressed them on Logan. "When you get some time, take a gander at these background reports I dug up on Rachel and Miss Georgia Peach."

Logan pushed the papers down into the pocket of her windbreaker. "Anything juicy?"

"Taylor shoots, and Rachel is a keen archer."

As a fiery red light crossed the eastern horizon, Logan held up her hand. "It stopped raining. I'll just be a minute. I need to get my cycling license out of the Jeep."

She dashed down the stairs, pulling up a yard short of her Jeep. Somebody had parked Jeremy's silvery truck alongside it. She circled around it, running her fingertips across the bumper a second time for flecks of teal or silver paint from her bike. A handful of faint scratches jumped out on the rounded curve of the passenger-side bumper. Behind her, Reilly shouted her name. She drew back her hand, crawled into the Jeep, grabbed her license from the glove box, and jogged up the stairs of the veranda.

———————

JAKE'S EASY CHATTER with the other cyclists reminded Logan of the promise she'd made to his brother. Today his tanned skin was unlined and unblemished and his manner convivial and carefree. His coal eyes gleamed like shiny obsidian rocks. With the hard work behind him, his laugh came easy, as did his handshakes. His laid-back demeanor contrasted with the obsequious man who'd unloaded her suitcase four days earlier and the one determined "to have his show go on" despite murder, mayhem, and mud.

She couldn't help compare Slade with his older brother—what had transpired on these lands that had left her man so selfless and this man so self-serving?

In front of her, Reilly handed Jake her licenses, while Logan lagged behind on the top step. When Jake slipped Reilly's credentials from her fingers, he held on a fraction too long to count as just friendly. Reilly pulled back her hand and stared stonily down at him as he went through the motions of comparing photographs of the woman standing in front of him to the real McCoy. He'd barely pulled the paper with her racing number from the box, when she snatched it from his grasp, wrote her name on the sign-in sheet, and stepped away to make room for Logan.

As Logan stepped forward, Reilly brought her hand up alongside her mouth. "Geez Louise—first you, now me. How can a man be so oblivious to a woman's animosity toward him?"

"Hunting is in his blood."

"And I've a license to spill it if necessary."

"Remind him if he gets too handsy." She pressed the torn card into Reilly's palm. "Here's that card you asked for."

Uncurling her fingers, Reilly peered down before zipping it away in her teal jacket.

Jake slid the sign-in sheet in Logan's direction. "Hey, beautiful."

She slapped down her licenses as his hand snaked out. Before she could pull back, his fingers trapped hers. Her anger flashed.

"Changed your mind yet?"

As his grip loosened slightly, she reclaimed her hand. "You're wasting your time. Reilly isn't interested either... so back off—and another thing, clean up the mess you've made of our lands, or I'll ban you from your homeland forever."

Behind her, Reilly's whisper bore terrorist-alert urgency. "Ready yet? We still have to eat and warm up."

What was left of the female contingency of Team Continental had converged on the footpath. "I'll chat up Allison while you're dealing with whatever," Reilly said.

"I'm done here. Wait for me."

As she scooped up her licenses, Jake gave her a flirtatious wink. Again her anger flared... until Taylor's giggle rose up behind her. She turned as Taylor mouthed "thank you" to Jake.

An irrational sense of relief flooded over her. Taylor and Jake were a match made in Hades, and one she'd do everything in her power to nurture. She seized up her race number and leapt down the stairs with a lightness of heart she hadn't felt in... well, in ages.

Reilly and Allison stood beside the bed of lavender, talking boisterously.

"Sydney's uncle helped her dope?" Allison said. "That's just plain bad uncle-ing."

"Would you reconsider your decision to quit if a team offered you a raise with a multi-year contract?" Reilly asked.

"Nope. All I want now is a clapboard house with a white picket fence and a brood clinging to my skirt."

Logan wrapped Allison in a bear hug. "Then have yourself a great last race."

Allison hugged her back. "You, too. Imagine—you and Slade. I didn't see that coming."

"Neither did I," she said.

Reilly wedged in between them for her own hugs. "Nobody did. You two watch out for each other when I'm not here—promise?"

They both crossed their hearts.

A high-pitched squeal hailed Allison from the veranda. Rachel leaned over the railing, waving her arms and making scribbling motions.

"I better go before Lilith explodes." Allison vaulted up the stairs.

———————

THEIR RACING BIKES stood in front of a third van that had moved in beside Grant's van sometime during the night. A canvas tarp fitted closely around each machine. A few feet away, Sabrina and Katy babbled excitedly in a language that blended the brutality of the Teutonic tongue with the harsh rhapsody of the steppe. The door to Simon's van was wide open, but their mechanic was nowhere in sight.

At their approach, Katy slipped a tarp off the tallest bike. "Look. Simon forget bottle cages."

"Is this your first time-trial race?" Logan asked.

Sabrina nodded.

"Simon never puts bottle cages on our gold bikes. It messes with the aerodynamics."

"You don't want anything on you or the bike to catch the wind," Reilly said. "Anything clunky, or that sticks out, acts like a rudder and slows you down, including bottle cages."

Logan ran a hand down the smooth edges of the seat post. "Even the edges of these tubes are smoother than those on our training bikes. Seconds, even fractions of a second, can cost you a place on the podium."

Sabrina's hard nod sent her dark curls twirling. "We get you. Nothing stick out."

"I lose this clunky water sac I load on myself, yes?" Katy said.

"Yep. Load up on fluids before the race," Reilly said.

"Tell us your race numbers," Logan said, "and we'll help you find your gold bikes."

"Gold bikes?" Sabrina gripped the top tube of Reilly's teal and silver bike. "Not gold... green and silver. Where are these golden bikes you speak of?"

Logan flipped over the tag twist-tied to the handlebars and pointed to the numeral 1. "This is Reilly's gold bike. We call our time-trial bikes our gold bikes because they're so costly."

Reilly pointed to the single front chain ring. "They're equipped with only one front chain ring instead of the usual pair to eliminate unnecessary weight."

When Reilly launched a homily that compared bike geometries, Logan sneaked out the background reports, careful not to rustle the papers.

Rachel had been born in Chicago, Illinois, the daughter of a physical-science teacher and an accountant. As a young girl, her grandfather had introduced Rachel and her twin brother Benjamin to the sport of archery. By age thirteen, Rachel and Ben had become accomplished archers, competing in statewide competitions until they graduated from high school. Rachel had also been a member of her high school swim team and collegiate cycling team. After receiving her degree in biochemistry, she'd attended medical school at the University of Michigan until she'd dropped out to pursue a career in pro-cycling. A few years ago, she'd enrolled at the Vanderbilt University School of Medicine to complete her medical training in the off-season.

She refolded the report and stuffed it back into her pocket. "Let's go." She tugged on Reilly's sleeve. "We've done enough damage for one race."

The Russians stepped away muttering about suffering dehydration during a race surely to be contested in a snowstorm or—at the very least—a downpour.

LOGAN HELD REILLY's bike upright as her friend gave it a final once-over. "I applaud your leadership initiative, but I'm happy we didn't pursue careers as diplomats. Our communication skills suck. We're getting as cynical as Simon."

Reilly pressed her thumb into the unyielding rubber of the front tire. "Ornery or not, Simon never lets us down. This tire is as hard as a rock."

The door to Grant's van flew open, and Simon skittered out. He detoured into his own van, returning with his toolkit. "Seat need fixing, Officer Reilly?" He slipped in beside Logan. "Got me tools right here. Be glad to fix her."

With Logan anchoring the bike, Reilly swung her leg over the top tube and slid onto the saddle. "Nope, it's fine."

"Fore and aft?" he asked.

Reilly spread herself over the bar. "Perfect."

"I gave you the fifty-four ring you asked for on this bike too."

"Super, thanks."

"Need shorter cranks? Help you spin faster if the wind kicks up. Got a set waiting on you in me van."

Reilly gave the pedals a quick whirl. "Not necessary. This pair feels just right."

Logan tightened her grip on the bike as Reilly dismounted.

Simon whirled around, tobacco spittle leaking from the seam between his lips. "Put titanium cranks on yours, girlie… and here's something else from my lips to your thick skull—don't bring this bike back all busted up like you did the last one."

Reilly cupped her mouth. "Looks like your grace period expired, girlie."

"I appreciate everything you've *ever* done for me," Logan said. "This weekend and every other day during the past eight years."

"Well, you can un-appreciate it. I didn't do nuthin' for you, I done it for—"

She clapped her hand over his mouth. "Fine, I un-appreciate it."

He shoved off her hand. "Frame ain't been made yet that can stand up to those muscles you're humping. Ain't right you know."

Reilly tilted her bike, elevating the rear wheel and then spinning the crank as she checked for brake clearance. "What ain't right?"

"Her." He jerked his thumb at Logan. "Womens are supposed to be the weaker sex."

"Don't you mean fairer?"

He ran a critical eye over Logan's dark hair and tanned skin. "She ain't that neither."

Logan removed the tarp from the next bike on the rack, gripped the top tube, and wiggled it backward, catching the brake lever on a truss. She gave it a yank. The handlebars jiggled but stayed put.

"Stop manhandling your machine, will you?" Simon wailed, flinging his toolkit onto the landing as he stomped up the stairs.

"Simon sure is an agreeable beastie today," Reilly said.

"Only to you and only because he bet on you like a bobtail nag."

GRIFFIN'S PANCAKE BREAKFAST was in full swing as all hundred-plus cyclists had disregarded Jake's rotating meal schedule and arrived in mass—some sitting at the tables, others standing at the buffet, still more lounging on the floor. Logan didn't blame them. A critical tenet of a good performance was figuring out how much—and when—to eat before a race. Too early or too late, too light or too heavy could spell disaster.

Sourdough pancakes stacked up in warming trays greeted them at the buffet. Oodles of butter in bowls and puddles of maple, cherry, and huckleberry syrups in carafes flanked them. Pitchers of milk and juice nestled in beds of ice. Griffin had also set out savory breads and muffins and an assortment of jams for those who didn't believe in the power of flapjacks, which included Logan and Reilly.

Reilly commandeered the toasters and began heating up a mess of sourdough and raisin muffins as Logan lathered her share with butter. While Reilly ventured into the kitchen to scrounge cottage cheese from Griffin, Logan set their trays down on a recently vacated table in a secluded nook near the fireplace.

Overhead, the winds beat the living daylights out of the galvanized roof. The poorly ventilated room smelled like one would expect with more than a hundred nervous racers packed armpit to armpit.

"Griffin hates me," Reilly moaned, slamming ceramic bowls, a quart of cottage cheese, and cups filled with milky coffee onto the tabletop in rapid succession. "First he said he didn't have any cottage cheese. Then he whined about how my predilection had ruined his special lasagna. Geez Louise! It's always *new* or *special* with your Magic Chef—never *old* or God-forbid *ordinary*."

Reilly threw herself into the opposite chair and scuttled her legs underneath the table. "When I told him the cottage cheese was for your *special* breakfast, he handed over a whole freaking quart without so much as a whimper." She tossed off her grapefruit juice with the same sour expression she conjured up when she drank down a capful of twenty-proof NyQuil.

Logan dumped cottage cheese into two bowls and then gummed her portion open-mouthed to show Reilly her full appreciation.

After they'd eaten, Reilly laid her phone next to her empty dishes. "One hour to relax before we start our warm-up." She pressed her forehead against the windowpane. "Goodness… this storm is going to clobber us."

"Look on the bright side… as the last two riders, we'll know what time we have to beat."

The crowd around the fireplace had inexplicably thinned, leaving them in virtual isolation.

Reilly brought out the torn card and set it between then. "Let's forget the race for a minute and talk about this."

Logan repeated Tim's explanation about metal alloys and bike frames. "But he lied. See this notation?" She pointed to the grouping $Ti84Mo3Al6.8C2(9)V6.2$. "That V is scientific shorthand for vanadium. Notice this 9 beside the $C2$?"

"Yep."

"Titanium, aluminum, carbon, and molybdenum are metals common in bike frames and parts. Vanadium is not, mainly because vanadium steel is too heavy for a bike frame."

"But that brake pad you found contained carbon and vanadium."

"Yep, and I'll give you house odds this Type Nine carbon is the one the sheriff is trying to source."

"What are you driving at, and how does it help us find the person who killed Julie?"

"Let's start with Tim."

"Tim killed Julie?"

"I didn't say Tim killed her. I said let's start with him because this card belonged to him, until Julie stole it along with Tim's formulations."

Reilly flipped to a blank page in her notebook and yanked out a pencil. "Consider this your official grilling."

"First, Theo/Tim was never afraid of what his German coaches back home were doing or not doing to his body. You said it yourself—'everyone lies.'"

"Romeo lied to us?"

"Or Theo lied to Romeo. He used that PED excuse to defect to America so he could work on his metal alloy, which he couldn't do back home. Romeo may have told us the truth about Tim's defection as he knew it, or he passed along Theo's lie for—well, I don't know why. Somehow, he found out about Tim's alloy—maybe in those notebooks he safeguarded—but didn't want us to know he knew."

Reilly ran a wistful finger around the inside of the cottage-cheese container, coming away with a white finger. "Now I see where you're going with this chemistry lesson. Julie wasn't a chemist, but Tim was... is. Julie's prototype is made from a metal alloy Tim dreamed up, and that's why she and Tim argued."

Logan drank off the last of her now cold coffee. "Tim helped himself to a pile of business cards from that jewelry store in Two Medicine. What I thought was a nervous gesture was really a bad habit. I'm reasonably sure this one is from a business in Europe—Ireland, specifically. We don't race in Ireland, but the men do."

"You lost me."

"Once upon a time, this card belonged to Tim before it didn't."

"Still lost."

"Team captains like you and Julie spend a lot of time together with their team coaches like Tim and Grant. You might be nosy, but even you have your own weird set of ethics. On the other hand, Julie was an unscrupulous snoop. It's possible she uncovered something in Tim's van—something *not* for public consumption?"

"Like his secret-decoder notebooks?"

"Now we're on the same page," Logan laughed. "Nosy Parker that she was, Julie flipped through them until she uncovered a page filled with some scientific mumbo jumbo and then scribbled those notations onto a business card from the horde Tim kept on hand without the faintest clue of their significance because that, too, was *so* Julie.

"How did she work out which of his formulations would build a better bike frame?"

"She didn't. We don't know when she got her hands on his formulations. Sometime last year, even two years ago. Armed with her scribbles, she hired a chemist in Europe to help her figure out which alloy to choose, and then she hired a fabricator to make it."

"Drake told Joe the truth—it wasn't his design?"

"It's a moot point. If Drake did design Julie's bike, and Julie stole his blueprint, too, he couldn't very well admit it without dire consequences."

"Ah, the blood-doping… I get it now."

"He also didn't want the sheriff to know he had good reason to kill Julie. With Julie dead, the rights to patent the design revert back to him, if it is his design."

"So Drake killed Julie."

"He had reason."

"Ditto for Tim, although he could've simply prosecuted Julie for theft and gotten the rights to his alloy back too."

"If Tim had exposed Julie as a thief, he might have had to bare himself as an illegal alien."

"It's also possible Julie didn't steal anything. Maybe Tim or Drake was her legitimate partner until she reneged on their agreement. Or the partner did. It's well-documented that people who lie assume everyone else lies too. Either way, it's a slam dunk. One of them killed her." Reilly lifted her phone.

She slipped it from her friend's hand. "Either… or… and it all made sense, until last night."

"Why… what happened last night?"

"Slade pointed out that Julie had been disagreeable for the better part of her life, yet the killer waited for this week to kill her—why?"

"The bike?"

"It always comes back to the bike."

"So this *is* about the bike."

"Have you not heard a word I've said? Or any of your own?"

"Apparently nothing that sunk in."

"The killer wanted Julie's bike but couldn't get his hands on it until this championship race."

"Why?"

"Why did the killer want the bike... that's the bazillion-dollar question. It couldn't be for the design. Once the bike showed up here, any Tom, Dick, or Harriet with a sketch pad could've copied the design."

"So, it's not the design... it's the alloy."

"What else could it be? More puzzling is how does Fay fit in?"

"The sheriff texted me early this morning. Fay is still refusing to help."

"I'm not surprised. In the short time we were together, I came away with the impression she hated Julie and blamed her for her illness. Whatever she knows, she'll take to her grave."

"Are you sure nobody overheard you talking to Tim in the jewelry store?"

"Yes, unless someone was hiding."

"What about when you were with Fay?"

"I passed a few hikers on my way to the greenhouse. Later, I was too focused on Fay to notice anyone. When she loaned me her helmet, anyone in the starting box could've overheard us—Reilly, Allison, Taylor, Davis, Tim, Jake, as well as two of Jake's cowboys—but the words we exchanged concerned her helmet—not Julie's murder."

"Where were Simon and Grant?"

"Simon went back into his van to pout after he gave me those papers, and Grant?" Logan shrugged. "He was around somewhere. He never skips a race."

CHAPTER 20

"REILLY LICKED COTTAGE cheese from her chops. "Chocolate milk?"

"Sure. Need help?"

"Nope. I'll tell Griffin it's for you. That man would walk through fire for you."

While Reilly went off to cajole the Magic Chef, Logan pulled out Taylor's background report. Unlike Rachel's middle-class upbringing, the want-to-be Sapphire Rose fashion diva had suffered through a privileged childhood on a 127-acre tea plantation in South Carolina low country. Taylor had reached the tender age of five when Missus Sherman had openly denounced her daughter as willful, ambitious, and self-absorbed. Taylor's personality hadn't mellowed much as she'd grown taller, and she'd come up empty at her debutante ball. To save herself future embarrassment, Missus Sherman had packed her only daughter off to the family's summer home in Minnesota with a generous monthly stipend.

Much to Papa Sherman's delight, Taylor had inherited his business aplomb. After obtaining an online degree in interior design, she'd built up a successful minority-owned business. She'd only taken up cycling to keep herself busy and skinny between gigs.

Also dabbles in biathlons, but she can't hit the side of a barn, Reilly had penciled in.

Taylor's only serious love affair had been with a local hotelier named Casper Lenon, a self-made entrepreneur from Vermont of thirty-three years. They'd met when Lenon had hired her to remodel all 113 of his grand hotels with the hope she'd pick one to settle down in with him. She hadn't. He hadn't given up.

She stuffed both background reports and the torn business card back into Reilly's jacket, fished out Reilly's notebook and sawed-off pencil, and scratched out a list of suspects. As Reilly's shadow fell over the table, Logan blotted out Allison, Griffin, Grant, and Romeo, leaving only two possibilities—Rachel and Taylor.

Reilly set tumblers of chocolate milk on the table. "Why do your friends get a free pass?"

"Because I don't throw my pals to the wolves."

"Why isn't Drake on your naughty list?"

"Logistics. He was miles away on the morning Julie died and a ghost on the day Jake held his time trial."

"Yeah, a ghost in the crowd." Reilly picked up the pencil and carefully wrote Tim's name beside Taylor's, then drew bold lines underneath it. "A minute ago Tim was Public Enemy Number One. Without him all we're got is eeny, meeny, miny, and moe."

Logan laughed. "We can keep him on the list with the caveat he was only an accomplice."

"An accomplice to murder is like a leaner in horseshoes—still worth prison time. So, who did Tim allegedly tidy up for?"

"My frontrunner is Rachel. If Tim told anyone about our meet and dump, it was Rachel. She was in the vicinity when I borrowed Fay's helmet. If she wasn't, Tim was—same thing. She went to medical school, and she had Jake's spare keys to the trucks. As an archer, she has good aim. Put a rifle in her hands, and she could've shot Fay. If the sheriff checks recent sales at the gun shop, he'll find that Rachel bought something... a box of bullets is my guess."

"It's feasible. The range of most rifles is more than three times the length of a football field. The sheriff figured the shooter stood about a hundred feet away, so he or she only needed to be a fair shot to pull that trigger, not Annie Oakley."

"Rachel has no alibi for Wednesday morning when Julie died or for Thursday afternoon when Fay was shot or for Friday morning when someone tried to mow me down—and Tim, hah! His excuses are as phony as a three-dollar bill."

Reilly penciled a few condemning words about Rachel in her notebook. "Rachel clucks over Tim like Mother Hen. It makes sense she'd try to get rid of anyone who wronged him."

Logan siphoned off her last drop of chocolate milk. "Only one piece of my puzzle doesn't fit. How did Rachel know Julie would be in that tunnel Wednesday morning?"

Reilly pressed a napkin to her lips. "The Julie we knew *was* all about bragging. We weren't with her more than fifteen minutes the morning she died, but even in that small window of time, she bragged on about her bike, her lunch date, and how she was going to whomp us. It's possible she gave her teammates the same earful at breakfast. If we're calling Rachel a liar, then let's go whole hog. Let's say she wasn't in her cabin studying as she told the sheriff but instead had taken her bike out and actually saw Julie and Griffin go into the tunnel. She waited until Griffin left, entered the tunnel, and found Julie. They argued, and Rachel killed Julie. Afterward, she phoned Tim and told him to hop into Jeremy's truck and help her clean up."

"Where did the hammer come from that Rachel used to drive in the spikes?"

"Most of the trucks around this place carry a toolkit to mend fences, corrals, barns, hot tubs—whatever."

"But according to Griffin, he had the F-250, and we know Jake had his Ridgeline."

"Joe can have another chat with Griffin to see if he can pinpoint the exact time he returned Jeremy's truck to the parking area."

They dumped their dishes in the bins, then headed toward the exit, hesitating in front of the gun cabinet, where Logan stared glassy-eyed at the rifles. "Hey wait a minute...."

Reilly trundled her from the snug dining hall into the shrieking winds. "It's time to warm up, so bottle up whatever make-believe is swirling about in your head, and we'll rehash it after the race. If by some miracle anything you've dreamed up this morning comes within a mile of the truth, nobody is going anywhere until after the race."

Inside Reilly's cabin, Logan stripped off her jeans, slipped on her warm-up pants, and fastened on her heart monitor strap. On their way outdoors, she tugged Reilly's spare yellow jacket over her orange one.

They pedaled east at a good clip with the wind at their backs. Thanks to Simon's diligence, the gears on her racing bike shifted smoothly, and Logan found several she could push comfortably at high cadences. Best of all, she felt no pain. The miles flew by as they made their way out to Jeremy's workshop.

On the return leg, they battled a ferocious headwind. Logan's racing bike felt light yet sturdy underneath her strong stroke and sliced through the blustery air like a sharp knife cutting through butter. They whittled away the miles in silence, drafting off the other's slipstream until they returned to the main entrance.

Sailing through the open gate, Logan slowed her speed and flexed her toes, accidentally popping open the Velcro fastening on her right shoe. She slowed her bike to a crawl, reached down, and tightened it. When she raised her eyes to the road again, a rock the size of a tortoise loomed on the pavement. With no time to maneuver around it, she jerked up on her handlebars to jump it, but the headset lifted off in her hands.

Time blurred as her front wheel spun left, and she pitched right, her feet still clipped into her pedals. She landed in a thicket of prickly brambles with her bike laying across her hip. More embarrassed than dazed, she reached down and forcibly hit her left shoe out of its clamp, then did the same with her right shoe. Then, she pushed away her bike and untangled herself from the bushes.

Reilly dashed over. "You okay?"

"At least my legs are working, which is more than I can say for this bike." She pointed to the handlebars teetering atop a rock where she'd dropped them.

"Holy cow! What happened?"

"My headset lifted out of the tube."

"You could've been seriously injured! It's very un-Simon-like to miss something like that." Reilly looked down the crowded roadway. Cyclists lined both gravel shoulders, setting up trainers, inspecting bikes, spinning wheels, guzzling Gatorade. Emergency vehicles now doubled-parked in front of the Craftsman. "Real estate is already at a premium. I'll find us a spot and set up while you deal with Simon."

He stood outside his van, dickering with a cadre of spare racing bikes.

Logan approached him, brandishing the handlebars. "Damnit, Simon! How could you let this happen?"

He recoiled. "Weren't me. I'd never miss nuthin' like that. I put your bike together meself, then checked it again this morning when I racked it, same as I always do."

"Did you see anyone milling around?"

"At o-stupid-hundred? You're barking up the wrong tree. You must've gripped the bars too tight to counterbalance the force you piled onto the pedals."

She tossed the severed handlebars at his feet. "That's bullshit, and you know it. Now fix it."

He beetled over to her headless bike and set his eye to the hollow tube. A moment passed before he pulled back his eye and inserted his finger.

"Well, bugger that!" He grabbed up her bike and wheeled it between them. "I told you it weren't me. Look-see for yourself."

She squinted inside the tube. The bolt that secured the handlebars to the cylinder was barely visible. "The inside bolt is shoved backward. Who could've unscrewed it like that? Wouldn't it take a special tool?"

"Nah, end-cap pops right off. Ordinary Phillips-head screwdriver will do her."

"Can you fix it?"

"Gimme two shakes."

Five minutes later, his "bugger off" sent her trampling across the gravel to join Reilly.

———————————

REILLY HAD SET up their staging area a couple car lengths beyond the starting box. "Did Simon own up to it?"

"It wasn't his fault. Somebody tampered with my headset."

"Geez Louise! Somebody really doesn't want you to race."

Logan checked the timer on her heart monitor, then lifted her eyes to the start box, where Slade stood beside the clock. "Hold that thought. I'll be right back."

She ran up the ramp and kissed him. "Thanks for coming." She downloaded the details of her latest mishap. "Somebody unscrewed the bolt inside the tube."

His face clouded. "I know how important this race is to you. Yet should anything unforeseen happen out on the course, do not panic. Trust your instincts and our lands—you are one. I will find you."

"How?"

"Our bond will lead me to you."

———————————

CHIEF BYRD WAS with Reilly when she returned to their warm-up area. Logan greeted him with a smile, hopped on her bike, and soft pedaled up her heart rate to a mild one hundred.

"Best see if Jake needs a hand," he said. "Be careful out there, ladies. The road is slick." He tipped his Stetson and strode toward the box.

At the sheriff's approach, Jake tucked away his clipboard, flashed his shiftless smile, and guided his cousin inside the open vestibule. She couldn't make out the words they exchanged, but the sweep of Jake's hand suggested he was concerned with the condition of the course.

She started Grant's warm-up with a five-minute strength interval, then breezed through her recovery interval, as a Montana Highway Patrol car drove up and parked just outside the front gate. She clicked the bike into a more difficult gear and began an eight-minute steady-state interval.

When her heart rate leveled off at 145, she turned to Reilly. "Do me a favor and check your bike again."

"I will, after I get back. That MHiP that just drove up is a guy I met at a conference last spring. I'll go say hi."

"MHiP?"

"Montana Highway Patrol." Reilly jogged over to the patrol car and greeted the sandy-haired officer.

Logan was into her second steady-state interval when the sheriff strolled over and joined Reilly and the MHiP. Hot and sweaty, Logan dismounted, stripped off her fleece pants, then Reilly's yellow jacket, and dropped both between the trainers. Loaded down with water bottles, she placed two between the trainers and drank off another before remounting her bike and adding resistance. As her muscles responded to the load, she increased her pedal speed until sweat beaded on her forehead. She tossed her orange jacket on the pile of castoffs as Reilly returned.

"Jake laid down a barrier of hay near the nasty turn," Reilly said. "Don't crash into it… and check your brakes again—pretty please."

Logan pulled hard on both levers at the same time. The back wheel caught and stopped spinning. The right amount of tension on the front brake pads was there, even if the front wheel wasn't. She released both levers and began a series of sprints while Reilly gave her own bike a final check, remounted, and continued her warm-up.

Logan abandoned her sprints and slow-pedaled, giving Reilly time to catch up. "Can you listen and pedal at the same time? It's important."

"More important than our race?"

"If attempted murder trumps a championship, then *yes*."

"Depends on the victim."

"Me."

Reilly's foot slipped off the pedal. "Go ahead, girlie. You got my attention."

"Taylor killed Julie."

"What happened to Rachel with a hammer and Tim cleaning up the corpse?"

"Same picture, only smudge out Rachel and paint in Taylor."

"Next you'll tell me her motive was that silly modeling gig. You do realize that's just plain wacko."

"Taylor is wacko and rich, and to people born and bred into money, enough is never enough. Losing that modeling gig meant losing millions of dollars."

"Was it something in the background report that sent you scurrying down this rabbit hole?"

"You told me to look and listen. Well, I spent too much time listening and not enough time seeing."

Reilly turned a sweaty face her way. "Whatever are you babbling about?"

"Dabbles in biathlons. Skiing and *shooting*. You said whoever fired that rifle at Fay didn't need to be a crack shot."

"Why would Tim tidy up for Taylor when he's engaged to Rachel?"

"That's the part I didn't see. Tim's engagement to Rachel is a ruse. The truth is he's about to become Mister Taylor Sherman."

Reilly choked on her water.

"TIM COULDN'T GIVE a fig about Rachel. I was so wrapped up framing Griffin, I failed to see my way through the breadcrumbs Taylor had dropped to lead me astray."

"What breadcrumbs?"

"Dancing with Romeo, flirting with Jake—when all the time it was Tim she cared about. Don't you remember the way he fawned over her in the starting box at Moriarty, then again at Jake's race? I caught them together on several other occasions, but what cinched it was the photograph I took from Julie's cabin."

Reilly held up a hand. "Back up. You stole evidence from a crime scene?"

"Nobody died in Julie's cabin, and it was laying forgotten in the nightstand. If I hadn't taken it, it might've ended up in the trash."

"Look and listen doesn't mean turn into a petty thief. What's so damning about this photograph anyway?'

"Tim's arm is around Taylor's waist."

"Since subtlety is not your strong suit, I assume you confronted Taylor?"

"She swore they were only a fling."

Reilly added her teal jacket to the growing pile of clothes. "Once again you've weaved another of your half-baked whodunits from nothing more than a few innocent situations."

"But this time I'm sure—well, almost."

Reilly clapped her hands over her ears.

She waved her hands in front of Reilly's face. "What other reason can Taylor have for turning down Mister Casper Moneybags?"

Reilly dropped her hands. "Oh, I don't know. Maybe it had something to do with a little thing called *love*."

"Taylor was already fuming about that Sapphire Rose contract and Julie's role in screwing her out of it, but when Tim told her Julie had stolen the formulation for his alloy, she went off the deep end. Have you ever known Taylor to place higher than fifteenth in the race of truth? Yet, she placed fourth in Jake's mock race two days ago—third if we discount Allison's time. She told me Tim's pillow talk included a new peaking plan for this race. Well, it worked. She's in top form. She admitted as much."

"What's wrong with that? So are we."

"What's wrong with it is we didn't use our fitness to kill anyone. Taylor could've easily covered the distance between the dining hall and greenhouse in less than eight minutes. With adrenaline on her side, maybe less than six."

"According to what—your magic math?" Shifting gears on the bike, Reilly began her steady-state intervals, staring grim-faced at the display on her heart monitor.

"The night I dragged you out to the greenhouse to see Griffin's poisonous plants, I timed our return leg. We fast-walked it in ten minutes. Taylor could've easily covered the distance from the dining hall to the greenhouse in less than six at a spirited run."

"Why in the heck would she need to... oh, I get it now... the gun cabinet."

"Yep. She grabbed up a rifle, shot Fay, then skedaddled, knowing I'd chose to help Fay rather than chase her.

"Okay... well, I'll go as far as a firm maybe... and you're lucky to get that. Remember that thirty-aught-six deer rifle I gushed on about Tuesday night when we first got here?"

"Your gushes are hard to forget."

"You might also recall it had only one bullet in its chamber. After the race, I'll ask the sheriff to run ballistics on all of Jeremy's guns. The big question is—why didn't either brother see Taylor running through the trees brandishing a rifle?"

"Because they arrived at the footpath after she'd returned the gun to the cabinet. It's also possible she took an alternative route. Or maybe she hid the rifle and put it back into the cabinet later."

"Fair enough, but even a super-fit Taylor couldn't have beat us back from the workshop, hopped in Jeremy's truck, and blasted onto the course to mow you down."

"No, that really was Tim. Taylor probably shadowed us to the workshop to give herself an unshakable alibi."

"They were a tag team?"

"It's the only way it works. Taylor killed Julie and shot Fay, and Tim helped clean up the nasty bits and tried to run me down as I suggested earlier."

"Back when you were framing Rachel."

"*We* were."

"There's just one itty-bitty raindrop on your parade. Tim's background report singled out the fact he has no driver's license."

"Really? Need I remind you the man is a chronic liar living a fake life under a false name? Yet driving without a license is the thorn in your backside? That's the least of his crimes."

"Okay, okay—then it's a solid I'll ask the sheriff to haul both of them in again after the race and turn up the thumb screws—happy?"

When Jake's voice blasted over the loudspeaker, they stopped pedaling long enough to hear him identify the incoming racer as well as her current standing. Although his voice was not as deep as his brother's, Jake's enthusiasm was contagious and his smooth jive appreciated by the crowd, who hooted, laughed, and cheered on cue.

As Reilly lowered herself onto her aero-bars, the hump of her Smith & Wesson stuck straight into the air like the dorsal fin of a shark. "Lucky for you Taylor is about to go off, or I'd cuff you to that squad car for your own safety." She waved to her MHiP pal. "Now, all you need to do is tell me a good lie to explain how you came by that torn business card."

———————

TEN MINUTES LATER, Logan joined the snaking line of cyclists waiting to use the toilets. Five minutes after that, she strolled leisurely back to the staging area, where Reilly had unscrewed her bike from the trainer.

"Let's meet back here after the race." Reilly fastened the clip on her helmet. "It's time to forget murder and mayhem and go win a championship."

CHAPTER 21

A FEW SNOWFLAKES floated past as Grant ambled over and rapped his watch. "Logan, two minutes—Reilly, three." Shouldering their bikes, he herded them over to the ramp, where Logan's minuteman posed in her stance waited for Jake to drop his arm.

"If you can manage it, pass Taylor before the turnaround," Reilly said, her cleats tapping a nervous staccato on the tarmac. "That'll take the wind out of her sails."

Logan laughed. "Good luck to you, too."

Grant threw them each a gel. "I'll wait for you at the two-hundred-yard marker."

Logan embraced him in a fierce hug. "Thanks for everything, Coach."

Taylor's sprint sent Logan and her bike up the ramp. Jake stood to the left of the start line, darting his eyes between the dial on the clock and the clipboard in his hand.

"Ten… nine…."

She brought her leg over the top tube and hovered over the seat.

"Eight… seven…."

Six brought her into her sprint stance. *Five* spun her pedals into position.

"Hay barriers are up the road… before and after the steep descent," Jake said.

"Four… three…."

She gave him a short nod and focused on her line down the ramp. "Two… one… you are off."

She blasted onto the road, lowered herself to the seat, shifted gears, and brought up her cadence. In less than ninety seconds, she'd jacked her heart rate up to race pace and relaxed into the aero-bars as the storm engulfed the ranch. What began as a few innocent snowflakes swiftly escalated into a curtain of blinding snow. Despite her hard effort, Logan shivered.

She'd trained her body to keep her heart rate steady to within four beats of her anaerobic threshold of 171. If she slacked off for even a few seconds, her heart rate would plummet, and she'd have to push that much harder to return her power output to race pace. If she went out too fast, she'd red zone. Snow or no snow, she kept to her plan, pumping her legs up and down and digging her elbows deeper into the rubber pads on her bars with each stroke.

Nine minutes into the race, she was cycling on grit alone, determined to make her last race her best one. Although the cold, heavy air was a formidable rival that added to her burden, the frigid weather helped stabilize her core temperature, leaving her body with more fuel to power her legs. She'd calculated her target time as fifty-four minutes, with a split of twenty-five minutes on the wind-aided 'out' leg, giving herself an extra four minutes to battle the headwind on her ride back in.

The section of rolling hills loomed after the six-mile mark. She geared into a harder cog and eased off on her stroke a quarter pedal. Her absolute power was well-suited to hilly terrain, and she pounded up and down each hillock, using the momentum she gained on the downhills to propel her up the steeper gradients. With half the hills behind her, the sun broke through the curtain of snow. The sudden blast of warm sunlight made the pavement slick but passable and lit up the road, bringing Taylor's familiar blue, silver, and black kit into view on the climb ahead.

Logan swallowed up the last hill at the same instant the timer on her bars flashed—she'd reached the bottom of the ascent ninety seconds faster than she'd anticipated. She returned to a steady-state gear and spun up her pedal speed to racing rhythm.

Midway up the climb, the roar of a truck's engine taking liberties with the closed course made her heart jump six beats. With each stroke, the clamor grew louder, setting her nerves on edge. She was within spitting distance of the summit, when she twisted around. A grayish blob stained the snowy horizon a quarter-mile back. For a fleeting second, anger consumed her, then she came to her senses.

Breathing was way better than bragging rights.

Cursing, she spun up her pedal speed and flew over the summit—but instead of turning left toward the turnaround—she geared down, charged into her red zone, skirted Jake's hay bales, and then accelerated east down the straightaway, her eyes darting left to right, looking for somewhere to hide—a rock, a crevice, a tunnel—any hole to melt into.

A half mile flew by, then a mile with the rumble drawing closer. The familiar wasp-riddled rocks rose on her left side, the road to the workshop on her right. With the truck chewing up the pavement at cheetah speed, staying on the roadway meant certain death. She scanned the jagged rocks looming in the distance, her heart pounding furiously. If she ditched the bike and traveled on foot, the plateau melded abruptly into a dense forest of towering pines and rushing waters—either would buy her some needed time.

Squeezing both brake levers as far back as they'd go at the same time, she locked the rear wheel and fishtailed the bike onto the gravel, twisting her feet from the pedals and softening her death grip on the aero-bars as it skidded to a stop. Her dismount came with a sudden blast of arctic rage that ripped the bike from her grasp, hurling it across the tarmac like a cigarette butt tossed recklessly from a getaway car. With no time to waste, she took off cross-country—going where the truck didn't dare.

She'd opened up a sizable gap between herself and the road, when she stubbed her toe on a rock, pitched forward, and hit the sand chin-first. Intense pain rocketed through her head. She shook it off. Pain was a familiar foe. The person behind the wheel of the truck was a deadly one.

She pushed herself to her feet and kept going... stumbling, then walking... zigzagging her way across a parched arroyo as the clamor of an engine sputtering, stalling out, revving, and then rumbling dangerously closer pursued her.

She whirled to her left. A silver truck charged up the arroyo, spraying sand forward and backward, left and right. A hundred feet out, the engine died, bringing the truck to a gut-wrenching stop. The door on the driver's side swung open with jarring fury. A jean-clad leg ending in a worn boot jumped down on the running board.

Her enemy had a face.

She bolted over the embankment and ran parallel to the cliff, leaping over rocks, scrubs, boughs, and bushes. Coming upon a granite ledge, she fell to her knees and crawled over its rough surface, not daring to look left or right, afraid if she did she'd black out or slip off the edge. At a half-frozen creek, she wrenched off her shoes and sloshed through the freezing water, ignoring the jagged pieces of ice slicing through her ankles and shins. The crackle of his footfalls through the brush made her lightheaded, and—as a cloud of hoary fog swept away her vision—her stomach knotted with real fear.

Trust your instincts and our lands.

Her last clear memory was a sensation of weightlessness as she plunged off the cliff into nature's frosty embrace.

BLOWING PAST THE 200-foot marker, the screams of the spectators urged Reilly on. Fifty feet from the finish line, she shifted into the last ring on her rear cog to master every watt of power Simon had conferred onto her machine and closed the gap at a ferocious forty-two mph, blissfully ignorant of the string of British idioms pouring from Grant's mouth as the wheel of her bike crossed over the sensor. The mere possibility of stepping onto the podium rippled shivers down her spine.

She'd gotten lucky. The swirling winds that had swept her out to the turnaround had circled around to usher her back in. Though she'd clipped Taylor's wings right after the turnaround, she'd never passed Logan—not unexpected since her friend was the better racer. Now, she scanned the crowd for Logan's familiar form, disheartened not to find her waiting. As Reilly steered her way cautiously through the sea of spectators, Grant weaved his way to her side.

"You blew 'em to smithereens, champ." His grin was the size of the Grand Canyon.

Champ! Her heart skipped a beat.

He offered a hand towel. "How does it feel?"

"I won... you're sure?" She jerked her cleats from the pedals, grabbed the towel, and mopped sweat from her face.

"By a whopping twenty-eight seconds!"

"No! That's not possible. What about Logan?" Lying her bike on the ground, she unfastened her helmet and slipped on the fleece pants he held out.

"Dunno. She's not back yet. Don't forget these." He slapped a handful of gels into her open palm. "Mocha—your favorite."

"Geez Louise... don't spoil me, or I'll never lose again." She slurped the coffee-flavored gels down like they were Jello shots, chasing them with a bottle of water. "What'd you mean she isn't back? That's impossible, unless...."

"Yep, puncture, I suspect... rotten luck."

"But that can't be! If she'd flatted, I would've passed her on the course—I didn't."

"Then she came in and slipped past me."

"With a time so rotten she didn't even place? I won't believe that. Have you checked the official's tent to see if she got flagged for a DQ? Or the trainers? Maybe she's cooling down."

"No and no—and stop worrying. She'll turn up—just not on the podium."

She placed her helmet alongside her bike and stepped out of her shoes. "Look after my gear, would you, pretty please? I'll be back in two shakes."

Leaving him happily clueless, she threaded her way through the throng with every Tom, Dick, and Harriet shouting unintelligible praise at her, clapping her on the back, and grabbing up her hand for a quick shake. When she passed the toilets, a few whoops rose above the din of the crowd noise. Simon stood beside a pizza vendor, jumping, hollering, and waving a fistful of greenbacks.

The sheriff's tall, lean form overshadowed the two trainers on the other side of the asphalt. She pushed toward him, the crowd parting to let her pass. At some point, she began to run, losing the ground underneath her feet when he scooped her up.

"Way to go, darlin.' You killed it!"

His enthusiastic greeting was the cherry on her sundae... the confirmation she needed to seal her victory. When he set her back down, a feeling of homelessness engulfed her. What was it about these quiet rocks that tempted her to stay?

She fastened on her sneakers as the remnants of the storm gulped down the eastern mountains. Shivering, she reached for her jacket in the discards.

It was gone.

She snatched up her spare and crawled into it. The thin fabric put up a meager fight against the lingering chill in the air, and her teeth began to chatter.

"Here." He wrapped her in his leather jacket.

"Thanks." She rose onto her tiptoes and kissed him. His strong arms welcomed her, and she relaxed against him, basking in his rawhide scent. "Grant says Logan hasn't come in yet."

"Any chance she got lost?"

"Not this time. I'm worried. What if...?"

"Don't go there. It's still too early in the hunt to start killing off the prey. We'll check first and worry later."

In their haste to get to the official's tent, they muscled people aside, stepped on toes, and apologized repeatedly. When they finally reached the marquee, she scrambled ahead of the sheriff and elbowed her way through a smaller crowd to an old man sitting at a table in the corner reading a computer printout.

"Did my minuteman come back yet?"

"You are?"

"Dawson... Officer Reilly Dawson." She waved her badge in front of his bloated face.

His knobby finger crawled down the names of the racers at the speed of an ant trundling a rotting grasshopper carcass. She summoned what was left of her patience, willed herself not to slap his hand, and darted her eyes down the list of names. No numbers glared back at her from the block where Logan's finish time should have been.

As a wave of frustration born out of helplessness washed over her, she whirled around and took a blind step, smashing into the sheriff's big everything. She stepped around him and rushed outside. One of Jake's ubiquitous carryalls sat off to the side, unfastened and gaping open. She seized it up. A shiny cog-set lay on the bottom. She counted the gears splined together into the unit.

Ten.

A HOP AND skip away, Rachel and Tim splashed about in a hot tub. Taylor leaned against a rock, repairing the damage to her hair. Katy, Sabrina, Allison, and Davis stood on the roadside, clutching cardboard cups of steaming coffee. Simon and Griffin sat on a bench eating paper-wrapped sandwiches. Romeo and Jake were missing... and Grant, along with her gear—eenie, meenie, miny.

The sheriff stepped from the tent and slipped the carryall from her hand. "You're shaking. What's wrong?"

"The carryall... look inside."

She dashed back inside the tent, jerked the pen from the old man's fingers, ripped off a sign-in sheet, and rejoined the sheriff, now down on a knee.

"Is it off Julie's bike?"

"I'm afraid it is." She knelt beside him and placed her hand on his cheek. "I'm so very sorry for what comes next, sir."

His jaw tightened. "You'll assume charge, Officer. The last thing we need is to give that bastard a loophole to crawl through." His hands shook as he fumbled out his phone. "Here. Meet me at the front gate in five."

She photographed the carryall and cog-set at all angles, then wrote out a somewhat intelligible description, annotated with the date and time. Zipping the paper away in her jacket, she seized up the carryall, wound the strap around her wrist, and jogged to the entrance where the crowds had thinned. The MiHP car was still parked alongside the ambulance, the sandy-haired officer seated behind the wheel.

She yanked open the passenger door. "Request another unit for assist—and start your engine." She set the carryall on the floor and slid over the seat as the sheriff and Slade ripped open the rear doors. "Drive, Officer Horner—and don't spare the horses."

CHAPTER 22

A MOUND OF soft chaparral broke her fall. Although every inch of her was battered or bruised, she was thankful to still be breathing.

A disquieting silence accompanied her landing. Thorny bushes blocked her egress on all sides. The cliffs lay to her right, the forest her left, the basin below her, and her safe haven back at the starting box. *Don't panic. He'll find you.*

She plunged through the prickly brambles until the sharp snap of a twig overhead sent her scrambling toward the end of the mesa. This time she didn't hesitate. She tucked her head between her knees and tumbled blindly into the thick fog, landing with a quiet thud on the soft sand. She allowed herself a few ragged breaths before she struggled up and sprinted north toward the mountains.

———————

THE SCENE REPEATED itself several times until she came upon the last set of cliffs. She tore off her helmet, unfastened her heart monitor, and climbed up the bluff. At the top, she hid her monitor in a foot-deep crevice. Her parents had given it to her the day she'd signed her professional contract—their last gift before they were gone too.

Dropping back down to the basin, she stripped off her clothes and sucked down the last of her energy gels. Then she scampered up an adjacent hillside and scattered her clothes. Despite the cold breeze, her fear kept her warm, and she crawled back over the rocks until she came to the river winding its way below the ledge. Drenched in sweat and dizzy from the strain of keeping her panic at bay, she dragged herself farther out on the edge, her temples throbbing.

With a last look behind her, she threw off her blanket of fear and dove in.

———————————

THE SHOCK OF the frigid water almost made her pass out.

In a matter of minutes she lost feeling in her hands and feet. As the river claimed her, she turned on her back, gulped air, and then rotated onto her stomach, moving her arms first, then her legs, then both at the same time, propelling herself forward.

In time, the clear blue waters yielded to grayish-green haze. As an odd solace eclipsed her, she relaxed and moved languidly along with the current. The diamond dust twinkling up at her from the riverbed was as inviting as the riches of Aladdin's treasure.

She dove deeper.

CHAPTER 23

LOGAN'S BIKE LAY east of the hay bales. The rear door opened even before Reilly could reach for the handle. "Officer Horner, call for an ambulance."

She swept her eyes over the imposing cliff of boulders that rimmed the forest. Slade's lanky form dissolved into a crevice a few hundred feet ahead. She stepped from the car.

Chief Byrd drew up beside her and cupped her elbow. "Come with me."

She jogged alongside him to the point where the rocks petered out and the ancient umbrella of trees began.

"You will find them underneath the cliffs by the river."

"How do you...?"

He kissed her with urgency. "Trust me... now go."

"Why... you're not coming?"

"In this you must act alone."

"I don't understand. Is it because...?"

His eyes softened. "The Great Creator brought you to us for this moment. Do whatever is necessary."

HE MOVED WITH economy to ensure his life force would sustain them both. At river's edge, her draw on him was so strong, he almost blacked out. He stripped off his dark-red shirt, jeans, and boots and dove into the icy water.

REILLY WEAVED THROUGH the canopy of leviathans. The hair on the back of her arms rose in anticipation. She slipped her gun from beneath her shirt and crisscrossed through the ancient land.

HER CLOTHES PETERED out at the summit. Sand stretched north to the cliffs, yet carried no footprints. She would not risk exposure on the slick rocks. Only one avenue remained, but even that would not keep her from him forever. He headed into the trees, pushing his lean body to its limit.

SHE WAS STRETCHED full length on the bank of the river, her bloody feet half hidden underneath the frothy waters. Slade lifted her gently, curling himself around her listless form. Neither his warm caress nor his lingering kiss aroused her. He crushed her against him as an excruciating pain exploded at the base of his skull. As darkness descended, he pitched forward, and in doing so, shielded his consort from death's swift hand.

JAKE WRENCHED HER from his brother's grasp—she *belonged* to him now.

HER HAND WAS as steady as that of a surgeon implanting a heart valve as she double-tapped the Smith & Wesson, framed Jake in the gunsight, and squeezed the trigger.

"For Julie."

The first bullet sank into his kneecap. He pitched forward, twitched, and jerked backward. With blood spurting from the mess she'd made of his leg, the sand around him turned rusty. He dropped to the ground and wiggled toward the river.

Her second bullet hit him in the shoulder, cutting short his journey. He folded onto the sand and moaned to an uncaring universe.

"For your brother."

His second attempt to slither away exposed his center of mass to the heavens, but she chose a more challenging shot, burying the third bullet into the meat of his thigh.

"For Logan."

CHAPTER 24

R EILLY SPRAWLED ON the lawn overlooking the hospital. "Your cousin?" she asked, welcoming the sheriff's intrusion on her vigil. He carved out a space beside a lodgepole pine. "No change."

"I have never known Logan to be so happy."

"The same for my cousin." His long arm overwhelmed her narrow frame. "Your story is now part of ours. Jeremy will ensure the heroics of the Desert Woman are not forgotten."

"Jeremy… how awful this must be for him."

"He knew Jake had chosen a dangerous path, but his warning fell on deaf ears."

"Why didn't Jeremy tell anyone… anyone who counted… like you, his own flesh and blood."

"Because the father chose a purpose that preserves our past, and his son one that paid forward. The human has not the eagle's eye, the moth's ear, or the elephant's nose. Our clarity, our decisions, our work—even those people we let into our inner circle—stem from our purpose. If chosen wisely, our purpose makes up for all we lack… an unstained spirit, a just heart, unclouded vision, an owlish mind. It serves as our guide, not our shackles."

"Where did Jake go wrong?"

He shrugged. "We've witnessed only part of his story—the part that touched ours. Perhaps his ending chapters will unfold more honorably."

He gathered her closer. "Logan got most of it right. She'd convinced herself—and you—the person who killed Miss Easton was someone who knew of the bike's arrival on the ranch *beforehand*, when in fact, it was the person who offloaded it from her SUV that realized its worth.

Jake's partnership with the aluminum plant had garnered him a working knowledge of metals and metal alloys. Coupled to Miss Easton's tendency to boast, he realized Julie's bike wasn't like the others he'd unloaded—the design, its weight. He went to work on her right away to find out why."

"And Julie being Julie give him exactly what he wanted and probably a whole lot more."

"No probably about it, according to my cousin. Once he had the patent in hand, Jake planned on teaming up with the aluminum plant to develop a manufacturing process and a line of goods that would reap them all a heap of money."

"I get *that* part. What I don't get is how he was able to seduce Julie in the span of two days."

"Women always come easy for Jake."

"What about his alibi? Jeremy swore Jake was in the stable at eleven thirty the morning Julie died."

"The big storm Tuesday night messed with the electricity. Clock was all wrong. Jake and my uncle worked on the fencing until ten thirty, not eleven thirty like the clock read. Jake told Jeremy he had other business to attend to and took off in his truck."

"How'd he know Julie would be in the tunnel at that exact time?"

"He'd met her there the night before. Miss Easton had suggested they meet there again, only he wasn't expecting her to have company. Got the shock of his life when he saw Jeremy's truck parked down the road. As far as he considered, anybody could've been in that tunnel with Julie. Curious to find out who, he waited until Griffin came out and drove away before he went inside. When he and Miss Easton started to get cozy, he seized his chance. My cousin isn't the *forever* type."

"How'd he get rid of the bike?"

"Jake carries portable welding equipment in the trunk of his Ridgeline. A lot of ranchers do. He didn't need the wheels, so he left them, and then torched the frame into bite-sized pieces. All he wanted was a sample for analysis."

"If Julie was that into him, an old-fashioned *please* and *thank you* might've gotten him to the same place with a lot less trouble." She gave her head a rude shake. "Hard to fathom he could drive the spikes through human flesh with the precision of a surgeon."

"Trouble with you city folk is you believe any man who prefers campfire coffee to Starbucks is a hick. We all went to university. Jake majored in physiology. He knows his way around flesh and bone."

"What was Fay's crime?"

"Miss White had to paw through more than one of Jake's carryalls to get Logan the helmet she wanted. One of those wrong ones was the one you found yesterday… the one with the cog-set off Julie's bike— only he didn't know it, and Miss White did. He only saw her horrified expression when she opened up his carryall. He realized then he'd made some kind of mistake that could link him to Julie's murder. What he didn't know was how much Miss White hated Julie. She'd sooner die than help put the man who killed her tormenter behind bars."

"She almost got her wish."

"Even without Miss White's testimony, we got my cousin dead to rights. Joe discovered Miss Easton's backpack and yellow jacket and your teal one with the torn card containing Tim Richard's formulation in the trunk of Jake's Ridgeline."

"A good defense lawyer will claim anybody with a spare set of keys to Jake's truck could've planted those things, and—according to Griffin— there's no shortage of keys on the ranch."

"Won't do Jake no good. If he weasels out of a murder one rap, we'll get him on three counts of attempted murder."

"Why didn't Jake destroy Julie's cog-set and all the rest of the incriminating stuff?"

"Time closed in on him. My call telling him to look after you and Logan the morning Julie died cut short his attempt to get rid of every trace of Julie's bike. He shoved the cog-set into his carryall. He had no clue Simon had seen that rear cog when he fixed Julie's bike Wednesday morning or that you and Reilly had seen it when you fixed her flat tire. He saw Logan hand you that torn card at the check-in table, and you put it into your jacket. He couldn't steal it until you were both on the course. After that, he had Logan to deal with."

"And the gun he used to shoot Fay?"

"Logan got that right. He grabbed that thirty-aught-six from the gun cabinet, dashed past the greenhouse, took the shot, jogged back, and cradled the rifle. Then he ran back down the road, only to meet up with his brother's fury. He knew Tim had forbid Miss White from riding her bike. Like I said, Jake had a way with the ladies. Wasn't hard for him to chat up that attractive Miss Sherman. She confirmed her coach had grounded Miss White and that she was in the habit of wandering the ranch. People with her illness usually embrace exercise until they're too weak to move. He figured he had a good chance of finding Miss White out and about—and if anyone saw him with a rifle—he could say he was out shooting quail."

"Small-minded me. I deemed no man capable of such super powers."

"Jake traded in his spurs for running shoes years ago."

"How'd your cousin know when to expect Logan at the turnaround yesterday?"

"Staged that mock time trial so he'd know when to expect her."

"Did he *really* loan his truck to Tim Friday morning?"

"Sure did. Guy Young's accident prompted Jake to put up a barrier at that sharp turn, so he hopped into Jeremy's F-250 and drove out to the turnaround to figure out how many bales he'd need. He chanced on Logan and seized the opportunity."

"So if Tim and Rachel are *really* an item, what was going on between Taylor and Tim?"

"Not a thing. Miss Sherman claims she's going to marry some damn Yankee."

"Did Jake admit to loosening the headset on Logan's racing bike too?"

"Yep. Sneaked out early morning."

"What did he have against Logan?"

"She chose his brother."

"Hardly an excuse to kill her."

"Oh, it wasn't her rejection of him that fired him up. Jake's no quitter."

"What then?"

"Losing out to his younger brother. You see, Slade *is* the forever type." He dropped a soft kiss on her cheek. "My uncle told me Josie has chosen you."

"Jeremy gave me his dog? Please thank him for me."

"It was not his doing. Josie believes you are her purpose."

"Am I such a basket case I need a guardian?" She held up her hand. "Don't answer that. Please tell your uncle I'll do my best by Josie." She raised her tear-filled eyes to his solemn face. "If it's not too much trouble, I'd like to stick around until...."

"Until you and I get to know each other better." He brushed away a stray tear. "Come on... we both could do with a chocolate milkshake."

She looked up at the top floor of the hospital. "What about your cousin?"

"Don't fret. He'll come back to us when he's ready. My cousin's got more lives than a whole brood of cats."

EPILOGUE

*S*HE SLITHERED AMONG *the grasses and released the seductive song of the Fates that would beacon the barbarous horsemen into the circle of the universe to await their judgment. They were five in number—four painted in the colors of his enemies, the fifth a dark turncoat, of the Warrior's ilk, but without his strength, courage, and compassion. They had reached the clearing when the band of blue light closed around them, making it impossible for them to escape. She melted into its whirling aura and—with the forest beasts screeching in frenzy—slay them where they stood. The traitor was the last to fall.*

———————

THE WARRIOR OPENED *his eyes to a night sky awash with twinkling stars and swaying shadows. Strange how alike this land of his afterlife seemed to his native homeland. A breath of glacial wind kissed his skin, and in the twinkling of an eye, the death arrows vanished among the grasses. As his wounds melted away, the air grew calm, and the shadows crept away.*

A maiden took shape beside him.

———————

By TWILIGHT, ALL that remained of their immortal bond was a ghost of a heartbeat shared between two. Moonrise brought the wind and the rush of the Merenale, washing his blood from the land out to the sea. Nightfall ushered in the return of the snow, a white burial shroud over the Blue Planet.

The heartbeat belonged to only one now.

She untethered his flesh and bone from the steel machines and freed his spirit to dance among the snowflakes. The silencing of his heart stirred a cry throughout the heavens.

First light shepherded in a feeble Sun cowering behind the mountains. Day's end surrendered the heavens to a pitch sky absent of a Moon to guide the mariners.

ON THE THIRD dayspring, the Blue Planet emerged from mourning lush with autumnal colors framed in snow-capped mountains and a brilliant blue sky.

Far to the north, an old Blackfoot and a snowy mountain goat climbed the sheer rock face up to an alpine meadow rich with grasses, sedges, mosses, and lichens. While the hairy goat grazed, the old man built a warming fire, huddled in his blanket, and waited.

THE ORANGE, PINK, and purple watercolors of Eventide yielded to a velvety canvas of twinkling stars. With the darkening of the sky, two of the brightest stars broke free and raced across the northern sky, chased by a halo of streaky blue light. As the band of blue light closed in around them, the stars fused into a wavy band of pink and turquoise light.

The universe hushed—and across the celestial sphere—the dancing lights froze.

Far below on the mountaintop, the old Blackfoot raised his head and held his breath.

His exhale harmonized with a renewed light show as the pink and turquoise lights skipped across the horizon, then disintegrated into circles of white light that floated softly down onto the Blue Planet.

As the Moon began its diurnal slumber, the Sun yawned itself awake.

The Warrior opened his fiery eyes to a soft, glacial breeze. The Maiden sat beside him, her emerald eyes bright and smiling.

Jeremy shrugged off his blanket. "Come along, my children. Winter is coming, and our journey is an arduous one. You will tell me of your adventures along the way."

ABOUT THE AUTHOR

PAM OWNS UP to liking only three things: thinking and talking about riding a bike, riding a bike, and writing about anything.

When she was five years old, Pam's mother walked her to the public library, led her to the mystery section, and said, "Pick out some books." Pam did. That half-hour began her life of crime.

Much later, Pam began writing for the Department of the Navy. Twenty-three years after that she stopped and turned to writing books about killing people in inventive fashion and riding a bike in standard fashion.

Since the mystery stories and people she enjoyed as a child were no longer with her, she began inventing both. Pam claims her stories are autobiographical in origin, outrageously exaggerated to the point of make-believe simply because her imagination runs more to the practical than the fanciful and not many would believe them as non-fiction if she offered them up that way.

At age 48, Pam began racing her bike and found out she was okay at it. She won two national championships, scaled Mt. Whitney from Death Valley, and became an expert-level cycling coach. Today, she still rides her bike—a lot, still races on occasion, still screams up and down mountains as a member of a Sunday-morning cycling posse. She still scripts out training plans and writes books about riding a bike in standard fashion while training the body in inventive fashion.